KACY RITTER

THE GREAT TEXAS DRAGON RACE

Illustrations by

PÉTUR ANTONSSON

CLARION BOOKS
An Imprint of HarperCollins*Publishers*

Libary of Congress Control Number: 2023930920
ISBN 978-0-06-324792-5

Typography by David DeWitt
23 24 25 26 27 LBC 5 4 3 2 1

First Edition

FOR KIT

SOMEDAY I'LL TEACH YOU
EVERYTHING I KNOW
ABOUT DRAGONS.

CASSIDY DRAKE'S DRAGON FIELD GUIDE

Scales change color with her emotions

Scars from the FC

POLYCHROMATIC DRAGON
(Name: Ranga / Rider: Cassidy Drake)

Piercing blue eyes

Sharp yellow and gold scales

QUETZALCOATL
(Name: Quetzal / Rider: Laura Torres)

Excellent eyesight for spotting prey above the mountains

CYAN MOUNTAIN DRAGON
(Name: Cash / Rider: Colt Meyer)

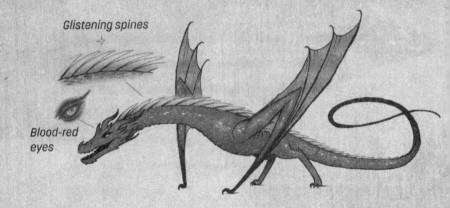

Glistening spines

Blood-red eyes

WINDSTRIKE WYVERN
(Name: Juliette / Rider: Ash Hook)

Vicious talons

FIREHEART WYVERN
(Name: Sergei / Rider: Nickolai Grigori)

Scary burgundy horns

Spikey, protective scales

DRACONIAN HYBRID
(Name: Scarlett / Rider: Valeen Grimsbane)

Loves Gran's disgusting sun tea

PURPLE LIGHTRAGE
(Grandma "Gran" Lynn McCoy's Housedragon)

Scales peek through its fur

Uses echolocation to find prey

MEXICAN FREE-TAILED DRAGONETTE

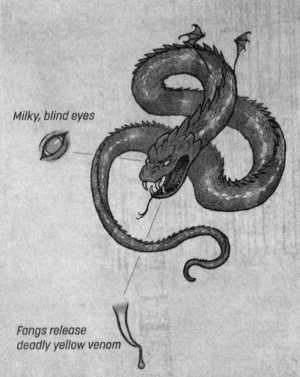

Milky, blind eyes

Fangs release deadly yellow venom

TEXAS CORAL VIPER

Bioluminescent eyes

Rows of serrated teeth

THREE-HEADED HYDRA

Frills retract to improve aerodynamics

NIGHTFRILLED RACING NESTERS
(Names: Jyoti and Jyotika / Riders: Rose and Viv Bhatti)

CHAPTER

This could be the moment I die.

Which is unfortunate, given we just blew past two wyverns, a one-eyed drake, and Ranga's best qualifying time on record. Who would've figured the only thing standing between us and the distant finish line was a three-foot tumbleweed?

"Ranga, no!" I cry.

But she's too unnerved by the tumbleweed to calm down.

Ranga's teal scales glitter in the brutal Texas sun, and we crash onto the desert floor like a falling airplane. Her pearly dragon wings flail and the wind whips my cheeks. Power builds underneath me and her skin heats up like coals. Reins pulled back, I struggle to hold on as fire erupts

1

from her sharp mouth. It blazes against the dirt, roaring the tumbleweed to ash.

Spinning into a fury, Ranga's massive body squashes cacti into green pancakes. With one hand, I clench the saddle horn. But I remember my training: keep your free hand on the emergency tracker. Her tail knocks me from my saddle and I gasp for air. Suddenly, I'm stuck under her feet as she pounds the ground, ivory talons clawing at dust and gravel. I can't move. My poor frayed lasso still dangles from her saddle.

My whole body screams, *Run!*

Too late.

Fire bursts from Ranga's belly and scorches everything in sight. Flames lick my arm as she takes off into the sky in a flash of turquoise. Even through fire-retardant clothes, it feels like my skin is melting, running off like citronella candle wax in the West Texas heat. As I wail, I click the GPS alert clipped to my belt, and my mind spins. How long will it take the medical team to reach me? I'm miles from the finish line.

But the pain rages on, and time condenses in a flurry of sound. As the world fades to black, I can't help but chuckle: Ranga is the only dragon I've ever met who's terrified of tumbleweeds.

CHAPTER

When I wake up, Grandma Lynn is standing over me, whistling Johnny Cash as she fusses with my bandages.

"Burning ring of fire, Gran?" I ask.

Gran shakes her head. "Cassidy Evangeline Drake, you have about as much sense as your mama did at age thirteen. Bless your heart," she coos. She's got that sugary southern way of speaking that lets me know she loves me, but she thinks I'm an idiot. "In my day, we would have tanned that dragon's hide for acting so ornery."

"She's a rescue, Gran." I try to sit up, but she presses me down with a strength that contradicts her AARP card status. "Ranga will never trust me if we go branding and cutting her."

3

Gran snorts, but I know she agrees with me. I shoo her off, and my tired old mattress squeaks. The cool bandages draped around my arm outline how far the burn has spread this time.

I draw in a sweet breath. Most people fear scars. They wrap them in long sleeves and cover them with makeup. But I'm not most people, and self-respecting dragon ranchers know that scars are proof of a hard day's ride. I flex my bicep and grin through the pain.

"After the Houston rodeo incident, the press will be on the lookout for dragons burning people alive." Gran leans over my desk and shoves aside plastic racing trophies and worn-out copies of Texas survival guides. She snips some dracaloe off the hundred-year-old bush on the windowsill and cuts it open. "You're a willful girl."

I run my fingers over her scarred forearm, which is decorated with a dozen turquoise bracelets. "Apple doesn't fall far from the tree, does it."

"Just don't let it get your face, you hear? It's all fun and games until you lose your cheeks. Or your hair." She tugs on my messy auburn braid.

Gran's got hair about as tall as the ceiling, which she says gets her closer to heaven—and my mom.

She hands me a glass of lemonade and 400 mg of

ibuprofen. I set the ibuprofen on the table and slug down the lemonade like a gunslinging cowboy from one of Gran's old movies.

The dracaloe soaks into my freckled skin and melts the scars into smoother lines, but that won't stop my non-dragoneering classmates from treating me like a leper. Dragon ranching is too politicized—and, frankly, too weird—for most people to understand. Many West Texans have had crops burned by wild dragons hunting for food. Others would prefer that wyverns and wurms be held captive in tiny zoos or put to work in mines. But I can't bother with what most people think. Dragons deserve a place in this world, and if winning deadly competitions is the way to raise cash for our dragon sanctuary, that's what I intend to do.

"Did I make the cut?" I ask Gran.

Gran hums and scoops up my open backpack, which is stuffed haphazardly with bleeding-red exam finals. A mess of lanyards from various reptilian sporting events jangles off the zipper. "You qualified despite that last run. Though I don't know why you even try. No matter how big the prize, there's no way your father will ever let you enter that adventure race. Speed tests are one thing. Wrangling wild dragons is another."

I wave her off and remind myself that I'll cross that bridge when I get to it. "Well, how long have I been out?"

"Not near as long as you'd like." She hands me my backpack and grins, the oily pink of her lipstick running at the corners. "No way you're missin' that final math test."

I frown. Pre-algebra doesn't pay the bills in this family.

Gran's 1995 Ford pickup kicks up dust as she drives me home from school that afternoon. The truck is a rusted beauty of red paint and sun-bleached bumper stickers that read, "I Brake for Tacos" and "Save the Rock Wyverns." Held together by love and duct tape, she's suitable for rides to Crockett Junior High, hauling dragon eggs, and that's about it. At my feet, a bogus "Suggested Summer Reading Material" list flutters in the breeze.

The brakes grind to a screeching halt at the front of our property.

"Sure you don't want to ride with me to Bobbie Lu's Quik Stop? These scratch-offs may make us millionaires," says Gran. She fans herself with two Texas Tango lotto tickets.

"And steal your thunder? No way," I reply. "Besides, a long walk is good practice for all the running I'll be doing in the upcoming race." I jump out of the car and lug on my backpack.

Gran shakes her head as if to say, "Good luck with that," and waves goodbye. The twang of Waylon Jennings lilts through the cracked window as she peels off, and I take the long, familiar dirt road home. It's hot as dragon's breath, but at least it's finally summer break.

Halfway down the road, I stop dead in my tracks and lift my sunglasses. A shiny black SUV is parked outside of our shop. It's too clean for Pecos—like someone's paid good money to have it waxed, but they've forgotten that they'd be driving unpaved roads to get to our ranch. It's the sort of car debt collectors and county tax assessors drive, and that's precisely what I don't like about it.

From my backpack, I pull out a jean jacket with an embroidered label that says, *Cassidy Drake, Drake's Dragon Ranch.* Careful to avoid the bandages draped around my arm, I slip it on and make for the shop.

When I approach, I discover a guy on our porch who's years older than me and miles taller. His hair is snowy from hydrogen peroxide, and under his name-brand sunglasses, I suspect his eyes are hard as ice. He kicks the small house dragon lapping from Gran's pitcher of sun tea brewing on the porch.

The dragon whines and bolts inside through the dog door.

7

"I'd like to see you try that once he's full grown," I snap.

The guy steps off the porch but doesn't respond. Instead, he takes out a piece of gum, tosses the wrapper onto the ground, and stuffs the stick in his mouth.

No one should mess with Texas, so I swipe up the trash and stomp to his fancy car. Reflecting his silence, I stand on the tippy toes of my red boots, lean over the hood, and tuck the wrapper underneath his windshield wiper. A chip in the windshield winks back at me. Probably from the gravel that lines our road. My lips turn up in a cherry ChapStick smirk.

Iceman glares as I take Gran's sun tea off the rail and make my way inside. Our shop's doorbell goes off with a *beep, beep, beep*. The conditioned air condenses on the pitcher of tea and fogs my sunglasses, which I stuff into my breast pocket.

I leave the pitcher and my backpack at the front and weave through glass tanks filled with domesticated, pet-friendly dragons: horny toads, iguanas, and bearded dragons. Strange, Jurassic plants with tendrils of green curl in the narrow rows of our run-down shop, and I brush against them as my boots click on the linoleum. I slap on my cheeriest, customer-friendly smile.

Near the counter, a customer with oiled, unnaturally

jet-black hair taps on the tempered glass of an innocent chameleon's tank.

My saccharine smile turns to a frown. "They don't like that."

The clean-shaven man raises an eyebrow and steps back from the terrarium. "My apologies." He's got a slick city accent that smacks of Yankee. "Is your father available?"

"My *pa* is busy." I'm sure to emphasize pa, so he knows he's an unwelcome foreigner. I lean against the counter and point to the crooked, dust-covered wall clock. "He's usually feeding the cows about this time." Dragons need a lot of food, so most ranchers like us tend cattle. And since dragon conservation donations have declined over the past few years, we sell the uneaten stock. It generates enough income to cover our steep reptilian-care taxes. Barely.

"Well, if you could tell him that Michael Carne, from FireCorp headquarters in White Plains, New York, came by with a proposition for your family, I'd be most grateful."

That's all he needs to say to tick me off. The bloodsuckers at FireCorp—a massive multibillion-dollar energy company—have been trying to buy our ranch for at least a dozen years. Most Americans know FireCorp as a gas station brand name, but I know them as fiends who exploit dragons for oil production. Michael Carne is their CEO, and he's accused of more draco-rights violations than just about anyone in the United States.

"You'll never get your grubby hands on our land," I say, arms crossed. "Or our dragons."

Folding his hands, he sets his elbows on the table like he's preparing for a board meeting power move, then nods at my fraying name tag. "Cassidy, is it? We could do great things for your family—remarkable things. Set you up for life. Send you to any college you want." He hands me a card that's got FireCorp's seal stamped on the front. Its desperate bright red foil screams "extensive marketing budget." "Give this to your pa." He talks slowly, like he thinks I'm some penniless backwoods hillbilly.

I smack the card on the counter. "Oh, don't worry. I'll be sure to tell him you came by. Uninvited."

He chuckles and smooths his fire-engine-red tie. "You're the biggest dragon sanctuary in the entire Southwest. Remember: great things." He spins back on his heel as he leaves. "Oh, and by the way—here's your mail." A sleek, platinum wedding ring dotted with diamonds glitters on his finger as he hands me a stack of mail. He's fanned the letters to expose the various "LATE" stamps on the outside.

I stuff them into my jacket and cross my arms. The

bandages peek out from the wrists, and the guy snorts. "Give it some thought. You could travel the world as a touring member of FireCorp."

Over my dead, burned-to-a-marshmallow-crisp body.

Most people who live in small towns like Pecos dream about moving to far-off places. They imagine fancy spring break vacations in Cancún and summers abroad in places like Paris. But I could give two squats about romantic European cultures or visiting stuffy museums with air pumped full of freshener. Nope. I'll take open fields and dragon's breath over a pee-soaked subway any day of the week.

Lifting my chin, I scoff, "My family has been here for nearly two centuries, and I sure as heck never intend to leave Texas. Crushing your New England lackeys in this year's race is going to be a real pleasure."

Michael Carne, corporate stooge, shrugs. "Suit yourself."

He saunters out of the shop and I toss the business card in the trash. No need to tell Pa about the fox in our henhouse. I hand-feed crickets to the traumatized chameleon and head back outside.

As the black SUV pulls out of the parking lot and heads back down the dusty trail to whatever corner of the underworld it rolled in from, a semitruck approaches. It curves around the rough driveway toward us, and I raise a hand to shield my eyes against the afternoon sun. Two visitors in one day is a rarity around these parts—the whole county of Pecos barely has a few thousand people in it—and the truck is unmarked. I walk to the edge of the porch as Pa rounds the corner.

"Who's in the truck?" I ask, squinting back at the fierce afternoon rays.

Pa's old John Deere baseball cap draws a shadow across his face. "Trouble, I bet."

The engine whirs loud, and the sun reflects off the windshield, so I can't see who's inside. When it stops, I brace myself and watch as Pa walks around to meet the driver.

Out of the cab pops Santiago Morales, a ranch hand from one of our sister farms in southeast New Mexico. I jump off the porch and run over to where he and Pa slap their hands together in a brotherly handshake.

"So, what have you gotten us into this time?" Pa asks.

A roar rattles the truck, which creaks and moans. I flinch only because I'm startled by the movement, not because I'm afraid of what's inside.

"Well, he's mean as a rattlesnake drinking hot sauce," says Santiago. "And I reckon that's exactly how they wanted him." He hands the invoice to Pa.

I sidle up next to Pa and peer over his shoulder. "What is it?"

He shrugs me off and puts on his drugstore readers. "A little room, please, grasshopper."

"Yeah, right." I push back in and lean over the paper. In great big letters, it reads: "MOTTLED RUBY-STINGER."

My eyes are wide as plates as I unsuccessfully try to snatch the paper from my dad's hands. "Seriously?" I run to the back of the truck and point at the fancy mechanical lock securing its doors. "C'mon—let's see him."

Santiago pushes up his wide-brimmed cowboy hat. "Look, kiddo—"

"Cassidy," I remind him. We've known each other forever.

"Okay, kiddo," he repeats. "The thing is, this stinger has no kindness left."

"We deal in rescues here, Santi. This isn't my first rodeo." I cross my arms and crunch a heel into the gravel. It's no lie. Most of the dragons at our ranch have been saved from one terror or another. "Let me in."

Pa sighs and shoves the old paper into his pocket. "He's muzzled, right?"

Santiago spins his key ring on his finger as if performing a magic trick. "If he weren't, I'd just about be dead. Before we open up the truck, I recommend bringing backup."

My excitement swells as we head to the cellar and enlist three dragons. They sense a new creature outside and trill as we saddle them. Only diamonds can cut diamonds, and dragons are no different. Riding mounts should de-escalate the unsocialized rubystinger.

Pa rides our fiercest dragon, a snarling bearded drogo with neon-orange frills, while Santiago takes the second largest, a horned snakeback with leathery indigo skin. I choose Ranga, ignoring the fact that together we are half the size of the drogo—or that she nearly killed me yesterday. She giddily wags her tail, and her pearly scales flash purple, aquamarine, and blue in the blazing sun. Because she's a polychromatic dragon, Ranga's coloring usually reflects her emotions.

Head held high, I slip my red boot into a stirrup. I sling up and take my seat on the saddle. "I'm ready," I say.

Pa nods stiffly.

Secure on our mounts, we guide all three dragons to the end of the truck. Santiago reaches into his pocket and pulls out an old machine that looks like an ancient garage clicker. He flips the safety cap off of it.

"You ready?" he asks.

Pa and I nod. I hold Ranga steady by her reins and settle firmly into the saddle. Confidence saves lives.

"One . . . ," counts Santiago. "Two . . ."

He slams his thumb on the button, and the back of the semitrailer crashes on the ground, revealing a mangled dragon hunched in the corner. The rubystinger's gem-like scales gleam a dull red, and he's thin in all the wrong places. His ragged gray wings heave up and down as he breathes.

"FireCorp did something awful to him," says Santiago.

My throat burns as I remember the oily man with his perfectly pressed, heavyweight business card. "He belonged to the FC?"

"Yep," says Santiago. "Check the brand on his shoulder."

A great big "FC" scar is etched into his skin, which twists a knot in my stomach.

"Must have been one they were using for steam injection—or maybe on the oil-refining line," Santiago continues. "His neck is raw from the chains, and I doubt he's ever seen the sun."

I shudder. Doomed to life as a petrol dragon is an awful fate. It means tiny cages, dangerous steroids, and continual cattle prodding during crude oil production. And when it comes to notorious dragon-rights violations, especially in the name of Big Oil, FireCorp is offender number one. When people fill their cars with FC gas, they don't imagine they're guzzling the pain of captive dragons. But just because they can't see it doesn't mean it's not real.

I lead Ranga closer, her steps tentative. "He doesn't look that mean," I whisper.

Ranga assumes a submissive pose and keeps her snout low as she nudges closer to the rubystinger. Step by step, I hum a soothing tune as we approach the back of the truck, the threat of flames tugging the back of my brain.

Chains rattle as the rubystinger pounces. Ranga jerks back with a yelp, and we barely avoid the rubystinger's daggerlike claws. I fall to the ground in a cloud of dust.

A shiver runs down my spine as the rubystinger chokes against the chain around his neck. Peeking out through the muzzle, his needlelike teeth drip with saliva. Pa bounds in front of me, and his dragon's shadow spills across the ground.

"Dagnabit, Cassidy!" says Pa. "Further back!"

Every time something like this happens, he thinks of Mom. What he doesn't know is that I think of her too. Not because I'm sad, but because I'm proud that I'm fearless, just like her. I stand up and wipe the dust from my tattered jeans. One more bruise to love.

Breaking away from Pa's protective stance, I pull Ranga close, reins in hand. The rubystinger's claws scrape against the trailer bed.

"We're fine, aren't we, Ranga?" I pet the curved magenta horns atop her head.

Body tense and scales rippling to gray, Ranga isn't so sure. I walk alongside her and nudge her forward, ignoring the pain in my rear and Pa's weather-beaten scowl.

The rubystinger growls deep in his throat, the sound muffled by his muzzle. Ranga's iridescent scales go dull, and her bright eyes warp into a vacant black—dark with the nostalgia of her past life. She flinches, but as I run my fingers along her scales, I coax the iridescent teal shimmer to return.

Santiago pulls a toothpick from his jeans and pops it in his mouth. "I think he's been doped on steroids. He'll be going through one heck of a withdrawal tonight."

Ranga trails behind me as I inch toward the writhing dragon in the trailer bed. He pulls against the chain and the spines along his back pulse with crimson. It lights his skin, which is marred with scars and puncture wounds.

"It's okay, baby," I say, drawing my voice to a low coo.

The dragon scrapes his nails against the sides of the

truck, and the metal creaks.

As I inch forward, I lock eyes with the rubystinger, and his breathing slows for just a second. I whistle gently for Ranga. She inches toward me, crawling along on her belly.

I grip Ranga's reins and peer into her eyes. "You're safe now. The past is the past."

She shakes her head as if trying to escape her reins. I grip them tighter. "This dragon needs you," I whisper.

Ranga grows two inches taller, her fiery heart rising to the task, and I loosen my hand to give her slack. She slides along the ground, exposing her belly to the rubystinger. Ranga's scars, visible reminders of potent invisible wounds, match the rubystinger's. In Ranga's presence, the chained dragon relaxes. I've been around dragons all my life, and I can't say I understand how they communicate, but there's a brief moment of understanding between Ranga and the rubystinger.

"I've never met a dragon that couldn't be made nicer with a little love," I say.

Pa grunts again. It's not a sign that he agrees with me.

As if on cue, the rubystinger growls through his muzzle again.

Santiago grinds down on his toothpick. "So, what do you think? You got space for him? The other Texas rescues are full, and you're probably the only one with enough square miles to keep him safe and happy. If that weren't the case, I wouldn't be coming to you—especially not when times are so tight."

I shoot a sharp glance at Pa, but he doesn't acknowledge me.

Many of our dragons are rescues, and most of them take more time, money, and energy than we can afford.

Pa sighs and gazes at the rubystinger. "There's always room for one more," he says.

31°03′26.0″ N, 102°43′32.5″ W
Drake's Dragon Ranch, Pecos County, Texas

The morning sun creeps through my window, lighting the faded patchwork quilt on my wrought-iron bed. I toss it off and throw on some old jeans and a tank top. Tacked up beside dragon classification charts, my calendar reads "Saturday." I mark it with an X in my fat black Sharpie. Only seven days left. Down the hall, a frying pan bangs on the stove, and the smell of bacon wafts through the outdated ductwork. My stomach growls as I race for the back door, aiming to cut through the kitchen on my way to practice.

"Missy, you give Ranga one day of rest," says Gran as I grab a piece of crispy, almost burned bacon.

Gran's sun tea–obsessed house dragon, a purple lightrage

about the size of a house cat, wriggles on the floor with clawed feet. He whines at me, eager for scraps. I pat the cobalt-blue horns peeking through his skin and he flaps his tiny wings.

"There are only two days in a weekend, Gran." I wolf down the bacon and give Gran a side hug. Her wide-framed glasses nearly fall off her nose as she reaches to keep me inside.

"Young lady, I don't know why you bother—your father will never let you enter that race. Not now, and not in a million years." She hugs me close with her superwoman grip, and it's no wonder she won the Texas triple cup—or that she's the Titebond glue holding our family together. "So, why don't you just stay inside and have some biscuits? You're already too thin as it is."

I'm a healthy weight, no question. But like a good southern grandma, she always seems to think I'm wasting away to nothing. I snatch a biscuit off the floral melamine plate by the stove.

"I'll enter that race if it's the last thing I do."

"If you enter that race, it very well may *be* the last thing you do." Gran shakes the pan of bacon, unintentionally enticing the whiny lightrage. She grabs my chin with her free hand and leans in. "But I suppose if there's anyone around here who might win that thing, it's you. Just like your mother." She kisses my cheek and releases me.

I wipe lipstick off my cheek and stuff half a biscuit into my mouth. "If you'd tell that to Pa, I'd sure appreciate it."

She shakes her head and waves me off with the spatula. "Well, go on—git!"

I feed my half-eaten biscuit to the squealing lightrage, wipe off my hands, and run outside. The screen door slams behind me.

It's one of those sweltering Texas days when the sweat melts down your back in a salty trickle and gets caught in the band of your jeans. The best type of day for riding dragons. And that's all I care about: Ranga and me blowing against the wind.

I swing open tornado shutters buried in the ground—the ones that remind me of *The Wizard of Oz*—and they slap back against the dust. Inside, a black cavern that looks like a coal mine stretches hundreds of yards underground. A string of industrial lights trails into the expanse, flickering as I descend into familiar territory. I can already smell dragon dung wafting up from the stables below. It's the smell that makes me think, *There's no place like home, there's no place like home.*

The heels of my boots dig into dry dirt layered with hay

and gravel. As I move, I hear the squeals, the screams, the roars—sounds that would scare the Crockett Junior High cheerleaders out of their clean, pretty tennis shoes. But not me.

"Cinder!" I yell out. "Bonnie! Clyde!" A fierce whistle flies out of my lips and ricochets through the mine shaft.

My babies howl back. Growls and chirps that sound like something out of *Jurassic Park*.

"Falkor! Ranga!" My dragons have the best names.

When I meet the end of the dust corridor, I press my palm into the security screen that reads my prints, and the doors fly open. We may be poor dragon ranchers, but that's mostly because we spend every cent we have on feeding dragons, treating their injuries, and buying tech to keep them safe. Beyond the doors, the air is hot and dry, thick with dragon's breath and hints of char.

Dragons love dark cozy spaces, and every sort of dragon under the ever-loving sun has a nest in this underground sanctuary. And each dragon has free access to our twenty-thousand-acre ranch, miles away from the fearful public eye. Not all dragons befriend humans, but ours are domesticated and friendly enough. Fun fact: In medieval times, dragons freely roamed the earth. But during the Industrial Revolution, people drove them to near extinction.

Most middle school textbooks don't mention that we've destroyed most of their natural habitat worldwide.

Straightening the red bandanna around my head, I saunter down the corridor. I run my fingers along the walls of wood and metal, so familiar and worn smooth. Technology has changed down here—we now have fingerprint scanners and a network of security cameras—but the structure has been passed down to Drakes for generations.

I round the corner, and the vision is spectacular. Dragons of all shapes and sizes turn to me, their eyes flashing: green and pink, blue and red.

"C'mon now!" I walk down the center of the underground barn, free-access stalls flanking me on either side. My outstretched fingers brush the metal walls as I greet various dragons, some that we've had for years and others that have come to us only recently.

I pass through the stalls, acknowledging massive wyverns, Rocky Mountain vipers, and basilisks as I move. My father may own this farm, but these are my dragons. And I'd do anything for them. The horned snakeback whistles at me; the golden drake sings. Not all dragons kill people, and only a few hoard gold.

As I round the corner, I find Ranga cowering in her stall like a sad puppy. In the pen beside her, the rubystinger growls through his muzzle—the sound mixing anger and agony.

"Poor buddy," I say.

I step up onto the first rung of Ranga's stable, and the points of my red cowboy boots peek through the metal slats. Warily, she slides along the ground and scratches her body against my toe. My arms dangle over into her stall and I reach down to say hello. As I stroke her fat, glossy scales, they flush with glittery color.

"I thought you would have made friends by now," I say, frowning.

Ranga huffs and the sharp angles of her jaw tighten. We may not speak the same language, but over the years, Ranga and I have come to understand each other the way only dragons and their riders can.

"You'll need more grit than that to win the race this summer." I lift the latch on Ranga's stall and curl up next to her in the corner. Her stomach is like an electric blanket turned on high, but I lean into it. She wraps a wing around me and nuzzles my arm like a shy baby dragon.

"Do you remember your first day here?"

Ranga blinks at me as if to say, "Don't remind me."

She knows what it's like to be scared. To be caged. I pet her scales and settle into her wing. "You were barely bigger than a miniature pony, and about as sad a dragon as I'd ever seen." I run my hands along a grizzly scar on her neck. Even years later, it's the reminder she was once a FireCorp bait beast—a weak plaything used to inspire confidence in the bigger dragons. Bait beasts are last in the pecking order when it comes to the oil production process. They make larger dragons even more aggressive and better for hard labor. We had no idea how long Ranga had been in chains before we rescued her, but when I look into her eyes, even now, I imagine it was probably for her whole life.

Maybe that's why she loves to race. Racing is freedom.

Lovingly, I scratch behind her aural lobes. "Of all dragons, you should understand the most. Who knows where he has been . . ."

We turn to the rubystinger, his prominent nostrils quivering.

He glares back at me with hollow yellow eyes and recoils, hissing. The steroids have worn off. I open my mouth and sing a tranquil tune, the best way I know to calm a traumatized dragon, and he sticks his head underneath his wings. Metal barbs protrude from his thick skin, a plastic surgery gift from whatever mean FireCorp sonofagun owned him before. Fleshy scar tissue has grown around the metal, and as he presses back into the corner, the metal grinds against the wall.

FireCorp thrives on broken dragons—ones with no fight left.

As I keep singing, I squeeze my fingers between the metal slats to pet him, but he growls. Heat rises from his nostrils, and this time, I'm the one to recoil.

I pull a pilfered strip of bacon from my pocket and halve it. I give a part to Ranga and toss the other half toward the rubystinger. He scrapes along the stall and licks it up through his muzzle.

Leaning back into Ranga, I take a folded sheet of paper from my pocket. It is worn with creases and dirty with oily finger marks where I've rubbed it thin. At the top, in thick lettering reminiscent of a novelty "Wanted" poster, it reads:

ENTER THE GREAT TEXAS DRAGON RACE
TEST YOUR DRAGON, YOUR GRIT, AND YOUR SKILL!

The Great Texas Dragon Race is the most prestigious amateur dragon-racing competition in the entire country: a weeklong event that's part speed race, part scavenger hunt, and part survival test. Anyone thirteen and up can participate, as long as you aren't a professional dragon rider. And since my birthday was two short weeks ago, I'm finally eligible. For the past five years, FireCorp riders have won. But when I look at Ranga, who loves to race and has earned her spot with enough qualifying competitions, I see a winner.

I settle into Ranga, who remains wary of the ruby-stinger. "I think we could win, Ranga. And together, we can remind the world that dragons should be protected, not enslaved."

Ranga wriggles onto her back, begging me to pet her underbelly. The little purple spines on her powerful hind legs gleam as she rolls onto the floor. A massive pile of charred bones clatters in the corner, knocked aside by her tail, which she hasn't yet grown into.

"Jeez, Ranga—with an appetite like that, you'd think you were a dragon twice your size."

She snorts at me, fierce and low.

I chuckle, pull a pen and the folded application from my pocket, then shut my eyes.

Behind my lids, I'm crossing the finishing line. As I rise and fall with Ranga's breath against my back, I imagine the win and what it would be like to take home the trophy and the fat check that comes with it. I envision Ranga and me in the winner's circle as the crowd cheers, *"Drake! Drake! Drake!"*

"Ehem."

Startled, I open my eyes. Pa peers down at me, brow furrowed as I shove the paper behind my back.

"What are you doing, grasshopper?"

"Not much," I say, scrambling for words. "Just talking to Ranga."

He raises an eyebrow, and I'm certain he can see right through me.

But Pa won't start an argument. That's the worst part. He won't confront me about the Great Texas Dragon Race because he knows that every argument fuels my hope and "reckless" desire to win, win, win.

I wipe sweaty palms against my jeans and pull the application from behind my back. "The race is only a few days away," I say. "All I need now is your signature so I can enter the qualifying tryouts."

Pa adjusts his hat farther over his face. With his gaunt cheeks and scruffy chin, he's sadder than a country song and a shell of the father who taught me to ride so high I can almost touch the sun.

"I don't have time to argue about this, Cass."

"I don't want to argue," I say. "I just want your signature."

He grunts, fiddles with the stall's latch, then leaves me with my thoughts.

Vintage relics, checkered vinyl flooring, and strawberry print curtains crowd our tiny, wonderfully tacky kitchen. Gran rules the gas range with an iron fist, never allowing us to help cook because she swears we "just don't do it right." Tucked in a booth excavated from an old diner, I pretend to scan social media like any normal junior high kid. The purple lightrage sleeps beside me and purrs.

"Is everyone at Crockett enjoying the first days of summer?" asks Gran.

Gran is always saying I need non-dragon friends, which I honestly couldn't care less about. Shielding my phone, I scroll through an online forum for the upcoming dragon race in West Texas. The message board runs wild discussing possible entrants. I grin, glad to find my name among the hopefuls.

"Sure looks like it," I lie.

Gran makes a sound like she doesn't believe a word I say. She offers Pa and me a glass of her gross, oversteeped sun tea. And like always, we both choose lemonade instead. No human besides Gran would dare drink that concoction. She shrugs and pours a bit in the lightrage's empty bowl. He jumps down, laps up the tea, and scurries off into the other room.

Propped across from me, Pa sucks on his lemonade as he flips through the mail. Many of these envelopes also bear the dreaded "LATE" stamp. Ugh. In Pecos, that means our neighbors will know we're struggling by the time church lets in at nine a.m. on Sunday. The thickest envelope, wrapped in glossy black paper, bears the Federation of Legal Animals and Reptilian Endangerment (FLARE) logo. My dad runs a thumb over the paper but doesn't bother to open it.

Gran sets a dish of mashed potatoes on the table and gives me a look that says, "Don't you dare ask about it."

But I was never very good at keeping my mouth shut. I snatch the envelope off of the gingham tablecloth. "How much is the tax this year?"

Gran coughs, a not-so-subtle recommendation to shut my mouth.

I ignore her. "Pa?"

Pa grimaces and pours extra sugar into his lemonade. "Never you mind."

I sigh and rip it open.

"Cassidy Evangeline Drake! He told you not to mind." Gran smacks the half-opened envelope from my hand with a rubber spatula that says "I love you like biscuits & gravy" on the handle.

It smarts, but I snatch the letter back up. If our ranch is failing and our dragons are at risk of being repossessed, I have a right to know. Inside the envelope, a paper states FLARE's catastrophic annual fee:

$98,000.

That's what it will cost to keep a big fat dragon habitat like ours "safe" from the public. The more dragons you have, the bigger the number. And since we always have room for one more, our fees are astronomical.

FLARE's protection is a necessary evil in a world filled with people who are terrified of massive, flying, fire-breathing reptiles. From fire-retardant shields on schools to draco-emergency broadcast systems, FLARE's technology protects the public from dragon-related incidents. In turn, our dragons aren't driven to extinction by angry mobs.

My lips go numb as I mentally tally our finances. I grip the paper, and it crinkles around the edges.

"Wish you hadn't opened it, huh?" says Pa. He takes off his baseball cap and sets it on the bench next to him. From years of squinting in the desert sun, his crow's-feet form a maplike pattern of tanned peaks and white valleys. "Maybe now you've had a taste of what it's like to walk in my shoes for once. That's what you get when you don't mind your elders."

"Well, what are we going to do?" I ask. "We can't afford that."

"How do you know what we can and can't afford?" It's not a question. It's one of those adult statements you aren't meant to answer.

But I purse my lips and answer anyway. "I'm not exactly a kid anymore. I know money doesn't grow on trees."

I also know what it's like to hang up on creditors and how it feels to wear hand-me-downs when everyone else shows up with new back-to-school outfits. So, I know what this paper means . . . It means that unless we can come up with the money, we'll have to sell dragons to make ends meet. I flex my toes inside my brand-spanking-new cowboy boots. It took me all year to save up for these red leather beauties, and now I wish I'd just given the money to Pa.

Underneath the table, I pick at a hangnail on my thumb. "We can't afford to ignore these letters. We have to act."

Pa grunts, and I am not sure if he's more upset about our bills or me challenging him.

Gran, who is perched over the stove, flips a pork chop in her cast-iron skillet with enough force to startle me. "Too many small farms are being driven into the hands of corporations." She snorts and fiddles with the pan. "And those CEOs are all crooked as question marks."

God bless Gran.

Rising taxes for dragon owners have knocked over dozens of small dragon rescues in the Southwest. The worst part is that when ranches fold, they're often gobbled up by greedy operations like FireCorp. And those corporations couldn't care less about dragon health, welfare, or conservation. All they care about is profit.

"The public is just wary since those diamond-tailed wingers started the Bastrop wildfires," says Pa. "They'll come around. People will remember dragons are worth saving. The conservation dollars will come back, and visitors will return with donations. And we always have the lizard shop and our cattle. We'll make up the difference by the time FLARE sends a second notice. Just you wait."

I cross my arms, because I've heard this before. "And if we don't make up the difference?"

"Well, then we just pray," he replies.

I've never been much for prayers, even though I'm a good Texas girl. As far as I can tell, hard work accomplishes more than most prayers.

I fold the paper back up and place it in the half-ripped envelope. "There is a solution." I inch forward in my chair, which creaks as I move. "Race tryouts start in three days, so there's still time to enter. I'm fast—and I can win the two-hundred-and-fifty-thousand-dollar prize." I sit tall, back pressing against the booth's broken springs. No matter what he says, I must remain calm.

"Do I look like I just fell off a turnip truck? We've already been over this. No means no."

"But, Pa—" The words come out like more of a whine. Calm isn't really my style. "Ranga and I have crushed every regional speed race. And I've been practicing Texas survival skills all year. The game designers can toss *any* ranching task at us, and we will ace it."

"Letting you sign up for a speed race is one thing. Allowing you to sign up for a dangerous Texas-wide scavenger hunt where you face wild dragons is another. People get hurt in the Great Texas Dragon Race every year."

Gran pipes up, "Someone died last year, if I'm not mistaken."

I glare at Gran, who is usually on my side.

She winks at me. "That said, I am sure that if anyone ever could win that race, it'd be our girl here." She slaps a pork chop on my plate. It's crusty around the edges, just like I like it.

"Lynn, will you let me do the parenting, just this once?" He rarely speaks to her that way. "She's too young."

"I'm not!" I say, pushing the plate out in front of me. "I'm finally old enough to compete. The boy who won three years ago was my age too. I'm twice as good as him. And Gran was only a year older than me when she raced."

"Ranga almost killed you because she's afraid of her own shadow. You're really going to race her for a week alongside strangers? Peanut, I appreciate your grit—but the answer is no. I'll not risk my daughter's life for money." He scoops up a spoonful of mashed potatoes and plops them on his plate. "What kind of father would that make me?"

Pa tucks into his meal and shovels potatoes into his mouth. He used to say I'd be the youngest person ever to win the Great Texas Dragon Race. When I was a kid, he'd make me medals out of tinfoil and call me his little champion. But after Mom died, he became cautious. *Too* cautious. Like he thinks every little thing might break me.

"Mom would have let me go," I snap, a brushfire sweeping through me. "Mom would have believed in me."

The mention of Mom makes him wince, and he clenches the edge of the table. "Dangerous people have a stake in that race, grasshopper," he whispers. "People you can't beat."

I stomp out of the booth, and Gran is hunched over, staring at the pork chop in the frying pan.

"Gran?" I ask.

She twists around, and her face is white as a bleached sheet. "You know, honey . . . I don't feel so good."

The grease-covered spatula falls out of her hand and clatters to the floor. I rush to her and catch her as she's about to keel over onto the linoleum.

"Gran!" I yell.

Pa drops his lemonade glass, which spills as it clatters to the floor, and bolts to Gran's side. He presses a hand against her forehead.

"She's burning up. Hold her." He clambers to the wall and grabs an old-school landline phone from the wall. The kind we keep because Gran doesn't like "newfangled devices."

"This is Paxton Drake over at Drake's Dragon Ranch. We need an ambulance."

A trickle of blood runs out of Gran's nose as I hold her tight. Her breath escapes in short spurts, and I rock her the way she did for me when I was a sick kid.

The smell of burning pork chop fills the kitchen. By the time the ambulance arrives, the pork chop is as black as a hockey puck, and the fire alarm is sounding through the house.

I'm so numb and terrified, I barely notice.

CHAPTER

As I swirl a plastic stick through my weak, hospital-vending-machine coffee, my reflection ripples in the Styrofoam cup. Eyes puffy from worry, I take a deep breath.

A solemn doctor with a cool-blue tie flips through the chart at the foot of Gran's bed. And as soon as he starts talking, my body goes numb, and he fades into the background.

A few uncertain diagnoses rise from the garble:

Vertigo . . . seizure . . . high blood pressure . . .

I wish I were watching one of those clever medical dramas where the handsome doctor always fixes the patient, but these yahoos have no idea what's wrong with her. My lips press into a tight line, and my feet are heavy in my boots.

As he drones on, Gran's face remains a motionless canvas of lines and sun damage. She's stable now, but far from recovered. I need to reapply her lipstick the next time she wakes up. I focus on the steady drip of the IV fluids attached to her arm. *Drip. Drip. Drip. Drip.*

"Miss?" says Doctor Blue Tie.

I sit up. "Sorry, what?"

"I know you like to be here when she's awake, but we need the room for a few tests. Then, hopefully, we can figure out what's wrong." He forces a smile, but the lines in his forehead say he isn't confident about the result.

I nod. "My coffee is cold, anyway." I set the cup on the table and leave Gran surrounded by a host of nurses.

My boots echo down the empty hallway. The disinfectant makes me long for the smell of dragon dung and hay. Only miles away, hundreds of people are lining up to try out for the Great Texas Dragon Race, and I'm stuck—trapped in Baptist Memorial Hospital while Gran gets poked and prodded by every doctor in a fifty-mile radius.

Sure, life's not fair. My mom's death taught me that. But this time, instead of being sad, I'm ticked off.

My sterile trail leads to the dreaded financial office. Beyond the pane of glass, Pa grimaces as he talks with a plump woman behind the desk. He pulls out a series of credit cards that she runs politely, one after another.

Rich people don't understand that when someone you love is sick, everything becomes a transaction. I search the internet and estimate the costs. Ambulance: $3,000. Diagnostic tests and imaging: $10,000. Hospital stay: $3,000 per day.

After three days of Jell-O and sleeping in an armchair, I estimate our costs have reduced the farm to nothing. And since no one seems to be able to figure out why Gran collapsed or why she can barely stand, I imagine we'll be poor as mud come Monday.

Pa comes out of the executioner's chamber and slips his baseball cap off his head, leaving his hair a furled mess. He sighs, low and heavy.

"What did they say?" I ask, eager to talk about anything other than Gran, even money. If I have to walk out of here without her, I might never stop crying.

Pa wrings his hunter-green hat and sets it back on his head. "We'll be okay, grasshopper."

There's enough tension in his jaw that I know he's lying. I imagine the next few months: lingering by Gran's bed as her hospital bills are sent to collections; helping around the farm like an obedient Texas girl while our dragons are sold off one by one. It stokes a burning desire to help deep in my stomach. The worn Great Texas Dragon Race application, with the promise of its sweet $250,000 prize, burns in my back pocket.

I slip it out and raise it up. "You have to let me help."

In my hand, I hold the key to solving our problems. Judging by my father's weathered face and the way his Adam's apple bobs, he knows it too. "You're a good kid," says Pa. "I—"

My heart pounds as "I know" forms on his lips.

He clears his throat. "And you being with family *is* helping. That's what we need right now." He plants a kiss on the top of my head as hope drains out of me. "I need to tend to the dragons. I'll pick you up later so we can sleep in our own beds tonight. I'll even grab fried chicken from Buddy's Fry Shop. Sound good?"

Buddy's fried chicken is just about the best in three counties, but my mouth turns to ash. I nod, knowing that a lie will be better than the truth, and the truth is that I will enter that race come rain or shine. Pa is a good man, but he's afraid. And I've had enough of his unending fear and restraint. With race tryouts ending just down the road in six hours, there's still time for me to say goodbye to Gran, pack a bag, and try out before nine p.m. All I need now is one last moment with Gran before I slip into the night after Pa falls asleep.

Some kids run away to join the circus. I'm going to run away and join the deadliest race this side of the Mississippi.

I make my way back to Gran's room and she's still fast asleep, her usually perfect hair mussed against the pillow. Legs heavy, I slump down into a chair and fiddle with strands from my braid. Nothing makes me more uncomfortable than inaction, and I struggle to keep myself from tapping my expensive red boots in time with the *drip, drip, drip*. I reach for Gran's hand, and she rustles awake.

"Where are my things?" Gran croaks. She takes a swig from the bottle of sun tea Pa brought her from home. "Good gravy, I can't get anything with these cords in my arms. I asked your father to bring my box."

I scoop up her bag from beside the bed and pull out a small wooden chest. She motions for me to set it on her lap, which I do.

Gran scooches up her pillow, takes an antique key from her purse, and unlocks it. She fumbles through various trinkets, yellowed notes on stationery, and Polaroids. Finding her treasure, she pulls out a tiny brass compass.

"Give me your hand, grasshopper." She sets the quarter-sized compass in my sweaty palm. "Turn it over."

On the back, obscured by scratches and a dull patina, an inscription reads:

Our choices reveal our character.

I thumb the lettering. "Where is this from?"

"The better question to ask is *who* is this from." She smiles, and the greenish hue in her skin seems to disappear for a moment. "Long ago, your great-great-great-grandparents—including your great-great-great-grandma Cassidy Jo—journeyed from Georgia with nothing but a wagon and three baby dragons. By the time Cassidy Jo made it to Texas, typhoid fever had claimed everyone but her daughter and those three dragons. As the legend goes, she followed this compass, and it led her to Pecos. She found other dragon riders when she came to Texas, and made Pecos home to keep her dragons safe." Gran folds the compass in my hand and squeezes my fist tight. "That's your namesake."

The metal presses into my palm, and I whisper, "You've never told me that story."

"Well, there's a right time for every story." Gran sighs as if releasing a heavy burden. "I gave this to your mother when she entered the Great Texas Dragon Race. So now,

I'm giving it to you."

I rip a fraying thread from the hole in my jeans. "But I'm not—"

"You lie like a rug." She coughs so loud I think she might lose a lung. "Cassidy Jo wasn't born a pioneer, but she became one. She protected her family and her dragons. I've been around long enough to know what this hospital stay will cost us. And I'd rather die than see our ranch end up in the hands of the FireCorp. I know you will make the right choice." She rifles through her purse and pulls out a red ballpoint pen. "Do you have that application?"

I slip it out of my pocket and Gran signs her name on the dotted guardian signature line. I hug her tighter than I ever have, avoiding the bouquet of tubes jutting out of her skin.

As I cling to her, she whispers, "When you're out there, remember who you are. Use your compass, but when all else fails, follow your heart. It will guide you."

Compass in hand, I rise to my feet.

"I will," I say. "I promise."

I encourage Pa to drown himself in one too many fried chicken legs during our feast, and he passes out on the couch. Working quickly, I stuff a canvas knapsack and plait my hair into braids of controlled chaos. I select my "Sunday best" flat-brimmed cowboy hat from the shelf. It leaves a gaping space alongside gold-plated trophies and worn stacks of *Sharptooth Junior* magazines.

Pack strapped to my back, I stroke a fraying magazine cutout glued to the vision board on my bedroom wall. With the race hanging over me, it suddenly seems like such a childish thing to have made. I shut the door to my room and vow to toss it when I get back.

If I get back.

Let's hope that's the darkest thought I have today.

My fingers rest on the handle for a few seconds, and I memorize the smell of home-cooked meals baked into our wallpaper. I creep down the hall, avoiding two notoriously creaky floorboards so as not to wake Pa. The house is dark, with not even a glare from the living room television. Framed family photos clutter the walls. Half of them have been knocked to crooked angles that no one's bothered to fix. I straighten a picture of my mom, her bright red hair hanging around her like flames as she leans against her dragon, Sol. Beside it is another of Gran and me running through a sprinkler in the backyard. Taking a breath, I reach into my pocket and palm the compass.

When I ride, I ride for her.

Outside, a cloak of stars looms overhead, and cicadas sing in a buzzy choir. Ranga and I fly with purpose, and my heart pounds in time with the second hand. Six minutes— that's all we have left. Rising from the uninhabited desert behind us, the desert arena glows like a beacon.

"Faster, Ranga! Faster!" Her scales glitter in the dark. I sneak a glance at my watch: four minutes to nine p.m. "Yah! Yah!"

Racing is all about communication, and ours is strong as can be. We move hypnotically as one, united against ticking time as we barrel toward the stadium. Dragons who didn't make the cut fly past me, away from the arena. They snarl and snap at Ranga, who narrowly avoids them while their riders pretend I don't exist. The rumbling growls and chirps of dozens of other dragons grow louder the closer we get. Bolts of fire shoot into the sky in the field beyond where those who've been selected to compete await their instructions. My throat dries.

Three minutes.

The stadium high beams kiss Ranga's scales, igniting their iridescence. We dive into the center. As we peel onto the field, the arena lights power down.

Three, two, one.

My stomach drops as the dark night swallows us whole.

Only the judges' box and the tread lighting between bleachers remain lit.

"Wait!" I shout, yanking on the reins. "One more—I'm here!"

Ranga roars and sends up a puff of spark and smoke. It illuminates the field and the empty stadium seating.

"Off! Off!" shouts someone over a megaphone. "Tryouts are over—we have made our selections. Move off the lawn."

I slide down Ranga's back so fast that my ankles hurt when I hit the ground. After stumbling to my feet, I rush to the stage at the back of the amphitheater and approach the judges as the megaphone blares: "Go on—git! Come back next year!"

"Excuse me!" I shout, waving my worn application like a flag. Frantically, I jump up and down to get their attention.

The head judge stands up on his tiptoes and stretches over the table. "Miss, the announcer is correct. I'm sorry, but the deadline to apply for this year's race has passed. Move on." He doesn't even bother to wave me off. He goes back to talking among his peers and shuffling papers.

"Actually," I say, "there are still two minutes left until nine o'clock. Technically the application deadline doesn't end until then."

"Ma'am, other people came and waited in line all day. If you think you can just show up here and do whatever you like on your own time, then you're applying to the wrong race."

"But I have my application!" I say. I dash up the side stairs toward the stage and approach the desk. A second judge takes my papers and reads my name.

"Drake?" he asks, his eyebrows raised. "Of the West Texas Drakes?"

I stand up a little taller and smooth my braids. "Yessir," I say, my words slurring together.

"Hmmm . . ."

They chatter among themselves, which goes on for far too long.

I squirm. "My mother rode this race and won," I remind them. "I think I'd make a good candidate."

The head judge lowers his spectacles. His salt-and-pepper hair says he's old enough to remember when Aurora McCoy (later known as Aurora Drake after she married Pa) roared past the finish line and became the first woman to win the Great Texas Dragon Race.

He grumbles, "Still doesn't account for your tardiness. We've already selected our fifty contestants. I'm sorry, little lady—"

"Women these days don't like to be called 'little lady,'" I interrupt. With a deep breath, I adjust my attitude. "Sir."

He noisily taps his papers into a neat stack.

A third judge leans over and nudges him. "People love a legacy story. The daughter of Aurora McCoy Drake will inspire juicy headlines—especially if we add an extra rider this year. Could mean more online viewers and higher ticket sales for the final event."

I want to argue, because good stories don't make for great races—that's what skill is for. But I hold my tongue and clasp my hands behind my back.

"Not a good enough reason. And not with a dragon that size."

No one talks about Ranga that way and gets away with it. I grunt and swing up onto her saddle.

We lift up, peeling across the arena as Ranga's stealthy wings whip the air faster than lightning. Gaining momentum, I guide her to the stands. Gasps rise as we barrel toward the judges, and the terror in their awed faces spurs me on. I pull up just as we get close, so close that Ranga's underside kisses the seats. The judges stare at us, bug-eyed, as we display our agility—something I'm sure no other rider would dare do with their lumbering lugs of meat and scales. As we move, I know a small pistol of a dragon like Ranga is a great advantage—no matter how much the judges may mock us: we are PR gold. Everyone loves an underdog.

It's not until I land in front of the judges' table that I realize how tight I've been holding the reins. In fact, my knuckles are white. I slide off Ranga's back. Wisps of hair that have fallen from my braids hang around my face.

The head judge reassembles the stack of papers that Ranga's wings whipped over the platform and sets my application on top. He reviews my paperwork, weighing over the input of his fellows.

Hands trembling, he flips through the pages. "Hmmm . . . consistent qualifying times. And it wouldn't be unprecedented to accept more than fifty riders." He consults my scribble. "Says here you turned thirteen a few weeks ago. And you won the Junior Trans-Pecos Marathon this year. Is that true?"

I open my mouth, but another judge answers first. "Sure is. And that hotshot dragon is a guaranteed crowd-pleaser, even if she is a skittish little thing."

"She's got a heart of fire," I snap, words drenched in vinegar. Remembering that flies—especially flies swarming news headlines—love honey, I smile and offer a weak half curtsy. "Sir."

The head judge continues his mental checklist. "No history of cheating or dragon steroids, I take it?"

"No, sir."

He confers once more with his peers, then clears his throat. "Your qualifying scores are good enough, and I like the idea of mixing it up. Welcome to the Great Texas Dragon Race."

I jump onto the ledge and vigorously shake each judge's hand. "You won't regret this."

"Head back that way, and you'll find the coordinators. They'll hitch your dragon for the night."

Proud but nervous that I'm jumping into the race without one word to Pa, I dash for the check-in area, Ranga in tow. Someone catches me by the arm. "Does your father know that you're joining this race?"

I whip around to find a tall beanpole of a man. A blue baseball cap obscures his brow, and the camera looped over his neck reflects the faint light beyond the stadium.

"I come from a long line of dragon riders."

"That was not what I asked."

I cross my arms and lean back on Ranga. "I don't think that's any of your business."

He strokes the full, well-kept beard on his prominent chin.

"Hmmm . . ." The man circles Ranga and runs a hand along her side. Her opalescent scales ripple gray at the touch of his strange hand. I wish she'd growl to push him off, but her years with FireCorp destroyed her trust in strangers, so she cowers. Encouraging her will be one of my greatest challenges in this race. She cranes her neck all the way around, muscles twitching as he circles her. He grabs her head and inspects it like she's a dog in a pedigree show, but she's too scared to bite. She huffs at him, and he fearlessly widens her lips to inspect her teeth. "She's rather small. Maybe the size of two elephants."

"Now wait a min—"

"I didn't say that was a bad thing. But entering with such a small dragon . . . You must have a story to tell. Care to grant me an exclusive interview? If you come out on top, I can guarantee viewers."

His fingers click across his phone at warp speed as he chomps on bubble gum. The screen glows onto his horse-like face, highlighting his thick brows and crooked nose.

"You!" I snap. "You're Thomas Karbach, right? You're the journalist who broke the story about our gyffilon destroying that burger joint."

This time, Ranga growls. She scrapes her claws in the dirt and raises her head over me in a protective stance.

He shrugs his lean, square shoulders. "It wasn't exactly a secret."

"That dragon was just hungry—and if those customers hadn't started shooting at him, he wouldn't have had to defend himself." I feel flecks of spit fly from my mouth. "Do you know how much hate mail we got after that piece was published? Our donors practically abandoned us after that." I wag a finger into his long face. "If I were you, I'd stay far away from me."

He presses on, unfazed. "I hear FireCorp wants to buy Drake's Dragon Ranch. What if I could offer you an opportunity to spin the press in your favor? Exclusive interviews, broadcast contracts. You'll make a great story."

Press against the FC is exactly what I want, but not from this vulture. I pull Ranga close. Even as a small dragon, she outweighs this lanky buzzard by tons. "Never in a million years."

Karbach types a note on his phone without breaking eye contact. "We'll see how you feel in a couple of days, especially once you realize that most big-network journalists don't care for unsponsored, dark-horse riders from Nowheresville, Texas." He slides the phone into his pocket. "Better get a move on, or the coordinators will assume you've chickened out."

Ranga's spines ripple along her tail and I push off her. Karbach's wiry arms are nearly the length of my legs, and he dwarfs me in everything but attitude.

"I won't chicken out," I say. "So, feel free to sit back while I claim my prize."

He blows a pink bubble. "You're certainly sure of yourself, aren't you?"

Before I can answer, Thomas Karbach slinks off into the night.

CHAPTER

31°31'02.4" N, 103°51'30.6" W
Schmidt Ranch, Reeves County, Texas

Ranga remains on edge as we pass through the arena's back doors. There, we find a rowdy collection of dragons snapping and growling in an adjacent field. Heat rises into the air in thick waves, a telltale sign of anxious dragons. Dozens of floodlights make my fellow competitors' massive wyverns, rockballs, and windblasts even more terrifying. I sing softly to Ranga as I sit atop her, but she flinches at every sound. I wonder if we should turn around and head home, back to our fate.

"Competitors only!" shouts a coordinator in a fresh "VOLUNTEER" baseball hat. "Rejects round the other side!"

"I *am* a competitor," I reply, standing up in the stirrups.

I slide off of Ranga, heave my duffel bag off her back, and flick an auburn braid over my shoulder. "Cassidy Drake, reporting." I stretch out a hand in greeting, but he ignores it. Instead, he rifles through his clipboard, then speaks into his headset. "I've got a Miss Cassidy Drake here—says she's been accepted—but I already have fifty riders who've checked in." His face twists at the response. "Got it."

"Sorry 'bout that, miss." He scratches his head with his pen. "We've rarely had more than fifty riders. And your dragon here is—er—a bit smaller than most."

Ranga spreads her wings as if to demonstrate her size, and I cross my arms. "Well, you know what—"

"No offense, of course." He scribbles something on his clipboard. "But I'd be careful if I were you—all eyes will be on you. Leave your dragon with me, then head on back for opening remarks and a room key for the night." He points into the chaos.

Ranga chitters, questioning, and I stroke her head.

"Are you sure you want to do this?" I ask.

She kicks in the dirt with her front legs.

"Okay, because once we're in, we're in."

She cackles to the sky, and I beam back. "Then let's show these knuckleheads how it's done. Go with this nice man. I'll see you tomorrow—I promise."

Her eyes flash black, but she soothes herself. Even though she loves to race, maybe more than any dragon I've ever met, a pang of guilt shoots through me as I leave her with a strange dragon handler.

Sucking in a breath, I weave through clusters of riders who exchange hugs and handshakes. Behind the polite smiles rests an uneasy tension and the whiff of death. Since young riders usually can't get parental approval to compete, and many racers turn pro by their mid-twenties, most riders are of high school and college age. Nearly everyone is older and taller than me. As visitors from across the United States greet one another with open arms, I suddenly feel like a very young foreigner in my own backyard. I imagine how much easier this would be with Gran by my side, cheering me on with pecan sandies and wisdom about facing your fears.

"Excuse me," I ask, tapping my finger on a boy's shoulder. "Can you tell me where to go for opening remarks?"

He spins around, controlled and smooth, and I'm grateful that he looks to be around my age.

I smile wide and adjust the duffel bag on my shoulder. "Howdy—could you tell me where I'm headed?"

He slings a black leather jacket over his shoulder and

dangles it behind him. "In this race, most people won't waste time answering questions for their competition." His words are iron wrapped in velvet.

My cheeks burn, and I drive my fingernails into my bag's worn leather strap. "Well, thank you so much for your help." I study him from head to toe—this time with pure contempt. He's clad in English-style riding clothes that reminds me of fancy horse races and old-money polo players. Clean FireCorp patches and winner's pins decorate his black jacket. "And welcome to Texas."

I take off before he can reply. That's the last time I ask anyone for help.

I meander through the crowd of riders and avoid the sheriffs hired to sniff out race violations. Even though I'm not breaking any rules, the sheriffs—our form of security during race checkpoints—seem menacing. A woman with warm brown skin keeps a vigilant watch, and I can tell, just from a look, that she takes guff from no one.

Hopefully, that extends to FireCorp.

Most competitors are costumed in high-end rodeo gear. As we say in Texas, some are "all hat and no cowboy." I wipe my dusty hands on my tattered jeans and smile, grateful for who Gran and Pa raised me to be. Many other young riders' parents will push them into top-tier dragoneering prep schools. But I couldn't care a stitch about some fancy academy. All I want is to win—to stand in the winner's circle, lift my voice in the fight for dragon conservation, and denounce companies like FireCorp for their crimes against dragons everywhere.

Avoiding contact with anyone else, I find the check-in area, a ramshackle platform draped in bunting, and wait as the rest of the competitors assemble around me.

"Good evening, riders!" shouts the presenter through a megaphone. He tips his giant cowboy hat in greeting. "On behalf of the Dragon Wrangling Association of West Texas, I'd like to give you folks a warm Texas welcome!"

Around me, the crowd of contestants goes wild. I edge forward, my palms growing clammy.

"It's an honor to host the hundredth annual Great Texas Dragon Race here in Pecos, and we couldn't be more proud. This year, we have riders from all over the nation—California!"

A group of Californians cheers and waves a white state flag.

"New Mexico!"

More cheers.

"Nevada, Montana, and Idaho!"

Cheers.

He lists a dozen other states. "And our very own Texas legends from across the Lone Star State!"

I erupt with a cheer so loud I can barely hear the others.

"We'd like to thank our silver sponsors, Titan Tack and Buckle and Grousewood Flight Gear, as well as our gold-level sponsors at FireCorp, for making this event possible."

I grit my teeth as dozens of people cheer. They're probably associates of the very corporations I'm here standing against. Not that I hate Titan Tack or Buckle & Grousewood. They treat their dragons well and are more like Olympic sponsors: in it to sell fancy saddles and leather gear more than anything else. FireCorp is in its own league of awful.

Behind me, the rude boy and his loser friends in their stupid jackets holler loudest of all. I hope they're sweating bullets in the summer heat.

"I'm also pleased to announce that, this year, we've expanded our race to include fifty-one riders. Accordingly, we're joined by a legacy from right here in Pecos: thirteen-year-old Cassidy Drake."

Icy chills spread down my body as riders scan the crowd. With my auburn hair and smattering of freckles, I suspect I'm the spitting image of my mother and that they know *exactly* who I am. Which means I've just become target number one. I shrink into my boots.

"Now," says the announcer, his voice calm and severe, "this might be a time for celebration and excitement, but I'm here to remind y'all of the sheer dangers of this competition. This adventure race tests the survival of the fittest. All you have is what is on your back, including but not limited to race-approved tech, maps, field guides, and rations. But the more you carry, the slower you'll be, so rely on your knowledge of Texas terrain and native plants, if you can.

"No communication devices or Web access allowed during the legs. A monitored phone line will be available to you at checkpoints. You've each been issued tracking devices. Use of performance-enhancing drugs is strictly prohibited. Unpredictable ranching tasks are located on every leg and are designed to test your dragoneering knowledge. Every rider who makes it to the last leg may invite their friends and family to join them for the grand finale celebration feast."

If I can make it to the final leg, I guess I'll be celebrating alone. No way Pa will ever forgive me.

The announcer whistles, which pierces through the megaphone.

Dozens of dragons descend from the sky and land in the open field beyond us. They're mounted by aggressive riders clad in tough leathers and full-rimmed goggles. The sounds of flapping wings and claws scrape along the ground and fill the cavernous space. A mess of spines and muscle, the dragons peck and roar at one another. The scariest half-time show in history. Smoke puffs out from nostrils as the riders pull back their mounts to hold off a fiery massacre.

My lungs fill with hot, dry air.

There, riding a colossal onyx dragon, is the slimy FireCorp CEO from my shop: Michael Carne.

The announcer motions to the snarling horde. "This here is your council, the legal board that oversees all matters in this race. They'll be monitoring your progress and joining us at all rest points. Some are affiliated with our generous sponsors. Others are the esteemed owners of world-class dragon ranches. Either way, each member has a personal history with this race. You'll even see some winners among them. That means we trust their judgment."

Michael Carne, who won the year after my mother, beams atop his windstrike wyvern.

Ugh. As if FireCorp deserves any more advantages.

Hopefully the other sponsors and ranch owners can over-rule him if he tries any funny business.

"So," the announcer continues, "you take an early start, they weigh in. You use undocumented or illegal tack, they weigh in. In short, we don't take nothing lightly out here in West Texas, and this group is here to be sure you don't either. Fair enough?"

The crowd is silent.

"Do I need to repeat myself? I said, 'Fair enough?!'"

This time we all shout back, "Yes!"

"Thank you!" He runs a finger along the brim of his hat. "Here in Pecos, we have a saying, 'Confidence is the feelin' you have before you understand the situation.' Many of you might be feeling pretty confident right now, but before you enter, remember: not everyone survives." The announcer clears his throat. "If you walk away, right now, we will consider you courageous for knowing yourself. But the moment you pass the gates, you're a rider. This is your last chance to leave."

Only a whistling wind fills the stadium. Pressing my shoulders back, I stiffen my resolve. I won't go down with-out a fight—not when I know that this may be the best way for me to gain a platform to promote dragon conserva-tion *and* expose FireCorp.

And to save my dragons.

The council's dragons huff as if threatening us to leave. Nobody moves.

"Good," the announcer calls.

CHAPTER

31°31'02.4" N, 103°51'30.6" W
Schmidt Ranch, Reeves County, Texas

As we all head for the pre-race search, I hear the other riders size me up and discuss my presence with their friends.

"Is *that* the legacy rider?"

"She's practically a baby."

"We can take her," they whisper.

"Cell phones, laptops, portable televisions, gaming systems—prepare to check them with an attendant!" shouts a coordinator, who also takes digital scans of our palm prints. "No communication devices! This isn't a new school race!"

Attendants pat me down and search my bags for anything that could be used to communicate with outsiders or other riders during the race. I pull my phone from my pocket. On the screen, I see a dozen notifications that say *missed call, missed call, missed call* . . . Each is from Pa. By this time, he's probably spoken with his contacts at the race and knows I'm here. I click off the phone and give it to the coordinator. I can't afford to question my decision. Aurora Drake wouldn't back out, and neither will I.

Beyond the stadium, a ring of mobile homes is arranged behind a chain-link fence that springs from the desert floor. The hot stare of my fellow riders burns into me as I pick up my room key. It's rusted and from the end dangles an unwieldy motel tag that says, *Everything's Bigger in Texas*, in retro script.

Once in my dorm, I heave my bag onto the foot of my twin mattress. Its old springs squeal. I fiddle with a hangnail and plop down on the squeaky bed to wait for my roommate. Will she be twice my age with eyes of steel . . . or worse, a sponsored rider, courtesy of FireCorp?

Cracks in the paint spread like spider's webs across the ceiling. It's a stark contrast to the vision of the Great Texas Dragon Race I've always had in my head. I'd always imagined a glamorous celebrity-filled event, with great dragon racers like Helga Olesen and Zeke Zeparterra watching us from the sidelines. But now, staring up at the decrepit old ceiling of this ramshackle mobile home, I realize there's far more decay than glamour.

A strand of hair sticks to my lip balm, and with an audible sigh, I wipe it away.

"Please don't tell me you snore," says a voice at the door.

I shoot upright as a dragon rider with long dark curls slams her things down on the twin bed next to me. She's decked in fashionable purple-fringed ankle boots and an El Paso Junior High School Debate Team T-shirt. No sign of FireCorp patches or gear.

"And what if I do?" I ask.

"If you do, I'll have my dragon roast you in your sleep." The girl smiles, perfectly white teeth gleaming back at me. It seems sincere. Friendly. "I'm Laura Torres. Nice to meet you." She extends a hand.

I reach forward and we shake. "Firm grip—I like that in the competition," I say. "Lets me know my victory will be hard-earned."

"You're the legacy, right? Cassidy Drake . . ." She taps a finger on her lip and looks to the shoddy ceiling as if trying to recall my stats. "From Drake's Dragon Ranch?"

I sit up a little straighter and beam back at her. "That's the one!"

"We own the herpetology store out in El Paso. And, I think you and I went to Big Bend's Dragon Camp for Girls, like, hmm . . . three years ago."

"Oh, that's right. Excellent memory!"

"We also bought a dragon from your dad."

I snap my fingers. "Oh, yeah! You adopted the quetzal-coatl, right?"

"That's the one—my pride and joy." Laura's eyes are bright and mischievous. "Best dragon out here."

"In your dreams," I counter. I sit cross-legged on my bed and start pulling out the other items from my pack. "But at least you're not one of the FireCorp bandits. Would've made this whole roommate situation very uncomfortable."

"No kidding," she says. "I can't believe Carne got a seat on the council—even with his racing record. A Grouse-wood employee is one thing, but Carne can't be trusted."

I nod enthusiastically. "Right?"

"The FC riders are totally obnoxious." Laura dumps out her pack, which is loaded with a mix of colorful clothing and sleek survival gear. "Just wait until you meet Valeen. Eyes like emeralds, a heart like coal."

"I'll be sure to avoid her, just like the rest of them." I jump out of bed and scoop up her high-tech goggles. Holding them to my face, I peer through the lenses and twist around the room. "Where did you get these beauties?"

"Northwestern Prep sent me those. They've been trying to recruit me for the eighth-grade racing team. My parents are pretty much sold on the idea, but I have my heart set on Drac Secondary."

I frown at my hastily stuffed pack and goggles with their broken magnification knob. "These make my goggles look weak." I gently set them back on her bed, then grin with a wicked smile. "But you'll need more than fancy goggles to win this race."

"Yeah, good thing I'm the best rider out here."

We gibe each other back and forth for a few minutes until she pulls out a tall votive candle plastered with a Catholic saint and sets it on the table.

Laura notices me eyeing the candle, and with a half smile, she faces the picture of the saint forward, exposing his illustration in full glory. The man pictured has a white cloak and a sharp goatee. "Saint George. He's supposed to be the patron saint of dragons." She pouts her lips, which are covered in a fantastic coral-colored lacquer. "I'm not much for this stuff, especially since it's 15.8 more ounces to carry, but I told my tía I'd bring it."

"No judgment." I hold up the James Avery cross dangling from my neck and swing it in the air. "Half the girls at Crockett Junior High have at least one piece of jewelry with a cross on it. This is from my mom." I pause. "We never really went to church, but it reminds me of her." I frown and stuff the necklace back in my calico shirt.

Laura wavers and slumps down onto the bed next to me. "Aurora McCoy Drake was legendary, even in my stretch of town. If it wasn't for her, you and I might not even be here competing for the title of First Rider."

I force a weak smile and continue to unpack. Silence stretches out until she breaks it.

"You know what?" Laura tosses down a pile of clothing. "I say we get out of here. Creep around the other double-wides, see where the FC is posted up. The sheriffs won't start cracking down on getting us to sleep until at least midnight."

My watch reads 10:47 p.m., and I consider my options: get some sleep and face my peers once the race begins, or break the ice. I didn't come here to make friends, but like it or not, the other competitors will be my campmates for the next week. And since the announcer has already branded me as the legacy, it'll be worse if I hole up alone. I remind myself that dragon riders are—or should be—my kind of people.

"Deal," I say.

CHAPTER

Wyverns howl in the distance as we exit to the courtyard, where a cluster of riders joke back and forth across a fire. To my relief, none of the FireCorp members have graced us with their blue-blooded presence. Sheriffs make the rounds, keeping an eye on us from a distance. A campfire zmey—an amber-colored, cat-sized dragon—sits beside the ring of stones, periodically spitting flames onto the wood. After the fire grows, a freckle-faced boy strokes the zmey and it settles into the dirt.

Across from him, a girl with pastel-dyed locks splays her hand out on a log. A younger version of her, dressed in a black T-shirt with glittery lettering that literally spells "TROUBLE," stabs a sleek blue knife between her counterpart's fingers in a rhythmic test of coordination. Normal kids may not be allowed to play with knives, but I guess anything goes when you're a dragon rider. Both laugh hysterically.

The older one elbows her knife-wielding friend. "Oh look, Viv, it's number fifty-one, the legacy entry."

Viv flips her knife closed and tosses it in the air. Her companion catches it and slips it into a tool belt of hand-painted pastel tools: a ball-peen hammer, a screwdriver, a flashlight.

"Can't wait to see if you're worthy of being a 'special case,'" says Viv.

The rest of the group faces me with curious expressions. Will I crack? How big a sport am I?

I hold my head high. "It'll take more than a few snide remarks to keep me out of this race."

"Challenge accepted," they say in unison.

"Ignore the Bhatti sisters. Rose and Viv are equal opportunity pranksters, so don't take it personally," whispers Laura. She leads me to a spot by the fire. "Guys, this is Cassidy. My new roommate, and probably the second-best rider here." She winks, accentuating her flares of eyeliner.

"Second best?" I ask, plopping down next to her on the log. "You wish."

My comment draws a few chuckles. Confidence rising, I snatch a marshmallow from the bag of Jet-Puffed Jumbos perched beside me.

"You gringas always think you do everything better." She snorts and hands me a coat hanger that's bent into a wonky metal stick. "My family has been here since the first Spanish mission settled in West Texas. And we have roots as far back as the Aztecs, who were, as you well know, the best dragon riders of all time."

The crowd gets noisy as we debate who the best dragon riders in history were.

"Are you Texas girls always so full of yourselves?" someone leans in and asks.

On the neighboring log, a high school–aged rider pushes a fresh white cowboy hat off his brow and winks at me. His eyes are blue as the sky, and they have a sparkling warmth that draws you in. Dimples form deep hollows in his cheeks. I smile back a little too widely.

"It's not arrogance if it's true," I retort, jamming the marshmallow on a coat hanger. "Though, from what I've learned about Laura today, she loves to vastly distort her greatness."

"So, you're the thirteen-year-old legacy rider." The boy offers up a hand glittering with heavy rings. "Colt Meyer, nice to meet you."

"Cassidy Drake." I shake his hand firmly.

"You'll have people after you the second we get out on the race." He says it with enough genuine midwestern heart that I know he's just teasing.

And because I'm not caught off guard, I have ammunition loaded for friendly fire. "It's tough to come from good stock with legendary ability."

He bursts with laughter, revealing pearly white teeth. I usually don't bother with making friends. What's the point of bonding with people who couldn't ride a royal amber-crest or a Harlem shellspine if their life depended on it?

But the Great Texas Dragon Race is not Crockett Junior High School. And most competitions I've been a part of are day trips at best, not weeklong death bowls jam-packed with other dragon fanatics. I lean into the conversation.

"Don't you worry," I say. "My mother may have been big on the circuit years ago, but my qualifying times are just as fast. Faster, in fact."

"Hmmm . . ." He scratches where a beard would be if he didn't have baby-soft skin.

The campfire-dragon-petting boy across the circle pipes up between a bite of his s'more. "Yeah, but your dragon may as well be a bunny rabbit." He snickers, and a couple of the others join in. "No offense, of course."

"I'll take small and fast over big and dumb any day of the week," I reply.

Again, the circle fills with laughter. Laura mingles, offering several riders warm greetings, and I'm a tad envious of their familiarity. I dip my marshmallow deep in the fire and let it burn. The edges turn black and I yank it out. Holding the coat hanger between my knees, I slap it onto a patty of graham cracker and chocolate.

I turn back to Colt. "Any chance you know the rest of these yahoos?"

"Yeah, I've ridden this circuit with most of them. That's Brayden Boone, from outside Las Vegas. The three blond ones dressed like they just rolled off tractors—Mikey, Gene, and Daniel—are sponsored by Buckle and Grousewood. They'll stick to themselves and are mostly harmless." He points at each one as he goes, then lowers his voice. "Annnddd . . . I can't really remember his name. Rion, I think?"

My head swims with names. "Got it. Your family owns Meyer Ranch in Montana, right?"

"Poison, Montana, to be specific."

"Poison, Montana? Sounds creepy."

"That's putting it lightly. Poison is a tiny town outside

of, well, nowhere. And technically, the locals call it Old Polson, not Poison." He pulls a marshmallow from the fire and smashes it into a graham sandwich double stuffed with chocolate. "But a small town like Old Polson is poison for gay cowboys like me. That's all I know."

I won't say I've met many out kids at my tiny, conservative West Texas middle school, and Colt's honesty makes me like him even more. I lift my s'more into the air, and we knock our melted treats against one another in a toast to mutual respect.

As we bite into our chocolaty grahams, our enemies worm their way into the courtyard. The energy in the circle shifts, and each of us goes on the defense. Even Laura's cordial cheeriness wanes. There are at least nine sponsored riders of various ages in the horde, and they're each dressed in FireCorp-branded tracksuits.

This must be the lamest group of gangsters this side of the Mississippi.

The zmey pushes itself farther into the dirt. I wring my marshmallow poker in my fist as they crowd our party, the arrogant boy who snubbed me leading the pack.

"Is that velour?" I ask, sticking my legs out so they can't cross any farther into our territory. The toes of my cowboy boots point up to the night sky. "Must've cost a fortune."

The Bhatti sisters giggle while fiddling with switchblades, which makes me sit a bit taller.

My now sworn enemy with dark hair approaches the fire and crosses his arms. "We came to introduce ourselves. Formally."

"No need. I think we know enough about you and your band of thugs." Battle lines drawn, I chomp on my s'more and stare him down.

An unidentified FC rider inches forward, and the dark-haired boy motions a signal of restraint like a crime boss holding back a drunken henchman. His defined upper lip curls. "You may not have noticed, but we're stuck with one another for the next week, like it or not."

Across the circle, the slim chestnut-haired boy named Brayden, who's been silently brooding during the entire exchange, pipes up. "Let me speak for everyone here when I say that would be an affirmative *not*."

The tallest, oldest rider in their pack steps up, lumbering right over my legs. I recognize him as the gum-wrapper-slinging outlaw from the shiny black SUV parked outside my house. Michael Carne's ride-along minion. His cool, nearly white hair is pulled into a tight bun at the back of his head. He snaps up a raw marshmallow and stuffs it into his mouth like a heathen who has no idea that he's sinning against taste. I decide I like him least of all.

I rise to my feet, the coat hanger a sword at my side. "To some of us, winning means more than another trophy for a suburban mantel. By the time you cross the finish line, I'll already be packed and on my way back home with a fat check and a smile as big as the sun."

Colt snickers.

I wring my coat hanger, imagining it's the dark-haired FireCorp boy's neck. "So why don't you all go back to bed. We'll see you at the finish line."

"I suggest you put away your 'better than' attitude and remember that these people may be your friends right now, but in the end, we're all enemies." His words cut through me like a blade of ice. Across the pit, my fellow independent riders squirm in their seats . . . because he's right. Unsponsored riders may be friendlier than FireCorp goons, but either way, we're all on opposing sides.

The FC boy nods to his gargantuan marshmallow-stealing lackey, who takes one last Jet-Puffed Jumbo. Mr. Marshmallow squeezes it in his fingers and sneers at the Bhatti sisters.

"Nice hair," he snickers. He flicks the marshmallow into the fire and turns on his heel.

The rest of the group follows, leaving the dark-haired

FireCorp boy, who casually slips his hands into the pockets of his velour tracksuit.

"By the way, Cassidy Drake," he says, "my name is Ash Hook, and I live on one hundred thousand acres in Connecticut. So the next time you want to take shots like I haven't spent my life on a dragon ranch just like you, do your homework first."

He rejoins his velour-draped companions. In the fire, the marshmallow sizzles and pops.

Once I'm sure they're gone, I set my coat hanger sword by the log and break the silence. "Jerks."

A few others mumble in agreement.

"Ash is right, though," says one of the riders.

I raise an eyebrow as he stands up. His combat boots are shined to a high gloss, and his posture screams "army." The firelight kisses his rich dark skin.

He offers a salute. "Rion Carter. Hollowton Preparatory School, Virginia."

Hollowton Prep is a boarding school for hardworking military families with dragon ties. At least it's better than Dragonscale, a private academy stuffed with FC riders. I manage not to roll my eyes.

"And before you ask," continues Rion, "no, I'm not a sponsored rider, and I have no allegiances."

He straightens his dress blues, then clasps his hands behind his back.

"Let me give you a quick rundown of the problems as I see them," he says. "*That* is a team of the meanest, most soulless riders this race has ever seen. I know because I've watched them all. Studied them like a football player studies game tape." He points at a rider across the circle. "You: Your dragon can't get over forty-two hundred feet without spinning out." He points at another. "You: Your dragon has a lazy eye that obstructs her vision." He finally points to me while gazing out at the crowd. "And her dragon is petite, to put it nicely, which won't help when it comes to brawls."

I pound my fist on the log. "If you have something to say, say it to me, not your audience."

"Okay, I'll say it. Your dragon is a liability. Small, scared, fast as a cartoon roadrunner but incapable of battling another dragon if it comes down to it."

I swallow hard, because in my bones I know he's right. But I'll be hog-tied if he sees any part of it. "You don't know what Ranga is capable of."

"So, what's your point?" asks Colt, who tugs me back before I can leap off the log and fight this guy. Even if he is years older than me.

Rion presses his shoulders back, and the metallic pins on his lapel flash in the firelight. "My point is that we have a lot of flaws, but together we could be a real force against the FireCorp riders, who are certain to work together."

Laura leans in as if ready to hear him out.

But Brayden grunts, drawing everyone's attention. "So, you want to team up?"

"And let me guess," I say. "You'd be the team captain?"

"I am skilled with tactical military training and war plans, and I am top of my class in Aerial Brigade, specializing in combat maneuvering and cavalry command. I've studied this race—and its rules—up and down. I know how to run an alliance while staying within the guidelines." He stands up straighter. "So yes, I believe I would be an effective leader."

Now, everyone except Laura erupts in laughter.

"This is a solo competition," I say. "And we're solo riders—we don't do teams."

"Fine," says Rion, taking a seat back on his log. His statuesque features reveal nothing, but his tone says it all. "Have it your way."

CHAPTER 9

A West Texas twang of guitar, harmonica, and drums swirls through the arena. My heart pounds as the crowd of visitors who've come to watch the opening ceremony cheer. They're joined by draggers: dragon-obsessed journalists who will report on the race as we ride. Excitement fills the air, and our dragons respond to it with rippling muscles and flapping wings.

I grin so wide that my cheeks feel like rubber bands ready to pop and fly off into the stands. With trembling hands, I pet Ranga's dull gray scales as Laura steps up beside me.

"Ready or not . . . ," she says.

"Here we come," I reply. Like we're two old friends about to take on the world.

But I have to prove myself to her as much as anyone. I don't want to be seen as a legacy admission.

The coordinators round us up and attach tiny livestream cameras to each dragon's bridle. They also give us an emergency beeper, which will send us notes about dangerous weather conditions.

The rider from Hollowton Prep who suggested we team up, Rion, is dressed in cavalry attire. His dragon—a sharp-mouth named Jet—is white as a cue ball, which perfectly offsets his rider's military blues. I smile at him, but his response is icy. Maybe I was too heavy-handed in shooting down his idea of teaming up. Just what I need—another enemy.

Not far behind him, a FireCorp rider with alabaster skin sits atop a draconian hybrid. The hybrid is a gorgeous creature with spiky onyx scales, and two enormous burgundy horns jut out from its head. The rider's FC gear reads "Grimsbane," and her oversize dragon flirts with the draggers. So, this must be the Valeen that Laura was talking about.

The crowd loves her.

Ahead, the smooth-as-butter FC rider named Ash Hook grins back at me and waves. He's saddled up on his titanic windstrike wyvern, which is a rich bundle of muscles and glossy black scales. Every move the boy makes reeks of confidence, as if he's never felt a moment of discomfort. He's probably never eaten a TV dinner or had his power shut off because his family couldn't pay the bills.

I whip back around and ignore him.

As I look out onto the dusty tracks, our dragons lined up and ready to take off, my breath catches.

My eyes drift down the hodgepodge of competitors as they fiddle with their tack and double-check their gear. The other dragons—especially the FC dragons—tower over Ranga. All of the other riders look older than me by years, and now it's not just Ranga who feels small. Every sponsored FireCorp rider bears the same setup: new saddles, fresh tack, high-tech gear. Yet another sign that they've invested thousands to demonstrate their might. On the left, Valeen snickers as her dragon peers down at mine. She lets it breathe hot on Ranga's back, and my nostrils flare at the threat.

I lean into Ranga, who crouches down. "We don't need size," I whisper as I stroke her scales. "We only need speed and our wits."

I soothe Ranga by humming a Dolly Parton tune and toss her a piece of beef jerky from my pack. There won't be much of it left to spare. She laps it up. As I scoot down to adjust the saddle tight around her, Ash saunters to the line, his slick black boots kicking up dust. Little flecks of dirt fly up at me, and I pretend to ignore them.

His wyvern snorts and takes her space beside us, her tail slashing to the side and brushing Ranga's legs. Ranga growls and beats her wings—smaller than the wyvern's by half—which forces Ash to step back. I stroke her in a signal of approval.

Ash glares back at me and runs a hand down his tyrant of a dragon, black as oil and mean as a viper. Her spines glisten in the bright afternoon sun.

I kick my boots into the dirt and set my sights on the starting line. One chance. That's all we have to qualify for the second leg and prove our worth. Only forty riders will make the cut. I grit my teeth as sweat beads form on my upper lip.

I will win this race.

A bullhorn gurgles with the announcer's call. "All right, riders, listen up!" He paces across a raised stage and adjusts his turquoise bolo. "There are four rest stops across the state, one at each checkpoint. Ten contestants will be eliminated at each checkpoint. But since we have fifty-one contestants this year, eleven will be eliminated in round one." He steps down from the stage, megaphone in hand, and makes his way to a black five-foot-wide disk with a big red power button.

"As you go along, you'll be searching for hologram platforms like these." He kicks the platform with a boot and it activates. Above the platform, a giant hologram crackles and comes into focus. It's a fifteen-foot-tall image of Marcello Russo, a world-renowned dracologist who famously died two years back while training an unruly acidsnout. "These hologram decks will deliver clues along the way. On my command, the air horn will sound, and the hologram will give the clue. Remember: To qualify for the next leg, you need to be one of the first forty riders to make it to the finish line."

Forty sounds like a big number, but it's the end of an epic journey for eleven people. And I cannot let it be the end of mine.

"Oh-kay then, mount yer dragons!" he yells.

I slip a red boot into the stirrup and sling around Ranga's body. She shivers, trigger-happy and ready to move. I crack my knuckles in my gloves and pull my bulky goggles over my eyes. The finicky magnification knob falls off in my hand and I snap it back in place.

On my left, someone whistles.

"Hey, Drake!"

I glance at Ash but immediately wish I hadn't.

Obnoxious riding crop in hand, he winks at me and sinks into his saddle. "See ya at the finish line."

I pull my handkerchief up over my relaxed smile and mutter, "Not if I see you first."

"Take yer marks!" yells the crackly voice in the megaphone.

I breathe in and out, reins trembling in my hands.

"Get set!"

I grit my teeth, waiting for the hologram platform to reveal its secrets . . .

"Go!"

An air horn blares and the hologram powers to life. The supersized image of Marcello Russo stands before us and speaks as if alive:

> *The cactus capital you must pass,*
> *for fifteen miles you'll ride.*
> *Head on north, round up your class,*
> *the sun's not on your side.*

Laura is first to shoot into the sky. I steady my focus.

> *The cactus capital you must pass,*
> *For fifteen miles you'll ride . . .*

I know this! Leather squeaks as I wrap my reins around my hands. FireCorp may spend months studying maps, but Texas is in my blood, and I know this state better than most.

"Yah! Yah!" I shout, urging Ranga into action.

She speeds past the line, quicker than FireCorp's slow lugs of meat. Beyond us, I see only open space. Wind lashes past me in a flurry of dust. I press my heels into Ranga, her mighty enthusiasm pulling us past the stands of cheering spectators. In no time, we pass Laura and her glorious quetzalcoatl.

All those Texas history lessons and rambling tales from Gran have been worth it. Now, I have one goal: ride to the first route marker north of Sanderson before the rest of the riders can. I crouch low to Ranga's body and kick into her sides. Somehow, I know she's smiling.

CHAPTER 10

The plains are vast and desolate, marked by spare cacti and green ocotillo plants that shoot up from the ground like witches' fingers. From Schmidt Ranch to Sanderson, roughly one hundred miles away, I see only lonely farms and swaths of ranchland. I settle into the familiar sights and sounds of the plain. The creosote bushes flick in the wind and the blinding sun hangs overhead.

The camera attached to Ranga's harness jiggles as it streams to spectators tracking our progress. After a few hours' ride, we jet over Big Sky Ranch in Sanderson. Crop circle patterns tattoo the dusty ground—telltale rock-dragon marks. I twist the magnification knob on my goggles. The hologram station comes into focus, and I see large pens filled with moving shapes. Belit dragons drag their fat tails, scraping geometric patterns in the ground. I gulp and grip the reins tighter.

"Yah! Yah!" Ranga picks up speed, her body taut as we pull up to the hologram platform.

I slide off Ranga and kick a large red button on the platform. The image of Marcy Townsend, the only person to win the Great Texas Dragon Race twice, sparks to life. She died in a belit stampede in Wyoming just four years ago. With a husky alto voice, her holographic image sings:

> *West Chihuahua, mountain mama,*
> *Take me home, country roads*

The melody hits me as I recall Gran blaring John Denver on an old 45 rpm record in her study. I scramble onto Ranga, no competitors in sight, and make a loop. There are fifty marked pens of belits, which means that if I weren't the fly in the ointment, there would be one for each competitor. This leg's instructions become clear: herd one pack of belits and take them to pasture in west Chihuahua. Simple. Except for the fact that the Chihuahuan Desert spans much of West Texas, reaches all the way up to New Mexico, and has several mountains that might be a good home for belit dragons. Oh, and belits are unruly herds. At best.

Not so simple.

I reach for my canteen and take a long drink of water. In dozens of separated pens, clusters of fourteen buffalo-sized belit dragons with tracking collars graze on loose rocks strewn across the ground. They crunch stones in their flat, bony teeth, extracting water and minerals from the hardened clay and feasting on lichens. A far cry from most dragons. They seem peaceful, almost docile, like herbivores in a family-friendly nature documentary.

That is, until you test them.

I clip the canteen on my saddlebag, dismount Ranga, and unlatch the nearest pen. The belits pay no mind.

Light-footed, I run along the outskirts of the fence until I am opposite the open gate and crouch down. From my fanny pack, I pull a whistle. I take a deep breath and let it blast.

Fweeeeeeet!

In every pen, the belits stir into a frenzy. They gallop and kick, spooked by the noise. I run full force as I blast the whistle, shepherding the belits as they peel out of the enclosure. In a mob of talons and teeth, the belits scatter across the plain. Their small wings lift them only for short distances at a time, and their heavy tails scrape the ground as they move.

I jump onto Ranga's back, and we launch into the air. Ranga knows this game, and she soars in a wide circle around our belits, pushing them in toward the center like a herd of scared sheep.

Just as we pull them into a tight ball, I glance over my shoulder. In the distance, a pack of massive black dragons, clad in FireCorp colors, soars through the air.

My heart drops.

Greeorrrwwww! Their unnatural roars echo off the dry earth like a gunshot.

My belits shudder.

"Hold them, Ranga!"

Rrrroarrrrrrgggg!

Ranga drops to the ground, cowering as the roars grow louder. Her scales dull, and the gray color change that spells F-E-A-R coats her vibrant spark. She must think the FC dragons are pursuing her.

"Ride, Ranga!"

She hesitates, eyes locked on the angry black dragons. Valeen's draconian hybrid puffs smoke as they approach.

Wwweeek, weeeeek, cry the belits.

My heart pounds faster as the wyverns chase us down.

Smoke fills my nostrils.

"Ranga, please!"

I kick into her until she launches—finally—into the blue sky. She transforms herself into a spinning cyclone around the belits. The herd assembles, held together by Ranga's authority. She ushers the belits as we escape the abandoned farmstead, leaving the others in our dust.

Like dark shadows, the FireCorp dragons and their belits haunt us as we barrel west for the tallest peak, El Capitan. I hope it's the site of the finish line. We race as best we can while keeping the belits in a steady group. Their tiny wings droop and my parched mouth screams, but we ride on.

Every so often, threatening growls pierce the air. Ranga picks up speed every time, pushing the belits faster than they've probably ever gone before. On the horizon, the sky bleeds burnt orange.

"Yah! Yah!"

As the sun sets, the belits begin to drag their tails as they trudge along the plain. No amount of urgency spurs them on. They're tired. We've pushed them hard, and it's starting to show.

Ranga flaps, her wings prickling, able to go only as fast

as they will let her.

El Capitan looms in the distance, becoming an ever more unreachable target as the belits wind down. FireCorp lags behind us, but Ash has pulled ahead of the pack.

"Come on, gang, almost there. Yah! Yah!"

When the sun dips below the mountain, the belits screech to a halt and settle on the ground, as if on automatic timers.

Panic floods my system. "What in God's name?"

Ranga lets out her most terrifying roar, but they don't budge.

I slide down Ranga's back and wipe sweat from my brow. In my loudest voice, I shout, "Yah! Yah!"

The belits ignore me and begin to snore.

Hands trembling, I rifle through my bag and bust out my whistle.

Fweet! Fweeeeeetttt!

But nothing. Lifting my goggles, I grit my teeth and glance over my shoulder. A few hundred yards away, a helmeted rider that I recognize as Ash Hook dismounts and unzips his leather jacket. His belits curl beside his wyvern, as immovable as mine. The rest of his FC troupe is nowhere to be found.

"Don't waste your breath!" he shouts. His voice echoes

across the plain, but my belit dragons scratch and roll around in the dirt, unfazed.

"Ignore him, Ranga." I flick her reins. On my command, Ranga roars at them to spur them on.

Nothing.

I brace myself as Ash, silent like a panther, walks my way, wyvern in tow. Ranga hides behind me, never taking her eyes off Ash's massive dragon. When he reaches our herd of sleepy belits, Ash pulls off his sleek black motorcycle helmet.

"Watch," he says, tucking the helmet under his arm. "Juliette!"

Ash snaps his fingers and his wyvern sits up, her long neck glowing with fire. With a blasting roar, Juliette pours a fiery breath over my belits. It pummels them, and the heat licks my face.

When the fire dies in a puff of smoke, crispy cacti and scorched limestone soil remain. But the belit dragons have barely registered the flame.

I wave smoke out of my face and scowl. Boys.

"If it were daylight, the belits would have scattered across the plain." Ash leans against Juliette like she's a Jaguar sports car. "These aren't your standard belits. Look at their lobes. They're diurnal belit hybrids—and they won't be moving until the sun gets up."

I don't acknowledge him, ignore the lobes, and pull down my goggles. With the night vision turned on, I scour the plains for signs of belits and fellow riders. An empty horizon stretches out in every direction.

When I lift my goggles, Ash is still there, stroking his sleek dragon. "Well, at least we're ahead of the others," I say.

"Unless they're using tactical gear to conceal their heat marks."

My jaw drops. "Thermal camouflage? That's military-grade tech. How is that allowed?"

"There's no rule against it. And we come prepared." He inspects the area with a slick pair of binoculars. "Half the military is funded by dragon money. Lockheed Martin, FireCorp, same difference."

I scowl and rip the goggles off my head.

"But," Ash carries on, "at least ten riders took off in another direction. I doubt we'll have much competition on the way to—"

"Don't try to bond with me." I frown and tuck the goggles into Ranga's saddlebag.

"I just figured, since we're here all night, we may as well make nice."

I snort. There's no point reminding Ash that I tried to be kind from the start. "City boys talk too much," I whisper.

I move to Ranga's side and untack her saddle, giving her room to breathe during the long night. She shudders and shakes off the tension as I plop the saddle on the ground.

When I turn back around and dust the dirt from my hands, Ash is still standing there. I cross my arms and stare at him, but he says nothing. The desert air ruffles the popped collar framing his face.

"Unless you need lessons on how to unhitch your dragon, I think we're done here." I flip a braid over my shoulder and lean back on my heels. Gran always says that nothing's worse for a self-assured boy than a girl who can take care of herself.

Ash leaves me to deal with dinner and walks back to his pack of dragons.

The nightly desert chill settles in around me, and I look at my watch with a heavy sigh. Nine hours to sunup, and I'm stuck in the wilderness with a ranch traitor. At least we'll get a good night's sleep before the sun stirs the belits again.

I pull off my tired leather gloves and flex my hands, already chapped from the long ride. My sore back moans as I stretch my legs and crack my knuckles. I bet my mom felt the same when she rode the race, and I smile through the pain.

Ranga refuses to hunt in the darkness with the FireCorp dragons on our tail and forgoes her meal. Like snakes, dragons don't eat often, but races burn calories, and I hope she'll kindle her bravery at the rest point. She settles near the sleeping belits as I rummage across the barren plain and collect scraps of wood. As I do, I'm reminded that summer days are meant for work and family. While the race looms large, I'm sure Pa feels I've left him to shoulder the entire responsibility of the farm alone.

Frowning, I assemble my sorry bundle of sticks and hover over it. It's barely enough to boil the water I've collected from a muddy creek, and my mouth is so dry even Gran's awful sun tea sounds pleasant. I pull an old Mexican blanket from my saddlebag and place it on the ground. As I lay the bright patterned cotton on the hard dirt, I imagine it's a magic carpet that can fly me home—my own version of Dorothy's ruby slippers.

With sore fingers, I scoop a handful of dried pinto beans stolen from Gran's pantry out of a canvas sack and put them in my aluminum pot. Beckoning Ranga, I whistle and point to the would-be firepit.

"Little help, girl?"

She lifts her triangular head, sleepy eyed, and breathes onto the sticks. Her breath is so hot it scorches them in seconds. I rush to place my skillet over the bundle before it fizzles away in a pitiful dance of red embers.

Dangit.

Across the plains, Ash fares better. His fire blazes nicely, the flame clinging to whatever chemical-drenched firelogs he brought with him. A pang of regret echoes through me as he waves at me from across the way. I crawl up next to Ranga with my pot of crunchy beans. With an old spoon, I pick through them as Ranga looks on longingly. It occurs to me that this is part of the FireCorp edge. Their legion is well equipped, and their dragons are probably trained to eat less and work harder.

But that doesn't mean we can't win. In my core, I know what I'm worth and what Ranga is capable of.

As the chill creeps across the desert, I unbraid my knotted hair. I run my hands through it and massage my scalp. The wild wisps hang down around me, keeping in the heat around my neck as I press into Ranga, her belly warm with the day's travels.

Barely full but proud to be ahead of so many well-trained dragons, I scoot down on the blanket. Overhead, the stars wink back at me in millions of sparkling points. I croon an old tune I remember my mother singing to me as a child, and Ranga purrs.

"Nice song."

His words startle me and remind me that I'm not the only one on this plain.

"What do you want?" I ask, propping myself up by my elbows.

Ash squats down, ignoring the unwelcome tone in my voice. I back up against Ranga's powerful body in response, and I half expect her to growl at him in my defense. But she doesn't. Instead, she makes a sweet throaty sound, which Ash echoes with a click of his tongue. She leans into him like she's suddenly forgotten her fear of humans—let alone FireCorp lackeys.

"It's hot chicken soup." Ash hands me a thermos. "I saw your fire, or what there was of it, and figured I could share." He keeps holding the canister out, but I don't take it.

I force a smile, just as I know Gran would have me do. "I appreciate the offer, but I'm just fine."

"Okay then . . . what about Ranga?" he asks. From his pack, Ash pulls a big strip of bacon. He holds it out and wriggles it in front of her face.

Ranga perks up and leans in to sniff the bacon. Her nostrils flare as she nuzzles the meat, and her round eyes plead with me like she's a pup hoping for a bone.

"You know, it's rude to offer somebody else's dragon a meal without asking first," I say, saltiness in my voice. Though I won't admit it, I'm angrier with myself that I haven't prepared for this race as well as he has. It's not that I don't want Ranga to have the treat—I just wish I were the one offering it.

Ash hangs his head. "I just figured you were both hungry. No need to be so proud that you won't accept help."

"As far as I know, there's poison in that soup, and that snack is laced with something that will kill my dragon."

He doesn't flinch. "Am I really that untrustworthy?"

"Why would I trust you? You ride for the brand!" I snap. A whip of wind pulls through the plain, and my dingy shirt wafts with it. I reel back my anger and soften my voice. "And you've been rude when you had no reason to be."

Ash's jaw flexes, and he twists his face to the stars. "You know," he says, ignoring the comment about his awful behavior when we first met, "not everyone can choose their fate."

"We can make our own fate," I say. "We can choose who we want to be."

Hungry and exhausted, I'm reminded I entered this

race to make my own fate. I chose to join, despite what Pa wanted. I left Gran, even though it hurts. And hopefully, all of these choices will alter the fate of my ranch—maybe even the fate of dragons everywhere.

Ash takes a seat next to me on the blanket, uninvited, and looks up into the stars again. He lets out a heavy sigh and folds his arms on the tops of his knees. I edge away from him. But, to my utter surprise, Ranga affectionately nudges his shoulder. She wobbles her head and blinks slowly, what dragoneers call "dragon kisses," and rests her head near Ash. He strokes the opalescent ridges of her triangular forehead.

Thanks for nothing, Ranga.

He keeps his eyes on the stars. "Some of us have allegiances we can't escape."

I snort. "I would escape FireCorp's clutches, no matter what. No matter how hard I had to try." I pause long and hard. "I would never let them be a part of our ranch. *I* have integrity."

Ash's face is cool, but there's darkness just below the surface. "What if FireCorp was your only opportunity to ride dragons?"

My lips turn down at the corners, and I can see the hurt in his eyes.

"When I was a kid, I believed I could choose my own path—and all I wanted was the freedom to ride. But when my parents got divorced and my mother remarried, everything changed. My destiny changed. Our family-owned ranch fell into FireCorp hands just like so many others." He pops the collar of his black leather jacket so it obscures his face. "And I watched my stepfather turn my mother into someone afraid of her own shadow."

"At least you have a mother," I clap back. I want to say that my mother died in front of me—that I watched helplessly as paralysis took her and she stopped breathing. I want to say that maybe, if my father hadn't been off selling dragons to pay for never-ending FLARE tariffs imposed by corporate lobbyists, I wouldn't have been a helpless six-year-old left alone with her.

But I don't. Because self-pity doesn't suit me, and he's not worth my story.

I suck in my breath as we hold steady in silence for a long time. My head reels as I relive the moment her lips turned blue and her eyes closed for the last time. In my heart, I know FireCorp isn't the only one to blame. If I'd paid more attention to my lessons, I would have known to administer antivenom, but . . .

"I can't choose to be rid of FireCorp any more than you

can bring your mother back to life," he says.

"It's not the same thing at all," I snap.

"That's because you don't understand what it's like to be me."

I rise to my feet then approach Ranga, leaving Ash on the blanket. I pet Ranga's scales with the backs of my knuckles and coo in her ear, "Okay, girl—let me show him."

Ranga relaxes as I run my hands down her neck to the place where her wings meet her body. I walk my fingers along the stretch of it, opening her wing and holding it back so that Ash can see the scars all along the underside of her body. If she weren't so oddly comfortable with Ash, perhaps she'd be more protective, but she freely exposes her scars.

"These scars are courtesy of FireCorp. Each one is a reminder that she was used as an FC bait dragon." My voice is clear and carries out over the plain. "Pumped full of drugs, she'd be left as a punching bag to train bigger, more aggressive FireCorp dragons." I release her wing and stand tall.

Ash folds his hands together and shifts uncomfortably.

"It doesn't matter how many times you look away, Ash Hook," I say. "This is happening to dragons worldwide because of gas companies like FireCorp."

Ash's shoulders bunch around his ears, and I stoop back to the ground to meet him. Ranga whimpers lightly, and I am not sure if it's from the sad remembrance of her time with FireCorp or to ease Ash.

"I will spend every minute of my life trying to ensure this never happens to another dragon," I say.

Ash clears his throat. "Not everyone who works for FireCorp treats their dragons that way."

"Maybe not—but evil persists when good cowgirls do nothing." I wrap my arms around Ranga. "And I wasn't built to do nothing."

"So, I guess I am the enemy then?" he asks.

I keep my lips tight and shrug. The silence hangs heavy around us. Shadows darken Ash's hazel eyes.

"Anyway, I guess I just thought you would understand," says Ash. He stands up, taking with him the thermos of soup.

Maybe because my stomach is growling or maybe because I just don't want to leave things sour, I call out to him.

"You know," I say, "I guess I wouldn't mind some of that soup."

Ash hesitates and the wind whisks around him. "I thought you were fine on your own."

I swallow and twirl the blanket's cotton tassels in my fingers. "But if you aren't going to eat it . . ."

Ash hesitates, body taut as if struck by lightning. He walks back and hands me the thermos. I nod but don't say thank you. Ranga watches closely as he walks away and then nudges me as if to say, "I like him."

Traitor.

The soup is bitter—a far cry from Gran's homemade stock chock-full of fresh herbs and spices. But it's warm and soothes my aching stomach.

I jolt awake to the sounds of belit dragons ringing through my ears. Chaos swirls around me and my head pounds, woozy with sleep. I blink, trying to press out the syrupy feeling and center myself.

My belits scatter across the plain, each one bounding in opposite directions.

"No!" I shout.

I rise to my feet, but I'm shaky and the world morphs in a kaleidoscope of color. Ranga roars and presses her head into my side. I steady myself against her as I feel the blood rush through my temples.

Holy mother-of-pearl. What was in that soup?

The belits kick up dust all around, and I can barely see

through the dirty haze. I cough and cover my mouth with my bandanna.

I punt Ash's stupid thermos into the chaos, then scramble for Ranga and jump onto her bareback. Her spine presses into my buttocks, but I ignore the bony scales. As we launch upward, something pummels into me from behind. I fall off of Ranga, back to the dirt. Cheek pressed into the sand, I lift my eyes. A FireCorp dragon soars into the atmosphere, the sun licking its onyx scales.

"What the heck?" I shout, choking on dust even through my bandanna.

I jump back on Ranga and we take to the sky. She flies on pure instinct, and tension runs the entire length of her body. Two FireCorp dragons circle overhead, whipping the belits into a tizzy. They spiral in panic, tiny wings flitting in the air.

"Happy hunting!" yells Valeen. She waves down at me with a gloved hand.

As Ranga and I speed up, the two FireCorp Dragons dart in the other direction. I watch in horror as Valeen and another rider take off toward . . .

It can't be.

Across the plain, Ash and Juliette stand tall beside three color-coded herds of belit dragons.

The bastard tricked me. Drugged me with bland soup and a sob story.

The two black FireCorp dragons meet Ash and their belits, and all three take off toward El Capitan for the final stretch. Their belits stay in tight formation, flanked by all three dragons.

And below me, on the ground, mine are scattered in several directions. Ranga and I fly as fast as we can to the edge of the unruly herds. There's no way I can reassemble the herd and get them to El Capitan before the others.

I grit my teeth, and my blood pumps hot. How dare Ash betray me? How dare he act like a friend?

Through my bandanna, I shout to Ranga, "Fire, fire!"

She lets out a bolt of fire that sends several of the belits back toward the center of the plain. The light is enough to hypnotize most of the belits and shock them into submission. They screech and chirp in fear and cluster into small groups across the plain—some as far as a mile off.

My only hope is that their small wings can't carry them too far too quickly. Dust cakes at the back of my throat.

In response to my subtle hand signal traced along her left shoulder, Ranga launches across the field, her iridescent scales glistening with purple. She's prepared to head off the herd, which keeps bolting farther from our camp.

She doesn't fly in a straight line but swoops across the plain in a wide curve. Her shoulders hunched and her spines pricked at attention, she flies in an arc toward a group of belits huddled at the far east side of the plain.

I let a piercing whistle split the air, and Ranga screeches to a halt. She dives down, fixing the apprehensive belits with a paralyzing stare. Frozen, they stare back as if bewitched like deer caught in blinding headlights. They are still, tense, and quiet. I feel my heartbeat in my ears, time racing through me in the seconds as Ranga establishes control. She steers the belits back to the center, like prey submitting to their predator.

Following my commands of gesture and whistles, Ranga keeps the belits at her side and maneuvers them to the next set of frantic dragons.

Wheep! Wheep! I whistle with two fingers pressed between my teeth. I feel the pearl buttons of my western overshirt pop open as we fly through the air.

"Go!" I shout, my voice burning through my throat. "Away! Away!"

Ranga darts into the air and circles like a sheepdog, driving the belits into a tame circle. Once they are calm, I jump from Ranga's back. I gather up everything I own and saddle Ranga, fast as ever.

"On, on!" I shout.

Ranga arcs to the west, guiding the belits to El Capitan. Her unwavering focus keeps them under her control.

Up ahead, the limestone ridge of the Guadalupe Mountains looms above the Chihuahuan Desert. We dart up the mountain ridge, not a hiker or camper in sight. The cattle-sized belits speed ahead, driven by Ranga as she hugs the wall of Bone Canyon, a steep ravine that slants down in a hundred-foot drop. Shards of flat rock clatter into the crevice as the belits drag their tails against the canyon ledge.

Miles pass, and the belits are under control but lagging. Ranga grows restless, sensing other riders at our back.

As we reach El Capitan, I spot a wide area cleared for the finish line. A shadow on the left takes my field of vision. I ignore it and lean down farther into Ranga's saddle, tightening my hand around the reins while yelling, "Yah! Yah!"

The shadow inches past us. A pair of wings knock against me on the right, and a gust of wind shakes Ranga. I press my calves into her and hold on tight.

My heart pounds. "Yah! Yah!"

And that's it. For short minutes, my life distills down to nothing but the win. Adrenaline surges through me, and I draw tight against Ranga's body. As I press on, my eyes trickling even with the goggles still in place, and I keep yelling, "Yah! Yah! Gee! Gee!"

I will make the cut. I *must* make the cut.

Failure loses the ranch.

Failure loses the dragon rescue.

Failure lands Ranga back with FireCorp.

"Yah! Yah!"

The handkerchief around my mouth smothers me, and dust clouds my goggles enough to make me question myself—Why did I think I could win with a small, traumatized dragon and a stupid brain that can't even remember who the enemy is? Gran would call it hubris. With my desire to live up to Mom's legacy and wanting to prove Pa wrong, I flew too close to the sun. Even worse, I actually believed that I—with my rescued dragon and heart full of naive Texas morals—could best and shame the biggest dragoneering corporation in the world.

Stupid, stupid girl.

Fists around my reins, I pull Ranga past the massive dragons flanking me, beyond the dust into the sky. I'll lose vital inches, but at least I'll be able to see. She careens forward, her nerves dancing on edge as the finish line comes into focus.

I yell out, "Dive, girl, dive!"

Ranga grumbles, and the fire in her belly warms my legs as she dives in front of two black dragons.

"Yah! Yah!"

She slides onto the finish line, and the FireCorp riders sneer at me from the winner's circle. Ash and his two other FC-loving weasels exchange handshakes in the center.

I catch my breath as the announcer names me the thirty-eighth rider to cross. Traveling draggers from various news outlets practically yawn at my arrival, and Karbach looks . . . disappointed. I may not have my phone, but I know that every message board is busy firing off the new favorites for the win. This time, I won't be one of them.

I throw my pack in the dust. How could I think I stood a chance of winning this race?

CHAPTER
11

The mountains rise from rough country, and our camp of forty riders and race coordinators hunkers down in our makeshift settlement around noon. The council members retreat to their own campground several hundred yards away, so at least I'm free of Michael Carne.

Preserved as one of only two national parks in the great state of Texas—the other, of course, being Big Bend— Guadalupe Mountains National Park is the "Top of Texas." The wind lashes the peaks and whistles through the crevices.

For now, our dragons roam free, protected by the miles and miles of remote land as they hunt for their food. The announcer tells us that, once fed, they'll be secured to massive hitching poles driven into the ground and closely guarded by the ranch hands. I hate the idea of being without Ranga, not just for my sake, but for hers.

Mandatory rest periods last anywhere from two to twenty-four hours, enough time to let the dragons recover vital energy, which is really the only way to guarantee they won't get ornery. Or kill people like they did in 2016 when a racing dragon escaped and burned down a San Antonio suburb. But aside from mandatory rest, we have no idea when we will be called up. It leaves the entire camp on edge as we scrape for food in the wilderness and boil whatever water we can find to stave off parasites.

Gran's dried beans won't last long, so foraging is the only way to survive. I hope that, as a Texas native, I know the land better than anyone. Sweat pours from my brow as I scrape in the barren landscape for wild onions and forest rose. Fire ants crawl up my legs as I traipse through the craggy brush, but I ignore the burning bites and remember that I may have only two hours to collect enough food to fill my starving belly. The pang reminds me that this is what I'm best at—surviving as a lone wolf.

My ears prick.

Hissssss.

A rattlesnake lunges for me, and I stamp it down with

my boot. That's the thing with Texas—you may be afraid of the wrong creature and forget what can actually kill you. But when you're used to dragons, snakes seem like child's play—even if they are venomous. Venomous dragons . . . that's something to actually worry about.

Luckily, the rattlesnake will make a protein-packed meal.

As I walk back to my camp, snake in hand, I pass the comm tent. It's the only place where you can access the outside world during the competition, because they don't want us to research or mine other resources. I'm fine with that part. I have no friends to speak of back home—well, none who could talk on the phone—and I know this state better than most. But the comm tent calls out to me, and this is my one opportunity to check on Gran for who knows how long. I drop my snake at my camp and hide its body underneath my pack. I can't afford to let anyone steal my food.

I stomp into the spartan comm tent, and the takes-no-guff sheriff in the corner sets me on edge. She doesn't even say a word and instead points to the bulky satellite phone on the table. Various forms of tech lie haphazardly on folding tables: drones for keeping watch; a mammoth pile of tracking collars from the now dispatched belit dragons; replacement batteries; thermal goggles; and God knows what else. The air sucks at the tent's canvas "doors."

"I just want to call my gran," I say.

The sheriff points again and crosses her legs. Slick black cowboy boots poke out of her pants, and she sets a legal notepad on her lap. The badge on her shirt reads "LAUDES" and flashes as she pulls a pen out of her pocket. She's going to take notes on my call.

Awkward.

The lightweight folding chair creaks as I pull up to the table. Taking a deep breath, I pull a slip of paper out of my pocket, brush away some lint, and dial the hospital number.

I curl my fingers around the phone as it rings. How many people have made uncomfortable calls from this comm tent? Has anyone ever called a sick family member?

"Hello?" A tired gruffness lingers in Pa's voice.

I wince because I'd hoped he wouldn't be the one to answer. "Hi, Pa," I say. My voice cracks, guilt seeping through the two short words.

I'm the one that should be at the hospital with Gran. Hopefully, someday, Pa will know this is my way of helping our family—and our dragons.

"I would've called the police if I didn't know exactly where you ran to," he says. No hello. No nothing. Just pure disappointment. "Lynn deserves a real piece of my mind for signing that application."

"We just completed the first leg," I say.

Before I can get more out, he interrupts me. "You should come home."

I grit my teeth and his voice scrapes against my nerves. Laudes scribbles something on her notepad, and I feel exposed before an audience. I mask my tone with confidence.

"Not yet . . ." I pause, wondering how much I should let on. "I did fine, by the way. I hope you'll come to the closing festival when I make it to the final leg." I don't mention that I was one of the last people to arrive this time. Or that it was my fault for eating drugged-up soup. Pa rarely follows these races, so I hope he hasn't tuned in to watch me fail.

The other end of the phone is silent, and I turn away from Laudes as if that offers some privacy. "Can I talk to Gran?"

"They just took her out for another set of tests," says Pa. "She should be back any minute."

"That means they still don't know what's wrong."

"They don't know what's wrong—yet. They're using every test at their disposal."

"That sounds expensive."

"It's not your place to worry about what's expensive."

A breeze wafts through the tent and licks the scratches across my knees. "I'm here because I care. And I am worried. I know you think I'm just a kid, but it's just us. Just the three of us: you, Gran, and me. And I intend to do my part."

Pa sighs. He moves past my heartfelt words in classic dad style. "I'm working on things that will help with the bills, so you don't have to . . . Some people have asked about the dragons."

Asked about, as in made bids on. "What people?"

"Kind people with solid track records."

"What dragons are you planning to sell off?" There's urgency in my voice. I immediately think of all the dragons I love, how long I've known them, and whether I'm willing to give them up. For every dragon that comes to mind, the answer is "no."

"How about you let me worry about that? Besides, the docs could come back later today and say Gran just needs a simple medication."

Pa was never very good at facing facts. Even in elementary school, I knew he couldn't internalize that Mom was gone. He never even said goodbye, and maybe that's why he never recovered.

The phone lets out a *beep beep* and Laudes motions for me to hurry up.

"My time is running out. Is Gran back yet?"

"No," he says.

"I just wanted to say that I love you both and that I'm doing okay."

"We love you too." I can tell it takes everything in him to say it. "Take care of yourself."

"I will."

I hang up the phone and slump into the rickety chair. If that was my last opportunity to talk to Gran, I'll shatter into a thousand jagged pieces. I stare at the folding table where the words "FC 4 Ever" glare back at me, scratched into the particleboard with a sharp object. Laudes coughs into her hand to get my attention, but I remain frozen, unable to pull myself to my feet.

A group clatters outside the tent, and bursts of laughter bounce off of the crags.

"Did you see her face, though?" asks a shrill voice.

"I doubt it could have gone any better," says another. "A fantastic show of FireCorp brotherhood."

"And sisterhood," says a girl.

They walk past the comm tent without noticing I'm there, hunched in my chair under Laudes's watchful eye.

I peer out past the whipping canvas. The small crowd of FC cronies laugh and share a pack of sour gummy worms.

"Well, at least we're further up in the ranks for now. We picked off at least five solo riders. Too bad it couldn't have been the Drake girl, though."

Ash chomps the end off of a magenta worm as the pack surrounds him. "She won't make it far with that dragon."

Valeen curls herself around Ash like a snake and hugs him. "I don't know. If you hadn't helped trick her, she would have shot up in the rankings." Ash steps back as she releases him. "Good thing you're a loyal boy."

I shrug aggressively at Laudes and gesture out the tent. Still, Laudes doesn't speak and shrugs back as if to say, "What do you want me to do?"

She's an authority figure, but there are no rules about tricking a fellow competitor. Using sedatives may be unacceptable, but I'm not about to bring it up, and I know the FC will never admit it. Even if Laudes wanted to take action, what *could* she do in a race where dragons regularly brawl?

As that sinks in, I sit up straight and pull back the canvas. Cowboy boots stomping on gravel, I launch out of the tent. Ash turns a sickly shade of green and nearly chokes on his candy.

"Oh no, don't stop your victory dance on my account," I say. Heat blooms in my ears, but I stand tall and cross my arms. My fingernails dig into my biceps, and I try to relax. I can't bear to let them see me lose it.

"Why, if it isn't Little Miss Texas herself. How does it feel to be at the bottom?" Valeen steps in front of Ash as the rest of the FC clique stands at attention. I've seen enough *National Geographic* to know they're like a pack of wolves, raising their hackles to make themselves look bigger and more terrifying.

I crinkle my nose at her cloud of designer perfume. "It doesn't matter if I'm at the bottom—all I need is one quick run where you guys don't cheat."

Ash remains aloof despite the accusation and takes a sip from an engraved Yeti Rambler that reads "AHC."

"What's wrong, Ash? Don't care to tell your friends how much we bonded out there on the plains all alone?" Valeen scowls as I dig my heels in. "No matter to me. Guess I'll just remember that you Yankees have about as much integrity as used-car salesmen."

"It's a competition," says the tall blond iceman, whose name I now know is Nickolai Grigori. A faint Eastern-bloc accent I hadn't noticed before lingers on his tongue.

"You're right—it is. And I can't wait to beat you by

playing a clean, honest game."

Ash cracks his knuckles, and I push past him.

"See you at the finish line," I call back.

They're long behind me when I remember how exhausted I am. Sweat trickles down my temple as I bend over, hands on my knees, to catch my breath. No matter how big I can act on the outside, it is not how I feel on the inside. My stomach churns, and I kick a boulder. Pain shoots up my toe, and I plop down on the rock and rest my head in my hands.

"Better be a bit more careful next time."

I lift my head and find Karbach clicking away on his camera. He spins the dial and, without even looking through the lens, snaps a photo of me.

"How are you even allowed out here?" I ask.

"If I were you, I'd be grateful. You never know what sorts of stories we can break, given the chance. I'm not just a drama-chasing reporter, I'm one of the good guys." Karbach gestures to the group of draggers busy comparing notes, fiddling with camera equipment, and typing up reports. Reports I wished I could read. Two sheriffs sit among them, monitoring their devices and making sure they don't share them with any of the competitors.

I glance back to Karbach, and he's already walking away,

sauntering back to his tent.

The camp bustles with fierce riders from across the country, and I try to imagine how my mom behaved during her race. I picture her cooking yucca on her own and ignoring the competition. She would never have made such a silly mistake as I did on the last leg. My watch reminds me that we may have only an hour left. Tired of sulking, I root around for firewood and head back to my snake. Lame twigs in hand, I kick a hollow in the dirt and crouch down to build a fire.

"You can share our fire!" shouts Laura from across the camp. She's crowded around a small blaze with Brayden, Rion, and Colt.

Without Ranga, I'll be stuck starting a fire with flint and steel. Socializing with the competition proved to be an awful idea with Ash, but time may be growing short, and this is the best group I've met so far.

The circle opens up as I sling the dead snake over my shoulder and head over to them.

"Have a seat." Laura smacks the ground with a stick before she tosses it on the fire.

I'm glad Laura made the cut, but part of me wishes she'd already been dismissed. She seems nice enough. But I can't imagine we will form any genuine bond. Especially now that I know that trusting the competition can mean betrayal and failure.

I add my twigs to the fire and set my aluminum kettle in the hot coals to purify the water.

"The FC cut me off before I even reached the task. And they tried to steal my belits," says Laura. Her face twists as she nibbles on unripe mulberries.

Relief spreads through me, but I'm too embarrassed to admit I was drugged. "Same."

Rion snorts, a passive-aggressive reminder that he already recommended we team up. "It's not against the rules to steal another player's task," he says. "You were both fair game. And easy, lone targets."

Ugh, he's right. Me and my big mouth. "Hey, look, I'm sorry about the other night," I say. "I didn't mean to shoot you down so fast."

Rion shrugs, then rifles through a handful of edible blossoms, checking for bugs before he pops the flowers in his mouth.

"Sharing a fire is one thing," says Brayden, scraping the bottom of his blackened pot full of beans. A trickle of sweat drips from his mop of chestnut coils and down his ruddy skin. "They can afford to team up—it's a part of their contract."

Laura and Rion share a silent exchange. I guess they both think alliances are the way to go.

"FireCorp gets brand awareness by sponsoring top riders, and the riders get the glory of riding with the FC," continues Brayden. "It's a fast track to the elite dragon leagues. I'm sure they could get older riders if they wanted, but they always use kids on their teams because they're easier to control."

"Pitiful," says Colt.

I fiddle with my snake and wonder if I should offer some to Rion as a peace offering. But none of us chooses to share, so I decide against it. At least rattlesnake is heartier than mulberries or forest rose.

Laura dusts off her hands. Somehow, her pink nail polish remains intact. "Forty-five minutes to potential start time. I'm boiling another canteen of water. Hand over your bottles."

I pull my bottle closer to my body. No way I'm letting another person contaminate my food. "I've got mine."

Laura raises an eyebrow. "Suit yourself. Rion, come with?"

Rion nods and joins her. Colt takes off in search of more food, leaving Brayden and me to watch over the fire.

On the outskirts of camp, a few dragons land, bellies full

from elk and whatever else they could scrounge up. I look to the locator on my belt, but Ranga is still far off. I click a red button that delivers a vibration calling her to return to the docking area where ranch hands will care for our dragons. I pray other dragons don't bully her—and that she gets back before takeoff. If we aren't at the starting line when the air horn blasts, it's over.

Beyond our circle, crouched together, the FC riders prep their own meals. Because their dragons dwarf everyone else's, they've brought all the comforts of home, including camper chairs and bottles of soda. Their camp makes ours appear pitiful by comparison, and it's as if the entire race is a joke to them. They ride for glory and status alone.

Ash and Valeen chat with a reporter while fiddling with tech. They keep looking over at me with a smile on their lips, and I know I am the butt of their joke.

I cut the head off my snake and toss it in the fire.

Brayden snaps his fingers in front of my face. "Hello?"

"Sorry—what?" My eyes flick over at Ash once more before I wipe my blade on an old rag.

Brayden spins around and notices Ash and Valeen. "Ah. Now I see." He clears his throat. "Just ignore them."

I cough, rip the innards out of the snake, and set them on a stone. Could be useful as bait. "Ignore who?"

He glances back at them once more. "I know that look—that feeling. Don't waste time hoping for their approval."

My ears are hot, and heat creeps across my cheeks. "I—"

Brayden leans in as he stirs his tiny pot of beans. "Besides, you're not the first person to be bullied by Ashton Carne."

My knife goes limp in my hand. "Ashton . . . Carne?"

"You don't know?" He stabs his beans and scrapes against the metal pot. "He goes by Ash Hook because he refuses to take his stepfather's name. But Michael Carne raised him. Married his mom when Ash was seven."

"How do you know that?"

Brayden churns over his thoughts as he sets down his bean-covered spoon, a little too rough, like he's pressing it into the rock. "I used to be a FireCorp rider."

My stomach drops and I have a sudden urge to take my kettle and run. But my legs are welded to the ground.

In the background, Valeen and Ash are fixed on Brayden with hard stares.

"Don't worry," he says with a dry laugh. He yanks his bean pot off the coals, and the embers spark around it. "That was a while ago, before I left Dragonscale Academy and my family moved our ranch west where land was cheaper and schools weren't so toxic."

I swallow a hard lump. "What was it like? Working with them, I mean."

He hunches over his pot and scrapes the bottom of it with a wooden spoon. "Great at first. Like family. I flew and died by red and yellow. But things changed. People changed. I changed."

The strategist in me wants to ask more questions—what their strengths are, how to beat them. His experience could hold the key to so many moves. But he's too sad looking to deserve a grilling from me.

I lay my hand on his forearm. "Well, I'm glad you changed. Because even if we aren't a team, we need you on this side of the fight."

Brayden creases his eyebrows and stokes the coals with a stick. "You don't need me as much as you think. After all, you're Aurora McCoy's daughter."

Hollow in my chest, I roast the snake until it's burned on the edges. I'm not hungry anymore, and the weight of exhaustion pulls me down, but this meal could mean the difference between thirtieth and thirty-first place on the next leg. Tough situations build strong people, or so I've been told. I want to live up to my mother's memory, save Drake's Ranch, and expose FireCorp for the heartless fiends that they are. But as I think of the terrifying moment the FC dragons descended on Ranga and me, I'm not certain *I* am enough.

Night settles in, but the horn doesn't call us, and I can almost taste the tension in the air. Our tentative alliance disbands, and each of us takes our own approach to prepping. Laura pores over a dozen maps by flashlight and takes a wealth of notes. Rion inventories and reorganizes his gear. Colt practices trick roping with his lasso. None of us knows where we're headed, and every passing second triples my anxiety. The only people who seem relaxed are the Bhattis, who spend time drawing Sharpie tattoos on a sleeping competitor's face.

Ranch hands rest beside hitching posts, keeping watch over the dragons beyond our camp. The dragons grow restless, begging for the skies. They set even the sheriffs on edge. Some howl as if in horrific pain, probably missing their riders. I can hear Ranga's whimpers above the cries, and each one shoots tiny daggers into my dragon-sized heart.

I lay my head down on a rock and shut my eyes. Sleep terrifies me—I don't want to be caught off guard—but riding hard on zero rest leaves me just as afraid.

31°52'38.3" N, 104°51'28.8" W

El Capitan, Guadalupe Mountains, Texas

A mighty roar echoes through the camp, jolting me awake. My watch reads two thirty a.m., and I shoot up, my body sore from sleeping on rocky ground.

Grooowwwwwuuulllllll!

Again, the mountains echo, and dust rises into the air. I snap around to find two huge verdant greatclaws—each with six powerful legs and thick, clubbed tails—looming over our camp. Wild and fierce, they puff with smoke and embers, perched atop two metal shipping containers like gargoyles sprung to life. Their green scales glimmer in the dull glow of dying campfires.

"Wake up! Wake up!" shouts the announcer over a crackling microphone. "Time for the next task!"

Holy crud on a cracker. Chaos erupts around me and I scramble to my feet.

"Rise and shine, cupcakes. Dragon ranching waits for no one!"

The campus buzzes and I expel a string of curses. Competitors tear down their tents and pour water on their fires, releasing clouds of steam across the camp. It mingles with the puffs of dragon smoke, and the two green dragons roar again. Their cries reverberate in my chest as I stuff my pack. Belongings secure, I dash for the area where our dragons are hitched. Other riders follow.

But a dozen people clad in silver fireproximity suits press us back. "Back! Back!"

"My dragon!" I shout, reaching out my fingers.

Most of my fellow competitors do the same, arguing with the alien-like suits. But Laura runs off in the other direction.

Ranga howls above the chorus of frustrated wyverns, goldenscales, and winged skinks. The piercing cry prickles my skin. I shouldn't have brought her here . . .

I struggle to rip past the defense of silver-suited ranch hands, but one pushes me back—hard.

"Ranga!" I yell above the chaos so she can hear my voice.

Ranga loosens a terrified yelp.

"Get to the starting line!" The ranch hand's voice echoes in the helmet, and I can't see beyond the orange glare of the aluminized hood. "Go!"

This time, Ranga roars and the ranch hand startles. The bunker suit is all that's protecting him from dragons begging for their riders. And nothing is protecting me.

The announcer's megaphone gurgles, "Two minutes, two minutes! Next leg starts in two minutes!"

More competitors abandon the defense line of silver suits and make for the announcer poised in front of the shipping containers. My heart pounds and my mind reels: Is this *really* a part of the game?

Dear dragons, I hope so.

I shout to Ranga, "It'll be okay, girl! I promise!"

Her whine rises above the choir of growls.

Leaving Ranga, I bolt for the announcer. Laura is already standing before him, waiting. The two monstrous greatclaws snarl through black teeth and flap their mighty, batlike wings. A rider is saddled on each dragon, and their thick, ragged talons grip the massive metal pods. Competitors crowd in front of the containers, keeping their distance from the strange container guardians.

The announcer, who may as well be our torturer, holds up a staff and whistles. One of the greatclaws bursts with fire and lights the staff. The announcer slams the staff into the ground. Shadows streak across the ground.

"In!"

At the announcer's command, the containers' metal flaps fall open and bang against the ground. Dust rises around us. On each side, the container reads, "FireCorp: Don't let your future go up in smoke." More sponsored gear for the race, branded with my least favorite slogan. I cough, and I'm not sure if it's because of the dust or my hatred for FireCorp.

The announcer bangs his hand against the sinister container. "I said, 'In!'"

Even though I know this is part of the race, crawling into a dark, windowless pod sends shivers across my skin. Leaving Ranga with strangers worries me even more, and it's as if I can feel her terror curling in my spirit. Even Laura hesitates. All of the other competitors stare at the shipping containers, motionless.

I step forward. "What are you going to do with my dragon?"

"You'll have her—just you wait."

The ranch hands and sheriffs are sleepy eyed, but there's a curious excitement in their faces. After clomping into a container, I find rows of school bus seats inside. I take a seat in the front row as the other riders follow. One of the oldest riders in the competition takes the seat beside me and Ash sits behind me. How lovely. I buckle my seat belt as the door slams shut on us.

The metal screeches with the sound of claws on steel, and the dragons lift the pod, swinging us in the air. We swing back and forth on our way to God knows where. I grip my pack and unzip the front pouch. In the darkness, I feel for my race gear: stacks of old Texas maps, field guides scribbled with notes, my canteen, my flashlight, and Gran's compass. Everything is there. I shine the flashlight around the pod.

A blaring voice crackles over a speaker. "The first drag-oneers traveled through dark caves and treacherous seas. They dealt with sleepless nights and hazardous conditions y'all can't even imagine. Turn that light out!"

I slam my back into the bus seat in protest and turn off the light. Darkness it is. My thoughts churn as the container sways. I imagine us plunging to our deaths, trapped in this pod, our bodies crashing together as it smashes into the mountains. I tighten my seat belt further and hope it will keep me secure.

As I sink into my spot, I worry about Ranga. I wonder how on earth she will be transported to wherever in tarnation they're taking us, and I pray she's not stuffed in a dark container too. Again, fear creeps up on me. Have I made a horrible mistake in bringing a traumatized dragon, no matter how eager, to a race like this? But in the cool dark, the swaying pod lulls me to sleep . . .

bwAAAAAAAHHHP!

An air horn–like sound blares through a speaker in the pod. It rings in my ears, and the entire group groans.

"No rest for the wicked!" shouts someone over the intercom.

The horn continues to go off every fifteen minutes, making sleep impossible. My bones ache, and I yawn more times than I can count. As time drags on, someone taps my shoulder.

"I know that you must hate me by now, but I really am so sorry," says Ash from behind me. "Please give me a chance to explain."

"There's no need to explain. It's a competition," I say. "Thank you for reminding me. Again." The darkness stretches out, and I hold my tongue. I want to tell Ash I'm not angry anymore—just hurt. I want to explain that I thought we shared a moment on that star-dotted West Texas plain. But I can't. Or I won't. My voice steadies as I whisper, "I'm not here to make friends."

Through the darkness, I feel Ash shrink back. And that's the end of that.

We fly for hours, periods of silence interrupted by the deafening horn. My ears ring. Twice, the dragons touch down, only to pick us up moments later. I spin the watch on my wrist over and over until my skin burns.

Near six a.m., the pod lurches to a stop, and I stretch my ragged body. With a deep breath, nerves on edge, I wait for the next leg to begin. The pod door slams open against the ground as an announcer gurgles over a megaphone.

"Welcome to the frontier!"

As his air horn blares, I scramble out of my seat and leap off the back of the container. Strange trees rise from cracks in a flat stone surface, and shallow pools of water reflect the morning dawn. The problem with Texas is that it's too gosh-darn big—this could be anywhere.

At the edge of the rock, I see our dragons, and relief spreads through me.

"Ranga!" I shout.

She cries and wriggles her head, and I run for her. But the other competitors aren't doing the same. The clue—I need to hear the clue!

"Hold on, girl!"

The early morning sun brightens the sky as I push

through the competitors to the hologram station. Rising from the deck, a hologram flickers with the image of Miles Drenteel, who won the race in 2003. He looks just as he did all those years ago, before he died in a wild dracurl-tail migration a few years back. The computer-generated Miles repeats a poem over and over:

Neither straight nor small,
with tales tall.
Glyphs in the earth.
Come find me.
We seem like pests,
where we now nest.
To my place of birth,
return me.

I snag a pencil from my pack and quickly scribble the poem on the back of an old map. I barely scraped by the last race, and I'm determined to do better this time. Doing my best to tune out the bustle, I saddle Ranga faster than ever before. I coo songs as I do and remind her how much I love her, but it doesn't stop her from trembling. Then, we take to the unknown skies. In this competition, intimidation is as much a tool as a map or compass, and I dare not let the other riders know I am clueless.

We rise, and the ground comes into focus; I recognize the dome-shaped granite mountain surrounded by trees. Enchanted Rock—which looks far less enchanted without a good night's sleep—rests in the heart of Texas. At least my Texas native advantage is panning out. Many others stay on the ground reading maps and speculating, but Ash, Laura, and Rion take to the skies. They all head in the same direction, so I follow them and unpack the clue as we ride.

Neither straight nor small.

So, something big. In the dragoneering world, that could be anything. Not helpful. I pull alongside Laura, careful not to outpace her and tip my hand.

"Time for a bit of nostalgia?" she shouts.

Nostalgia? Why would she—

Oh, wait. *Neither straight nor small* . . . Of course. Big Bend National Park!

In Laura, I suddenly see the same bucktoothed kid who attended Big Bend's Dragon Camp for Girls with me years ago. My heart races as a smile tugs at my cheeks. "I wonder if we'll see any Dragon Scouts."

Laura winks.

Behind us, black dragons cluster in the pale blue sky. "Looks like the FC riddled it out."

"But do they have the power of the Junior Draco Trekker Badge?" Laura pulls out a faded map with the Dragon Camp's logo imprinted on the front. Dang—this girl is prepared. "I hope you kept yours!"

"There are dozens of glyphs in the park, so that kiddie map won't help much." I chuckle as Ranga pulls on the bridle. Perhaps my speed can outpace Laura's quick wit. "That said, I don't suppose you want to share?"

"I think I've said enough!" shouts Laura, smiling.

Friendly competition—my lifeblood. "May the best woman win!"

I grip Ranga's reins and grin, my goggles pressing deep into my cheeks.

Big Bend is one of the greatest natural wonders in Texas, a sprawling national park of mountains and rivers. And for those worth their salt, it's the perfect place to find petroglyphs left by ancient dragon handlers. But even if you're familiar with historical dragon sites, it could take days to search all of them. Finding a needle in a haystack might be easier.

"Hold steady, Ranga!"

The excitement of riding rushes through her, and her scales morph into vibrant colors of purple and teal. Following Gran's compass, I shift my track south to where the first green hints of Big Bend creep across the state.

CHAPTER 13

Hours later, Laura and I separate as we approach the park. Let's hope she doesn't have a better idea than I do. As the sun pours down, I consider dragons native to Big Bend who might be considered pests:

Spiny crevice dragons: Killed a rider in Big Bend last year.

Sandclaw toothless dragons: Notorious for their mountain lion–like appearance.

Spike-toed wyverns: Often mistaken for UFOs.

I consult my field guide and visit dozens of dragoneering monuments around the park. But even with hours of searching, I can't find any clues—no hint of pesky dragons or this leg's goal.

As the sun dips below the horizon, I land Ranga on an exposed cliff side. A unique geometric pattern is etched into a huge rock formation.

"This one's called Bee Mountain Cave," I say. "What do you think, girl?"

Ranga sniffs the air as I run my toe through footprints in the gravel—I'm not the only person to have come this way today. Did they check this cavern? Did they find anything? With a frown, I prop my tinted goggles on my head. Panoramic mountains chock-full of ancient cave dwellings, abandoned cabins, and run-down mines tower around us. Knowledgeable riders could easily stage an ambush from these hidden landmarks. Perhaps my fellow competitors are lurking in the waxing shadows.

Feeling exposed, I squat next to the formation and search for the caprock, just as I did with my parents years ago. With calloused fingers, I pry the stone from the rock and reach my hand into the crevice. In the back of the hole, I feel it: a set of gears. I spin the gears like a locker dial. With one glance over my shoulder, I yank the gear, and it pops out an inch. As it does, a door made of stone scrapes along the mountainside, sliding back with a series of pulleys. It creaks and crumbles, whining through the crags.

Ranga ripples with gray and presses into the rocks. I ask

her to stay, and she settles in.

I slip my flashlight from its holster, click "ON," and shine it down the cave.

"Hello?" My voice echoes to the back of the cave.

With my light, I search the wall until I find a familiar wooden steering wheel mounted on the rock.

I turn it, rolling the rock wall closed. Flashlight piercing the dark, I dash through the narrow cave. As I approach the tunnel's end, the beam uncloaks a shadowy figure beside an official route marker. Ash raises a hand to shield him from the blinding beam of my flashlight. The light illuminates fire-red spray paint scrawled across the cave wall behind him:

WATCH OUT, DRAKE. WE'RE
COMING FOR YOU.
WITH LOVE, FC

The crude words send a chill through me because this is the confirmation I've been waiting for. FireCorp has me— not Laura, not Rion, not Colt, or any one of the dozen other unsponsored riders—in their crosshairs. The question is why . . . *Why* would they choose me to oppose? I'm not one of the top competitors. I haven't challenged them in any real way (yet). Did becoming the fifty-first entrant make me a target? Or are Carne's creatures trying to make sure I walk away from this race penniless so he can get our ranch?

My flashlight bears down on Ash like an interrogation lamp.

"It wasn't me," he says.

"Like crickets it wasn't." I push past him to the route marker, a West Texas Dragon Wrangling Association insignia above a large orange button. I press it, and a hologram appears. This time, it isn't a person, but words blinking like an old neon sign:

STILL LOST?
PERHAPS YOU'RE LOOKING
IN THE WRONG PLACE.

The clue mocks me, and I scribble it down, gripping my pencil like a weapon. My mind is too tired and overloaded to think through this nonsense—this total lack of a clue—with Ash staring at me. Heels grinding into gravel, I march out of the cave.

Ash shouts back, "I'm not who you think I am."

The words echo down the stone corridor, flicking

through the reaches of the cave like a long tail.

I stop dead in my tracks as it clicks . . . *Not who you think I am.*

I'm searching for the wrong sort of dragon.

I've wasted time on mountaintops and windswept peaks when what I need to do is drop low. We are searching for wurms. It's the obvious choice. The huge, serpentine creatures fled from their usual mountaintop nests earlier this year. Since then, they've been responsible for dozens of Big Bend wildfires. With rocklike camouflage that mimics local grasses and lichens, they will be hard to find. But at least I know what I'm looking for.

Holding back a smile that could give away what I've just worked out, I keep on the track out of the cave.

Night has fallen by the time I make it back to Ranga. As I do, I feel my legs giving out. Soreness pounds through them and reminds me I've gotten only two hours of sleep in the past day. But I can't give in. The warning written in red spray paint is etched into my mind as I rifle through my pack for a map of Big Bend.

When I reach Ranga, she's snoring and her body is twitching as if she's dreaming. I click my tongue as I approach, my voice calm and steady.

"Ranga?"

She bolts upright and snarls, knocking me over. My pack flies open, scattering its contents to the ground.

"It's just me, girl." I keep my voice soft and relax my arms so she knows I'm not a threat.

Ranga growls but squeaks when she notices who I am. She lays her head back down as if to say, "Please. Just one more hour."

I frown and pet her. She sighs deeply and ambles into a ready position for the next leg.

"I'm sorry, girl," I say, collecting my scattered things.

I gingerly climb atop Ranga and lean my head against her. Even the moon and stars seem to sleep behind the wall of clouds drifting across the sky. I close my eyes for a quick moment and imagine curling up in my own bed. After savoring the thought for too many seconds, I pull myself upright, ignoring the soreness in my back and thighs.

We make for the mountains just above the cave, free from Ash, where I can regroup and mull over my clues in peace. Dry trees reach up from the ground, crying out for the rainwater they've missed during the local drought. Not the most ideal situation for a skittish fire-breathing dragon, but that's our lot in this game.

Ranga and I take refuge by abandoned cabins tucked into the rock. The network of old buildings will camouflage us so I can read my map without the flashlight creating a target for the FC.

"Stay here, girl. I'll be right back," I whisper, so quiet that my words evaporate in the air.

Leaving Ranga beside the decrepit cabin, I grab my pack and blanket and search for the darkest corner inside.

The scent of sulfur and arsenic—remnants of a hot spring—leaks up into walls and mixes with the musty smell of the Rio Grande. Map in hand, I pull my blanket over my head and flick on my flashlight. The strange West Texas wind swirls around canyons and whistles through the empty buildings. I recall scary legends told at Big Bend's Dragon Camp for Girls and my skin prickles. As I shift, the boards underneath my body creak.

This is no time for ghost stories—it is time for survival.

Map sprawled across the ground, I beam my flashlight on the paper, searching for low-lying areas where I might find wurms. From tales in *Ranch Times*, I know the locations of a few wildfires started by wurms. From inside my pack I whip out the scribbly clues I wrote and compare them:

To my place of birth,
return me.

and

Still lost?

I turn the words over until the task becomes clear. *Lost!* We need to return a wurm to Lost Mine Peak. Surveying the map, I circle Panther Junction, the biggest site of wurm-borne wildfires. Then I draw a line to Lost Mine Peak. It's only a few short miles. This has to be it.

I dig into my pack for Gran's compass, but it's not in its usual spot. Panic sweeps through me as I rummage around for the compass. It isn't there. I dart out of the cabin and back to Ranga, heart pounding as I retrace my steps.

"Ranga—help," I say, knowing she can't. I push her to the side, sweeping the flashlight underneath me, less afraid of the FC than losing Gran's gift.

It's nowhere to be found among the thirsty leaves and parched rocks.

A chill races down my spine as I shut off my flashlight and rush to the edge of the mountains. I push through the unruly brush, and dry branches scrape my legs. Below, a small band of FC riders has gathered—no, swarmed—outside the marker. I don't see Ash or Valeen, but the crew looks equally awful.

My compass must be there, trapped among them where my pack burst open. Recalling the red spray paint, I swallow. Their four gargantuan dragons snap at each other as the riders start a campfire. Clouds swirl overhead, obscuring the stars, and even if I could use them as a guide, I can't bear leaving without the compass.

When southerners talk about being up a creek without a paddle, this is exactly what they mean.

I wait for nearly three hours, hoping for a break in the clouds or for the riders to leave, but they don't. Ranga's ears prick.

My blood runs cold. "What do you hear, girl?"

A low rumble echoes from the cabins—a lionlike roar mixed with hissing.

Dragon murmurs.

It suddenly occurs to me that if I scream, only the FC will notice. There's not a single kind soul around to hear my cry. As leaves rustle in the dark, I whip around and press up against Ranga. She growls deep in her throat and lowers to the ground, ready to pounce at the lurking threat. If we're being hunted, I must act now.

Summoning my courage, I jump onto Ranga's back and flick the reins. "Go, Ranga! Now!"

And that's when the thing—no, another dragon—attacks.

Ranga bucks like a rodeo bronco, and I'm left pinned to her, trying to regain control. What's worse is that I can't tell what sort of dragon is attacking us, so I don't know how to stop it. I jerk back and forth as my core tightens to keep me in my saddle.

The other dragon hisses at us as it grapples with Ranga and knocks her to the ground. I'm crushed underneath her as her body grows warm. With one breath, Ranga could spark a park-wide wildfire.

"Ranga—s-stay calm," I grunt. "No fire!"

She rolls more on me, smashing my body as the other dragon continues to attack. Trapped underneath her and struggling to get away before the other dragon kills her or me, I try to shout. But my voice is pressed down to a sharp whisper.

"No fire, Ranga—no fire—t-too much wood—"

But she doesn't stop, and as the flame heats in her body, light leaks into the area.

"Stop!" commands another voice, calling off our attacker.

A blinding high beam flashes into my eyes. The leaves rustle, and a shadowy figure appears. A shimmering quetzalcoatl, illuminated by the flashlight, leaps back. Ranga rolls off of me, leaving me squashed in the dirt.

"Are you insane?" says a familiar voice.

I hold up a hand as the beam pours into my face. I squint, and the beam is lowered. Laura grabs my hand and pulls me up.

"Thank God." I toss my arms around Laura and she hugs back. Catching my breath, I wipe leaves and dirt from my clothes.

Quetzal and Ranga back away from each other and whirl around in a flurry of gold and teal scales. Like always, Ranga maintains a beta position, lower to the ground, and cowers despite Quetzal's friendly and open posture. I sing a nonsense tune, and long cords of tense muscles relax in Ranga's neck.

Laura's mouth gapes as if she's never seen anyone sing to a dragon to calm them. She reaches up to stroke Ranga, and Ranga blanches before allowing Laura to run slender fingers along her sharp cheekbones. Ranga's scales pulse a dull gray, and Laura backs off, her hands in the air signaling to Ranga that she means no harm.

I take Ranga's head in my hands and stroke the underside of her chin, coaxing the vibrance back into her scales, which flicker in the pale moonlight.

"Sorry for the attack," says Laura, "but I had to stop you from taking off and ending up in the FC's clutches."

Quetzal proudly puffs up his chest, which is lined with

ribbony scales of tangerine and canary. He regally lifts his head, and I must admit, with his angular jaw and piercing blue eyes, he's one of the most handsome dragons I've ever seen.

Laura guides me to the edge of the crag and points down at the FC. "That's a bona fide war troop. FireCorp's B-team is trained to guard the entrance and ward off anyone searching for the clue. That way, the first string—Valeen, Nickolai, Myra, Trevor, and especially Ash—maintains the lead. It's how I lost first place at the Salt Lakes Tournament last year." She smirks and leans back on a boulder. "I know you're an 'every woman for herself' kinda chica—but I can't stand by and watch your stupidity reign supreme."

I grit my teeth. Overhead, the clouds mock me, still shielding the stars. Without them or my compass, I'm flying blind. And even if I weren't, I can't leave without arousing suspicion. Laura will be hot on my tail. "Do you think they'll leave soon?"

"Not until we're several hours behind their cronies." A competitive edge thins the usual bounce in her voice. She backs away from the cliff and lowers herself to the ground. "No chance you already have a clue?"

I hesitate. "No—you?" My mouth feels dry wrapped around the lie.

Laura shakes her head. "Well, unless we want our dragons to lose a few wings, it's best we wait." She doesn't reference Ranga's size, which I appreciate. "But the B-team will get restless—even though they've been paid off. Eventually, they'll leave and we'll find an opening."

We sit in relative silence for the better part of an hour, both of us waiting on the ledge for the team to leave. Ranga and Quetzal curl behind us like the Secret Service, each one protecting their rider. Laura lovingly cleans Quetzal's nails with a set of shears as we wait, and their sweet exchange makes me feel worse about lying about the clue. This is a girl who treats her dragon well. The sort of person I root for when watching a race.

It's a competition, I try to remind myself.

The FC doesn't budge, and the clouds keep swirling. Every second pulls us further from the finish line.

Laura whips her hair up into a fresh ponytail and unzips an organized backpack. Even after a hard day's ride, she's a picture of glamour and confidence. With her color-coded field guides and fresh manicure, she could pass for a prep school valedictorian. Or worse, a member of the FC.

I clear my throat and push the fear deep inside myself. "The truth is, I—I lost my compass."

Laura unpacks her accordion folder of maps and rifles through them. "And?"

"And I'm wondering if, maybe, you'd let me use yours."

Laura flicks the neon tabs on her folder, then pushes back into Quetzal's broad chest. Neither of us knows how far behind the pack we are. There may be only one spot left. "What use is a compass without the clue?"

I bite my tongue. The part of me who sees a sister allied against the FC wants to operate with fearless honesty—but there's a darker part that can't bear the idea of Laura winning if I can't.

"So, you lied," she says.

Heat creeps across my cheeks as I clench my flashlight. "It's a game."

"It's more than a game." Laura settles into Quetzal and crosses her arms around her folder. Her bangles jingle around her wrist as she gazes past the trees and up into the dark sky. "Sure, for some people, this race is about money and fame, but it's also about scholarships to good schools. And it's about proving that anyone can win." She smacks her file folder on the ground.

I pull my scraped knees to my chest. "It'd be nice to prove that you don't need fancy riding gear and pricey training to win," I reply.

"That's only half the story, Cass. The FC has a long history of barring people of color from their collectives. And you know what? No Latina has ever won this race—and I mean *ever*. You can blame it on fate or fortune, but it's more than that. It's about inequalities in the whole system. Something you can't begin to understand."

I fiddle with a scab and nod. "I guess I never thought of it that way."

Quetzal cups his great, amber-colored wings around his human, lending her his strength.

Silence hangs in the air between us, interrupted only by that crying wind. With her curated file of Texas maps and the pink polish disguising calloused fingertips, Laura percolates with fierce determination. In her, I see everything she stands to gain from the race.

"I don't just want to win because I want fame and glory." I clench my fists. "Or because I hate the FC."

"Then why? And not a half-truth—give me a good enough reason to hand over my compass. A good enough reason to trust you."

Ranga whimpers behind me and nudges my back. It jostles my body, and I shoot up straight as she pushes her head underneath my arm.

I open my fists and find crescent-shaped marks in my palms. "My gran is sick. And we don't have the money to cover the medical bills."

The words escape from my body like a rushing river set free, and I relax into Ranga's warm skin. I've wanted to appear confident and secure this whole time, but I can't hold this in any longer. I stroke Ranga's forehead and launch into the tale of how our donors stopped giving and how Michael is now vying for Drake's Dragon Ranch. I explain Gran's mysterious, sudden illness, our mounting bills, and my father's unwillingness to face reality. I lean my head against Ranga's and take a deep breath.

Laura traces the long ridge of scales trailing down Quetzal's elegant wings. "So, I guess we both have a reason to be here."

I pull my map from my back pocket and spread it across the ground. "Wurms," I say, my voice heavy. "'We seem like pests, where we now nest.' . . . We are looking for wurms. Specifically, I think, the wurms who sparked the wildfires in Panther Junction just outside Chisos Basin." I point to the affected area on the map.

Laura hunches over the map beside me and runs a finger along its timeworn edges.

"And we have to return them to Lost Mine Peak."

Quetzal spreads his enormous orange wings in a deep stretch. As Laura rises, I notice the heavy circles under her eyes.

"We make for Panther Junction together?" I ask. My heart is heavy because I know this means leaving the compass and carrying on with my best chance. But I know Gran would tell me to soldier on.

Laura touches the toes of her purple-fringed boots with a yoga-like grace. "And after?"

"In the end, there are no teams."

CHAPTER 14

Around us, charred branches twist from the ground, and a smokiness hangs in the air. The sky is a dark morning blue as we reach the outskirts of Chisos Basin. I lean into Ranga, and we dive—down, down where the wurms are hiding. The wind ripping across my skin feels like heaven. I could spend my life in the air, alone with Ranga.

I yell out to Laura, "Do you see any?"

The ashy air circles Quetzal as Laura scans the earth, her fancy goggles lowered. I catch the hint of a smile underneath them. "I'm not sure . . ."

Ranga and I swoop low, pulling in a tight formation next to Quetzal. My tone light, I shout, "You lie like a rug, Laura Torres!"

"Every woman for herself?" She's requesting permission, and I have to give it.

"Every woman for herself," I confirm.

She peels off on Quetzal, disappearing into the smoky valley.

"Consarnit," I mutter, flicking the reins against Ranga's back. "Follow her!"

We dive into the canyon and whoosh past dozens of jagged rocks, the perfect camouflage for a dragon hiding where it shouldn't be.

It's immediately clear: other riders have figured out the clues too. At least a dozen of them swoop alongside the rocks, searching for wurms.

Wurms are well camouflaged on a clear day, and the layer of ash covering everything makes them even harder to spot. Through the ashes and pale morning light, I cannot distinguish their lichen-like scales, yellow teeth, bulging eyes, or pointed claws. I pull out my lasso and lower it so it runs along the rocks. My breath hitches as I wait for a dragon to wake up, tickled by the rope, annoyed as if I am a flea on a dog. Other riders dart up and down in flurries of dust, searching for their own wurm.

A gust of wind hits me, stale and hot. Dragon's breath. Spinning sideways, I follow the jet of air and shout,

"Down, Ranga! Down!"

But I am too late.

A wurm emerges from the ashes, and a rider clad in FireCorp branding trails it. His brutal obsidian-and-jade dragon nips at the wurm's tail, and it screams, the sound echoing through the canyon. I cringe at the bloodcurdling cry and hold fast to Ranga, my hand tight around her reins. The other rider and the lassoed wurm take to the sky like a flare, disappearing into the smoke of dawn.

As they vanish, I allow the lump in my throat to pass. My spirits lift as we careen into another crevice. Ranga angles her body, allowing me to reach the walls of rock. My fingers graze a rock—and it stirs under my touch.

"Ranga, hold!"

But as I reach for my lasso, another dragon knocks me to the side.

My head whirls around to find FC rider Tanner Bright, who descends on my wurm. "Son of a bacon bit!"

Tanner pulls a long whip from his satchel. "It's only a game!"

With a menacing smile, Tanner slices his whip, which is lined with dragon scales, through the air.

Crack!

The cord licks the wurm so hard the noise pierces my

ears. Rocks, dust, and plants erupt in a shudder as the wurm's stonelike body springs to life. It rises the length of two school buses, ready to attack Tanner. Its huge green eyes bulge, and its razor-sharp teeth snap at the air. But Tanner's leather cord snaps the wurm once more, and it slams against a tree. Branches scatter to the canyon below, and the other trees creak as the wurm tries to escape.

Crack! Crack!

Tanner's biceps ripple underneath his FireCorp polo as he lashes the wurm. Its unnatural cry—like rusted nails on a thousand chalkboards—sends shivers through my body. Green blood runs in a sad stream from the creature's tail as the poor thing thrashes, unable to escape Tanner's relentless whip. The emerald liquid, hot and metallic, spatters across my face. I wipe the slick from my goggles.

Ranga's turquoise scales flash a chaotic pattern of dark purple.

I try to intervene, my body pressing into Ranga as we attempt to knock them out of the way, but Tanner's ruthlessness and the size of his dragon are too great a match. The wurm's tail droops as they take off into the sky. The creature will be lucky to make it to Lost Mine Peak alive.

The heat inside me burns—how could someone do this to a dragon? They may be snarling and terrifying, but no creature anywhere deserves this sort of treatment. I breathe through the desire to chase after Tanner and free the wurm. But as I look at his giant dragon and long whip, I know there's nothing that Ranga and I can do. With a heavy heart, I guide Ranga in the opposite direction.

About a hundred yards away, rocks skitter in a writhing patch. As fast as I can, I flick Ranga's reins, and we make for the spot. We push harder. Faster. Nearly all the other riders have already taken off, so I keep pushing.

"Yah! Yah!" I shout at Ranga, whose wings beat against the air.

A titanic wurm wriggles in my line of sight, and I reach for my lasso. I spin the tightly twined rope overhead as we bear down, the wurm's breath growing stronger with every inch.

But just as I'm about to release the rope, Laura dives, spiraling from the haze.

"No!" My voice ricochets across the canyon.

My heart sinks as I lock eyes with Laura. Quetzal subdues the wurm with his hind legs as Ranga dives down after him.

Ranga rears up. I press my heels into the stirrups—stuffing my rising tears and the crack in my voice. My body sings with exhaustion, and more important, I need this wurm. "She's mine!"

"I'm sorry, Cass—but I've been working this wurm for ten minutes." Laura holds her head high, and the sun gleams down on Quetzal's sharp yellow-and-purple scales. "We agreed . . . it's every chica for herself." She hesitates, then barrels off and corners the wurm in a crevice.

My face falls, and my body tenses as I pull back.

It's a game, it's a game. Challenge her.

But I waver too long. As Laura struggles to control the wurm, a cyan mountain dragon peels into the mix.

"Yah! Yah!" I recognize Colt's voice. He wields his lasso and spins it overhead. It's some of the best ropework I've ever seen from someone his age. The lasso loops around the wurm's neck, and the serpentine creature jerks back.

"Blast, Colt!" My voice echoes off the cave walls. I don't know if I'm angry for myself or for Laura. Both, maybe.

I'm not the only one with a dog in this fight.

Quetzal lets loose a blaze of fire, burning through the rope holding the captive wurm. Laura knocks past me, ropes the wurm, and takes off.

A tear falls down my cheek as, bitter and more alone than ever, I chase after Colt. A heaviness settles in my bones, and I snap Ranga's reins.

"That wurm wasn't yours!" My eyebrows press together,

165

and I kick my heels into Ranga. Her wings flap in a dangerous defensive motion.

"Touchy, touchy. If you think I'd go down without a fight, you're living in a dreamworld." He tips his hat, silver rings flashing, and makes for the skies.

There are no alliances in the Great Texas Dragon Race.

My mouth tastes like acid as Ranga and I skim the canyon. Still rocks stare back at me. Silence fills the void—all the other riders have already taken to the sky with their dragons.

I hang my head as fear and regret creep through me. Fingers numb, I run a hand along Ranga's skin as if the gesture can comfort me—wash away the ache.

Whack!

Something knocks us hard against stone. I struggle to hold on to the saddle and bear down into the stirrups with my ruby-red boots. As I pull myself upright, Ranga turns. We are face-to-face with a gargantuan, snarling wurm. Its lichen-covered body tremors, then it swings toward the bottom of the canyon. Reins tight around my hands, I falter, then guide Ranga down, remembering Mom's moves from old recordings. I'm as agile as her—I know it. Ranga tenses as we dive, but she stays the course. She is a warrior, and I am her companion.

But when we reach the bottom, the earth scatters around us, and the mossy wurm peels back and forth before turning on us. It pants in heaving breaths of fire.

Ranga recoils and shrieks.

"Come on, Ranga!"

Tentative, she puffs embers.

Thrashing, the wurm attacks as if we're a mosquito ready to be squashed. It smacks Ranga and me, cutting my thigh with its serrated scales. We struggle to land upright, and I'm tossed from the saddle onto rocky ground. The fall knocks the wind out of me. My thigh bleeds. I clamp down on the biggest wound with my hand. The wurm crushes Ranga's wing underneath its belly, trapping her as I scramble in the dirt.

My goggles fall around my neck and dust stings my eyes. Hot air swirls around me, rank and powerful. I wipe the dirt from my face and look up.

The savage wurm prowls closer. Its bulging green eyes narrow.

ROARRRR!

Like a tornado, the strength of its breath presses me back against the ground. As if it will help me, I cover my head but glance up through the cracks between my arms. Rows of serrated teeth gleam. They drip with saliva, which pools onto the ground.

The wurm bears down, inching closer and closer. And at that moment, I imagine how upset my father will be if I don't come home. I imagine what will happen to Gran when I am gone. People say that before you die, your life flashes before you. But as the wurm licks me with its tongue, that is not my experience. Instead, I see flashes of the life I will never live: going to eighth grade; running the dragon ranch; winning the Great Texas Dragon Race.

All the things I've never done in my short thirteen-year-old life.

And so, because I can imagine nothing else, I start to sing. I'm a poor western Dorothy trying to get back home. Instead of ruby slippers, I have ruby cowboy boots. My song escapes with choked vibrato as I press back tears:

> Home, home on the range,
> where the deer and the antelope play;
> where seldom is heard
> a discouraging word,
> and the skies are not cloudy all day . . .

Halfway into the second verse, the wurm stops. It sucks in a hot breath, and wisps of hair fly around my face. The wurm cocks its head like a dog listening to a strange whistle. The rims of its pupils seize, flickering from green to blue—a sign that "it" is actually a "she"—then recede.

Straightening my body, I continue to sing "Home on the Range," and the more I sing, the calmer the wurm seems to be. I rise, lift my hands in a shaky suggestion of surrender, and walk toward the wurm. Heat rises from the wurm's mottled body, and I run my hand along her scales. She is hot—hotter than she should be. Her body craves the mountaintop, where the wind can kiss her skin. She isn't a barbarian—she just wants to get back home.

I scratch underneath her chin as she edges into my hand. Ranga creeps toward us, her steps light.

"Good girl," I say to the wurm.

The other riders have already flown off with their prizes. Unless I can urge this wurm to speed up, I doubt we will make it back in time. But as the wurm's mouth gapes, I know that spurring her on with lassos and whips will only harm her. She deserves a slow and steady ride, even if it costs me the win. I stroke her mosslike scales.

"Would you let us guide you out of here?" I ask.

The wurm's pupils flash. That's good enough for me.

So, we ride on with the wurm in tow.

****

"Ladies and gentlemen, may I present the riders who saved Big Bend from another fire!" The announcer stomps across a platform, bullhorn lifted to his lips.

The reporters and local fans cheer as my heart pounds. Members of the board are there, including Michael Carne, who lifts his head to the adoring crowd. Scratches trace my thighs where the wurm's scales cut through my jeans before I got her in line. But my overwhelming disappointment dulls the pain. I safely delivered the wurm to Lost Mine Peak—and I'm proud of that—but I've missed the cut by one. *One.*

As the reporters' cameras click away, I focus on my breath and fight back the tears welling in the corners of my eyes. I stand tall nonetheless, hoping that no one can see what I've lost. Laura stands next to me, and I don't dare look at her. Despite our run-in with the wurms, I want to be happy for her.

But wanting to be happy and actually being happy aren't the same thing. Not even close. I've abandoned my family and disappointed Pa for nothing.

"Now, as you know, only thirty riders can advance to the next leg of the race. Riders: If you are one of the thirty who arrived first, please step forward."

They step forward and their shadows stretch across me. More cheers. More shame.

The announcer pulls a paper from his back pocket and slaps it on the podium. "Usually, placements in the Great Texas Dragon Race are determined by time and time alone. But as you know, dragon care and health is a top priority for the West Texas Dragon Wrangling Association. Unless the dragon threatens human life, we expect our riders to operate with conservation in mind."

The ambient humming of his microphone pops with feedback as the announcer clears his throat. I lift my head to the noise. Beside him, Michael Carne stands motionless alongside the other members of the council.

"And unfortunately, one competitor nearly killed their wurm and violated these sacred guidelines."

With bated breath, the crowd of reporters goes silent.

"Tanner Bright has therefore been disqualified from this portion of the competition. This means that Cassidy Drake—who treated her dragon with exceptional care and is the thirty-first to arrive—will move on to the next leg of the race. Tanner, please step back. Cassidy, please step forward!"

I hesitate as outrage lifts from the section where dozens of FireCorp groupies have gathered in the bleachers. Michael Carne's dark features clench together and form a wall of stone.

"This is an outrage!" shouts a random FC fan.

"Tanner is first—Tanner is the winner!" shouts another FireCorp-clad rider, foaming at the mouth.

I stare back at Michael, wondering how much sway he has over the competition. But the announcer is unfazed.

"I'm sorry. We have deliberated this as a council, and our decision is final." He waves me forward. "Cassidy Drake, take your place."

The sounds of whoops and cheers from unsponsored riders and a handful of reporters rise into the sky. I step forward, my head held high. Beside me, Laura beams, her rosy cheeks stretched from ear to ear, revealing her dimples. Down the line, Ash is stone-faced, and my joy rises.

Tanner, however, does not step back. His ears are red, and he stays locked on Michael, whose jaw is clenched tight. He's obviously already advocated for Tanner, and lost.

Two sheriffs step into the winner's circle and approach Tanner. He holds his ground until they grab him by both arms. He fights back and punches a sheriff in the face. But the sheriff, his head the size of a watermelon, drags Tanner to the ground and restrains him. The surrounding crowd wails with a mixture of cheers and boos.

I press my lips together, holding back a smirk as they take Tanner offstage.

"Just you wait, Cassidy Drake!" he screams. "We are coming for you! FireCorp is coming for you!"

I lace my fingers behind my back and do not look his way. I've placed. And that is all that matters.

"Ladies and gentlemen," says the announcer, "I present to you the official winners of the second leg of the Great Texas Dragon Race!"

CHAPTER 15

We set up camp in a valley below Lost Mine Peak, and the thirty remaining competitors scatter across the tree-dotted terrain to collect food. Again, the sheriffs outline the designated area we're expected to stay inside. The ranch hands recharge our livestream cameras and assemble a generator with dozens of extension cords, creating a hub for us to juice up whatever approved devices we've brought along. I dare not leave anything plugged in, lest it gets stolen, so I dash off to change my T-shirt and search for food. Meanwhile, ranch hands perform medical checks on the dragons—to Ranga's displeasure—some of whom were brutalized in the rough ride. That will cost their riders in the long run.

This time, they offer our dragons a pasty, nutritional supplement. It should ensure none of them goes on a terror storm during the next leg. Sweet burning bacon, I hope they give us at least a few hours of sleep.

Solo riders greet me with rushed pats on the back and handshakes as we scavenge the plains. I want to call Pa to gloat, but I ignore the comm tent like the plague.

There's not even a puddle in sight, which means none of us can replenish our canteens. I shake mine, which is only half-full. Scrambling, I set my sights on a cactus patch and hack off nopal paddles with my bowie knife. Nopales and prickly pear will make a nutritious meal.

Careful not to prick my fingers on the spines, I stuff the paddles in a canvas bag. Angry whispers lilt through the tents as I rush to the campsite. The sharp tones bounce back and forth, and I can't help but lean in. I hide behind the makeshift infirmary tent and listen, eyes closed.

"You can't ignore me forever," says the first whisper. Her voice is familiar. Yes, it's—

"You're lucky I acknowledge you at all."

Bam. Something clatters to the ground.

I step out from behind the tent and prop my hands on my hips. Valeen whirls around. Her sleek bob brushes her chin and her cheeks blush red. A glassy-eyed Ash lingers behind her, scrunched up against a drooping juniper tree. His engraved Yeti lies on the ground.

"Trouble in paradise?" I ask, staring back at them like a U.S. marshal with pistols at her sides.

Valeen purses her burgundy lips and loops the leather strap of her toiletries case around her shoulder.

"This is none of your business, freckle-faced Lizard of Oz."

Such a strange insult coming from a fellow dragoneer, especially since she's the Wicked Witch. "I'm sure the press would love to know that everything is not as it seems at FireCorp."

"Pfft." Valeen's expensive perfume, which hardly covers her sweaty stench, hangs around her like a noxious cloud. "I'd race a few more legs before claiming to know how things work around here, newbie."

The heels of her English riding boots crunch through the dirt. I keep her in my crosshairs until she disappears into the bustle of camp.

Ash's cold hazel eyes catch my attention. "Can we talk?"

I cross my arms and scowl. He's dressed in onyx riding gear and carries a long nylon riding crop at his side. "Snobby" doesn't even begin to cover this outfit.

"Unless you plan to apologize, I'd rather not." I spin on my heels and swish through the brush toward the generator. Nancy Sinatra's "These Boots Are Made for Walkin'" jangles in my head.

Ash glides up behind me. "I have something for you."

Beyond the campsite, someone's diamondfin screeches, sending an eerie echo across the plains. Neither of us startles, which I find wildly annoying. Boys that scare easily are less of a pain.

"I can just about guaran-darn-tee that's not the case." I twist my digital watch, its rubber band hot from the midday sun. "Now, if you don't mind, I have things to do."

"You're insufferable," Ash mutters. He reaches into the pocket of his black breeches and pulls out Gran's compass. It dangles from its familiar purple ribbon.

I burst with excitement and cup it as he suspends it midair. "Where did you find it?"

"I found it on the ground outside the cave, and remembered seeing you with it at the last rest stop." He drops the compass into my palm. "Please, just let me explain. I'm sorry about the soup. Truly. And I promise I'm not the person you think I am. It's just this race—and what I'm bound to do."

As I part my lips to speak, Michael Carne interjects and

waves Ash aside. His colonial, high-fashion garb, complete with a silk ascot, makes Ash look like a commoner. Michael snatches the compass from me with a gloved hand.

"Ah, give us a minute, *son*." Michael says "son" as if he is Gollum and Ash is the precious.

The color drains from Ash's face. I feel as though I'm watching him implode like a planet in a sci-fi movie. Ash angles his jaw to Michael before walking off, and I'm not sure if I sense anger or fear in his gesture.

But I'm not so easily intimidated. I step closer. "Isn't it convenient that council members are allowed at rest stops. I suppose you're busy giving your cronies gear and tips for the next leg."

"We're searched and quarantined this entire race, Miss Drake." says Michael. "Council members are bound by the honor code, just like you."

"You have no honor."

Michael ignores the comment, and his black glove forms a militant fist around my compass. "I'm pleased to hear that Ashton retrieved your compass. A family heirloom, I take it."

"I'd like it back, please." I hold out my hand.

But he opens his hand, turns it over again, and seems to drift into meditation. "When I was a child, I was just like you," he starts. "Small-time dragon farmer from a poor background—following the bucolic path laid out for me."

I reach for the compass, but Michael dodges me. He plucks off his glove with hyperbleached teeth, revealing a network of scars on the back of his hand that trails into his sleeves. With a marred thumb, he caresses the compass. "The night Ashton's mother and I got married, Ashton's biological father rode to our house, drunk, on the back of a pearly nightgrave. He nearly killed Ashton with that fire-spewing dragon. I pulled Ashton from the flames, and that's how I got this."

He holds up his hand and waves his fingers. Words cool as ice, he continues, tone level as if disconnected from reality. "No one deserves a father like that. I would know. I will do anything to protect Ashton. And I will work hard to provide him with every opportunity I never had as a young boy. Dragons have the power to change lives and unite nations. They are FireCorp's path to greatness—Ashton's path to greatness."

Ugh. "You do know you sound like the evil henchman in a graphic novel, right?"

"Someday, maybe you won't simplify everything the way that I once did." He clears his throat. "I respect these animals as they are. Not like those of you who would coddle them and tuck them away in rural ranches. They thrive, like children, in the fist of discipline—just as they did hundreds of years ago when the greatest dragon riders in history ruled by might and mercy."

Usually, this brand of hate speech is kept in dark web message boards or private clubs. To hear dracosupremacy spoken out loud, in public, sends shivers down my spine.

"What a charming thought." I reach for the compass once more as the clock ticks away. Again, Michael withholds it.

"I know what it's like to grow up on the verge of poverty with a father who won't make tough decisions to save his family. Wouldn't you give anything to know you are taken care of?"

My heart twinges. Michael's words echo my deepest disappointments.

Michael must read the hesitation on my face. "I've struck a chord. So, remember this: one day, we will rise up with our dragons—trained, armed, and ready to lead. We will be unstoppable. Indestructible. We will take our rightful places as leaders of energy and industry." Michael presses the compass into my hand and clutches my fingers into a fist. "You choose where you fall in that order."

I rip my hand from his and glare up at him. "I would never choose a path where dragons become slaves for personal gain."

"Make no mistake: this is a competition for personal gain. Dragons die in the Great Texas Dragon Race, just like humans. I've flown this race—I know. Even you entered with a small, skittish dragon who must be terrified of the tasks set before her." Michael raises an eyebrow and refits his glove over his scarred hand. "How different are we, really?"

I squeeze the compass so tight the glass could break. Beyond him, obscured by a heat haze drifting from the shrubby desert floor, Ash lingers, watching us like a buzzard. I'm not sure which of us is the carcass.

Michael wipes a bit of dust from my shoulder. "At some point, society will try to snatch our dragons from us. It is our job to make sure we alone command these creatures. Dragons deserve more than provincial ranches and wilderness."

I straighten my cowboy hat. "Funny thing to say, since FireCorp is a huge lobbyist for the FLARE tariffs."

"I lobby for regulations that keep dragons in the hands of those able to support their needs."

"You mean the wealthy."

"I mean those who've stopped blaming their problems on circumstance and society. Those who've taken up the call to—as you say in your world—pull themselves up by their proverbial bootstraps."

"It's physically impossible to pull yourself up by your bootstraps. But I will tell you this: I *am* going to beat you in this race—and I won't need to harm dragons or have a representative on the council to do it." I nod toward the sponsored riders whispering as they clean dragon tack and exchange maps. "Please give Tanner my regards."

I brush past him, spirits soaring. My rump aches and my thighs are sore, but the sweet knowledge that I've beaten one of Michael's pets radiates through me. I've made my first statement in this race: treating dragons well trumps cruelty. I stuff the compass in my pocket as Ash peers back at me with hazel eyes that say, "I'm sorry for whatever he said to you."

For a moment, I consider hearing Ash out. But my feet lag, and Valeen drags him to the FC's fire. Which is just as well.

Ash and I will never have much to say to one another. I don't need him to explain that he's lived a hard life under the thumb of a narcissistic monster. And I don't want him to justify his obligation to ride hard for an oppressive organization. He's returned my compass, and the gesture reminds me I have only so much space for hate in my heart.

With time ticking away, I dash for the generator in the center of camp.

I grimace as Karbach conjoins our paths. He blows a bubble, then shoves his gum to the side with his tongue.

"FireCorp keeps taking the bridles off their dragons." Karbach clicks away on his phone as he walks alongside me. I try to ignore him, but with his lanky legs, he out-paces me. "Our cameras aren't catching anything—which seems suspicious. I'd pay attention if I were you."

"Excuse me?"

"You heard me."

He waves at a passing fellow reporter as I pick up the pace. In my head, my wheels are turning. What has he learned from weaseling around this camp like a spy? What is he trying to say about FireCorp?

"I have it on good authority that your father isn't too pleased you joined this race. Bad for you, good for your story. Viewers love a rebel." Karbach cuts me off as I object to his prying in my life. "But I'd clean up and shine that belt buckle if I were you. People prefer their rebels buffed to a high gloss." He smacks his gum once, twice, three times. "Anyway, I hope you will invite your dad to the final feast. That is, if you make it that far." He peels to the right to bother another contestant.

What a donkey.

I find Colt underneath a piñon tree and toss my canvas bag of nopales on the ground beside the extension cord he's commandeered.

"That's no way for a champion to behave," says Colt, who nurses a small fire. A shadowy outline of dirt surrounds the areas where his goggles and bandanna covered his face.

"Sorry. I just hate these doggone draggers."

"Enjoy your success while you can. I saw the FC's message for you in the cave. And after Tanner, they'll be gunning for you every second until this race ends."

After sliding off my backpack, I take out my devices: my fritzy goggles, my game-issued GPS locator, and Ranga's emergency call device. I untangle a wad of cables and plug each into the beat-up extension cord. I gingerly lift the nopales from the canvas bag.

"Did you find any water?" I ask, changing the subject.

"Not a drop." He flicks my nopales with his forefinger. "Cactus will have to keep you going."

Rion joins us at the cord and murmurs something about

me having too many devices plugged in, which I ignore. I scrape the cactus with my knife and shave off the prickers. But my finger catches on a cactus spine as an argument starts on the other side of the generator. Nickolai slyly pushes Ash, and Ash stumbles as Michael chats with a reporter, oblivious. Neither Valeen nor any of the other FireCorp riders says a thing.

"It's a dangerous game they're playing," says Rion. "They can get disqualified for violence during pit stops. Everyone should leave their personal business at home."

I cut the sticker from my finger with the knife as Colt hums a little tune, suggesting he disagrees with Rion. "Having a brother isn't easy," he says.

"Brother?" I ask, flipping the nopales over to scrape off the rest of the spines.

"Technically, Nickolai is Michael's ward—brought here years ago from Moscow. Ash and Nickolai were raised together. They're roommates at Dragonscale, even though Ash is fourteen and Nickolai is seventeen. Who knows how they managed that."

Nickolai towers over Ash as he says something I can't hear. The sheriffs inch forward. I grin, knowing that perhaps FireCorp isn't entirely untouchable.

"I actually think that Ash might not be half bad if it

wasn't for Carne breathing down his neck. Nickolai, on the other hand, is mean as a copperhead," says Colt. He dabs his forehead with a colorful bandanna.

"How is your brother?" asks Rion.

"So-so." Colt skewers ground cherries on a stick and leans them over the fire to get a nice char. I join him and do the same with my nopales. Colt sinks into his seat. "My brother, Reid, was always the chosen one," he tells me. "You know, the responsible kid born to be a famous dragon rancher. Last year, he burned half his arm off while riding a grisly sparkhide during the Mesa Race."

"Holy chicken mole," I say. "That's right. I read about it in *Sharptooth*."

Rion's face twists. "I was there—it was awful."

"Meanest dragon I've ever met, that's for sure." Silver rings flashing, Colt fans himself with his cowboy hat.

My collection of nopales is puny, but I offer a piece to Colt. I want him to know I appreciate his willingness to share this story with me. I also offer Rion a piece, and he hesitates but accepts. He gives me a sip of his canteen in return, and because he's been drinking from it, I welcome the gesture. Maybe I'll manage to smooth things over with him before this race ends.

"My brother was in line to take over the ranch so I could

move to Nashville and become a musician." Colt offers me a ground cherry.

I pop the fruit in my mouth, and the sourness reminds me of tomatillo salsa.

"But the injury broke his body and his spirit," says Colt. "Our ninety-thousand-acre ranch is now my responsibility, whether I want it or not."

A pang of jealousy runs through me. "Sounds like a high-class problem, if you ask me."

Colt takes a tiny sip of water from his canteen. "I'm not saying others don't have it worse—but I want more than the life laid out for me." He looks wistfully into the cloud-streaked distance. "There's a tribe out there for everyone, and a place for me away from the Montana-born boondock rednecks that don't appreciate who I am. Or what I represent."

I cock my head. "What's that?"

"Someone *different* . . . even if I am clearly fabulous." He pretends to flick dust off of his shoulder, then blows on his nails as if to express his undeniable fabulousness.

Rion and I laugh. I stuff prickly pear flesh into my mouth, and the berry-sweet juices trickle down my chin. "Clearly."

The sun bears down through the piñon tree, warning

us that the day will be hot and long. Laura and the three milk-skinned Grousewood cowboys join us at the extension cord. We share jokes and meager rations, then rest our heads. If we've learned one thing, it's to grab shut-eye when we can.

CHAPTER

16

After four hours of poor daytime sleep, the third leg begins. A hologram of Chayton Dukes, a famous Mescalero dragon rider I recognize from old sepia-toned photographs, spouts the clue:

> You heard me before,
> yet you hear me once more.
> I die till you call me anew.
> Not April or June,
> not a garden or dune.
> Just follow the butterfly through.

Certainly cryptic enough.

You heard me before, yet you hear me once more. That part is definitely about an echo, so I am guessing the next location is a cave. *Not April or June . . .* May? A cave named May? Everyone around me appears just as stumped as I am. I refocus and recall a lesson from Texas history class about a cave called the Mayfield Cave. Mayfield Cave is part of a bigger cavern, but I can't remember its name. I bite the inside of my cheek. *Just follow the butterfly through.*

The butterfly. The butterfly. It sounds so familiar.

Wait! The Caverns of Sonora! That's where Mayfield Cave is. Of course. Complete with a crystal formation called the Butterfly, the Caverns of Sonora must be home to the next task.

Ranga and I launch into the air as the sun beams down like pure gold. Several riders take off in the other direction. Usually, that would worry me, but not today. I've got this clue nailed.

"We'll have the jump on everyone headed north," I say to Ranga.

She picks up speed, pulling against the reins with an infectious excitement that reminds me how much she loves to fly. We rocket through the air, and the dry wind whips my mustard-colored tee that reads, "Hold Your Horses."

Ranga's scales gleam like Gran's turquoise jewelry.

Once I reach the Caverns of Sonora, I waste time testing several hidden entry points, but my spirit remains high. Touching down at a third craggy entrance, we find Valeen's mean black-and-burgundy dragon, Scarlett, hitched outside. Ranga shudders and hovers above the earth, too scared to land. Scarlett senses her uneasiness and scratches her wine-red talons in the dirt.

Reeeeekkkkkchek! Scarlett warns.

Ranga jerks and my tailbone slams into the saddle so hard that I might cry.

"It's okay, Ranga." I fumble with the reins. "She won't hurt us. The cameras are watching."

Scarlett roars again as if to disagree with me, and saliva drips from her pearly white teeth.

Ranga's scales flash a dull gray and her translucent wings beat the air.

"Dagnabit, Ranga, hold steady!"

But Scarlett roars again, and Ranga spirals away, nearly bucking me off her saddle. Eventually, I manage to land her a few hundred yards out. Ranga's entire body ripples with hot, anxious energy.

I slide off her back, stomp over, and grab her bridle. "Ranga, you know what, I love you, but I need you to try harder," I snap, peeling off my gloves and tossing them to the ground.

She cowers and draws her head low in a beta position.

"No. Don't cower. That's the problem." I circle her and tap the underside of her pointed jaw, forcing it upward. "Sit up straight. You're better than this."

She whimpers.

"Don't whimper at me. I'm the human and you're the awesome fire-breathing dragon who survived the trauma of FireCorp!" I shout as my own inborn fire rises to meet hers. For a moment, I don't mind if she lashes back and burns me alive. In fact, I would welcome it. "You're strong, Ranga . . . and you're faster than every other dragon in this race."

She chirps, which is Ranga's way of asking me to stop, but I can't. And I won't. My mom gave me a thousand of these pep talks, and now it is time for Ranga to have hers.

"I don't care how big those other dragons are. It's not the breadth of your wings or the size of your teeth that matters. It's how much fiery courage you have in your blood." I pound on my chest with a bare fist as if to motion to my own heart. "You survived FireCorp, and you have more untapped courage in your baby claw than their entire team combined. Accept who you are. Survivor. Fighter. *Warrior.* You are the best dragon in this whole stinkin' race. Stop acting like you're beneath everyone."

But Ranga cowers, and despite my best argument, she refuses to return to go near Scarlett. I leave Ranga in the mountains and drag my feet back to the cavern.

Scarlett's bulky neck tightens as I approach, and she glares at me with slitted pupils, catlike as Valeen herself. There are no distinctive markers and I can't find the hologram platform. Under the watchful eye of Scarlett, I kick up dust, scouring for a clue. Panting, I flip over rocks and dried wood.

Valeen appears from the cave. She pulls her goggles down around her neck and simpers.

"Funny seeing you here." An evil grin twists her porcelain face. "Oh, how awful this must feel."

I rest my hands on my hips. "And why is that?"

She flexes her hands in her soft leather gloves. "My apologies." Her voice is acidic and mischievous. "I thought you'd already figured this one out. Ha! So, your last win was a fluke, wasn't it?"

My fists ball at my side. "Cut the crap, Valeen."

Valeen holds a finger in the air. "Let me see." She walks to a boulder with a faint X chiseled into it. Valeen directs

Scarlett to move it. It scrapes along the ground, revealing a shallow pit. The hologram platform rests inside it. "You might want to see the hologram."

I drag my feet to the pit. "I don't need your help."

"Oh, but I wouldn't miss this." Valeen beckons me to press the red button. "Go ahead."

I kick the button, and the hologram flickers to life. My blood runs icy as a familiar image stands before me.

My mother.

She says:

> Red touches black, safe for Jack.
> Red touches yellow, kills a fellow.

Her face is fresh and lovely in the digital projection, and my stomach turns sour. She looks much like I remember from home movies and faded photographs, but there are small things I don't recognize: the way her lips move when she speaks; the timbre of her voice. And she's shorter than I remember. Short, just like me.

"Stunning, isn't it?" asks Valeen. "At Dragonscale Academy, we're taught everything we could ever want to know about the past winners of this race. Including your mother. If I'm not mistaken, it was a Texas coral viper that killed her, wasn't it? Such a morbid choice by the game designers to choose dead riders for the holograms."

But fear fills my heart instead of rage. As I peer into my dead mother's image, I can't think of any sassy comebacks.

Valeen grins like a panther after a meal. "Oh, perhaps *this* is why they let you enter as number fifty-one—because I must say, the look on your face is priceless. Let's hope Scarlett picked it up on her camera. I'm sure the draggers will go wild with this latest development." She lifts a vial filled with milky liquid and shakes it in front of my face. "I'm certain you're positively built for this task."

My eyes sweep back to the cavern as Ash descends on Juliette. My stomach unknots as he hitches his dragon and stalks toward us. He lifts the visor on his helmet, which casts a long shadow over his rigid face.

"Ash, how nice to see you. Sorry, I can't stay—races to win." Valeen puts her goggles back on and tightens the velveteen riding helmet around her head.

Ash doesn't respond, and it strikes me as odd that she doesn't stay to share strategy or give him any clues. Perhaps there's more to the FireCorp story than what the press are selling.

Valeen makes for Scarlett, then spins back around and offers one last unsolicited comment. "Oh, and Cassidy, I know so much more about your mother's history. Let me know if you'd ever like me to enlighten you about who Aurora McCoy Drake *really* was." With a casual hand, she blows Ash a kiss.

Ash recoils as if the gesture burns him. He stares Valeen down as she and Scarlett fly off in a mighty gust.

"Where's the clue?" he asks, emotionless.

Too rattled to ignore him, I point at the boulder. My fingers tremble.

Ash hits the hologram deck, and again my mother appears. And again, I can't do more than stare at the life-like hologram.

Ash shakes his head, and the way he fumbles with his wyvern's reins tells me he's uncomfortable. People are always uncomfortable when the subject of my famed dead mother comes up. Let alone when I'm standing before a spitting image of her.

After looping a pack on his back, Ash grabs a lasso. "I'm sorry," he mutters.

Like a puff of smoke, he disappears into the cave. I'm wasting time, but a powerful desire to hug this counterfeit Aurora Drake consumes me. I approach the hologram and stretch out a hand as if I could touch her. But my hand distorts the empty image with flickers of red and green.

Even though it's fake, and even though it does nothing more than repeat the chilling poem, a part of me can't bear leaving it behind.

"Goodbye, Mom," I whisper, withdrawing my hand.

With a deep breath, I leave her and pass into the crevice. I take small, calculated steps as if every ounce of cowgirl courage has left me. The floor is wet, and the cave smells like sulfur and mold. Glowing luminarias made of paper bags and battery-powered votive candles, the type usually reserved for cheery outdoor Christmas decorations, light the tunnel, marking my path and leading me through narrow passages. The haunting glow turns the space into an ancient tomb. The ghost of my mother lingers in every shadow, and she calls to me in the air whistling through the abyss.

The twisting passageway terminates in a damp, musty chamber. A low supernatural hum grows louder with each step I take. I breathe in the stale, mildewy air. Rocks skitter under my feet and echo down the cave. Consarnit.

A vicious dragon wriggles in the shadows, and I slam against the wall.

With stripes of red, black, and yellow, the viper's slick reptilian skin ripples along pounds of lithe muscle. Its sleek head is more snakelike than anything we've seen so far, and it bobs like a cobra in some old movie. Delicate and hypnotic and covered in crystal-shaped scales, the viper is almost beautiful as it glistens in the glow of torches.

Terror coils in my belly, and I skirt the cave wall, hidden in the shadows and careful to give the dragon a wide berth. Ash is nowhere to be seen.

Though it's the length of a water slide, size isn't what makes a Texas coral viper dangerous. No. As it growls, ivory teeth retract from the roof of its mouth and shimmer with glorious danger. The translucent fangs, long as golf clubs and twice as thick, drip with deadly dragon venom.

Images of my mother flash through my mind: the way she looked when the toxin paralyzed her; the way her breathing became ragged. The worst part was that we had the antivenom. She just couldn't tell me where it was. Pa wasn't home, and I was too young.

The Texas coral viper that killed her was a FireCorp rescue. It had been too traumatized to trust my mom. And it wound up killing her.

In the corner, underneath a shining cave lamp, rests a wicker basket. Under cover of shadows, I creep to the basket, lift the lid, and read the inscription plastered on the underside.

One for each. Collect, but don't drink. Return the venom to Silver Spur.

Below the plaque are several large Pyrex test tubes capped with thin plastic. The same kind that Valeen had taunted me with. I count them up. Twenty-three. An ounce of relief washes over me. At least I'm not the last to arrive. I grab the tube and discover it's attached to a muslin bag filled with three wheels. Curious. Goods in hand, I creep round the bend, keeping low.

A lump forms in my throat as I peer at the viper between stalactites. Following my mother's death, Pa transferred the offending dragon to a herpetological park in Idaho and never spoke about Texas coral vipers again. I haven't seen one since. And though I've watched naturalists extract venom from snakes on TV, I can't remember how to lull coral vipers into submission. Sweat forms under my hand, sandwiched between calluses and Pyrex. I take calculated breaths to soothe the anxiety building within me.

I know, deep in my bones, that if I die by this dragon, my father will never ride again.

I crouch down and scour the scene for Ash. With years at Dragonscale Academy, he's probably milked a viper before. And since my only hope is to learn from someone else, he is my ticket. I manage to make him out through the shadows across the cave, but he doesn't budge. Dang it. I guess we're both stuck waiting until someone else makes a move. My heart races as the minutes drag out.

I steady my breath as the sounds of falling rocks fill the cavern. The viper startles but settles back into her sleeping position as the humming continues its haunting echo.

Someone rustles in the cave, catching my attention. My spirits lift as I watch Laura kneel by the basket. Part of me wants to call out to her and ask for help. But I keep silent, reminding myself that there are no teams in this race. *Be courageous, be strong, be a Drake*, I chant in my head.

I stay pressed against the stone as Laura gathers her test tube. Without hesitation, she steadies herself and grabs her lasso. She tethers the rope around a stalactite and forms a primitive pulley system from the wheels. Of course! Using the pulley will make it easier to wrangle the dragon with our own weight. After securing the rope, she twirls the lasso overhead. It slices through the air, capturing the viper's attention. Milky eyes glistening, it sets its sights on Laura.

But Laura Torres is as quick as she is smart.

She lassos the viper, pulls it tight with all her might, and forces the dragon into submission. With its head wedged against the ground, she ties it in place with a set of fancy knots. The viper hisses in the corner, warring with the rope and stalactite.

Fearless and determined, the purple fringe of her boots dancing, Laura strides to the dragon. I catch my breath as she stoops beside the hissing viper. Quicker than a jack-rabbit, she shoves a fang into her test tube and pets the creature's ear. It blinks slowly, then leans into her caress. Yellow liquid oozes down the edge of the glass.

Laura stands and holds her prize up to a soft, flickering lantern.

Beyond her, the viper begins wrestling with its muzzle again. It cries out and my fingers tremble. Across the cave, Ash unhooks his lasso, ready to make his move. I'm not ready to face the task, but I can't let him get to the viper before I do. Time is running out. So I hastily dash out into the landing before Ash can beat me to it.

As I dart forward, the tethered viper thrashes against its muzzle and screeches. My entire body tenses with fear and I fumble, slamming into Laura. I knock the precious test tube from her hand and fall to the ground. It spins in the air as the viper shrieks. Laura slides across the wet stone, barely catching the vial before it shatters.

She clutches it to her chest and yells, "What is wrong with you?"

The viper jerks at its muzzle and releases a loud, hissing noise. It flails and whips around the space. Its immature wings beat the air, which echoes back through the cave.

"After everything I've done to help you so far?" says Laura.

My breath catches in my throat. "I—I didn't do it on purpose—"

"This may be a game, but I never thought you'd sabotage a fellow player outright." Laura grips the test tube like it's a lifeline, then slips it into her pouch. "At least I know where we stand now."

She grabs the nylon rope securing the writhing dragon and wags the end at me. "I know your mother died facing a Texas coral viper. When I heard the clue, I honestly felt for you. If you'd asked, I would have left this lasso tied up for you."

"I swear I didn't—"

"But I guess you were right. In the end, there are no teams." Laura flicks open a switchblade and saws through the rope. Strands pop until it's holding on by a few delicate fibers, and she darts back into the cave. Horror spreads through me as the viper screeches and snaps back, breaking the cord.

Hissssss!

The dragon rises from the rocky garden, body sleek and

muscular. Slithering, it lurches overhead and stretches up between the stone shafts around us. Eyes milky with blindness, its head darts back and forth, listening—waiting. From its venomous mouth flits a burnt yellow tongue, tasting fear and sweat. The deadly fangs scrape the air, dripping with fatal venom.

Left alone, vipers can live for a month off one meal. But now it's awake, angry, and ready for blood. My empty test tube feels heavy in the satchel at my side, and my eyes tear at the corners. Only a few people stand between me and a win, so I try to push my interaction with Laura aside and breathe. In through the nose. Out through the mouth.

I crawl back into a shallow crevice, safe in its darkness. Gran always says good cowboys know when to take a break, but I can't stop. Not now. Hands trembling, I thread my rope through the wheels.

In. Out.

I make for the flailing viper as its red, black, and yellow snakeskin pulses. Heart in my throat, I secure my cord and prepare to launch from my hiding place. But another lasso loops around the viper's neck.

Across the cavern, Ash stands like a ghostly figure.

"No!" I cry, leaping from the shadows.

The coral viper snaps in my direction. A long white fang nicks my forearm, sending a shock through my muscles.

The tingle of venom trickles up my arm as I fall back and squeeze into the tight crannies of the cave. My lips grow numb with fear.

Ash reels in the viper with powerful arms, rushes to my spot between stalagmites, and hovers over me. "Why didn't you keep your big mouth shut?"

"I—I don't know. T-this task . . ." I feel claustrophobic, as if the narrow cave is closing in on me, and I suck in a sharp breath. "I'm so s-stupid."

"Shhh." Ash rips a flap of carmine fabric from his FireCorp polo and binds the wound. "I don't mean to scare you, but you have to go. *Now.*"

I shake my head as a tear rolls down my cheek. How could I have screwed up this task so much? "The race. I—I have to finish." My hands are numb. I woozily stumble to my feet and stagger across uneven ground to the captured dragon. I jam the viper's fang into the test tube. But my legs begin to give way, and the viper hisses as I drop to the murky earth beside it, test tube in hand. I manage to stopper the vial, even though my hands are shaking.

Ash hovers over me, and the stalactites form a chilling cathedral above him. "We should call the medical team to come and get you. We can send word via livestream and—"

"W-who knows how long that will take. I can make it to the checkpoint."

"You have about an hour before paralysis takes hold."

"You mean before it kills me."

The viper screeches and it echoes through the cavern.

"Stop talking," says Ash.

Ash scoops me up and runs me outside. The sun glares down on me, growing brighter with every moment. Nickolai Grigori touches down as I guide Ash to Ranga. She rushes to Ash and whimpers.

"Ranga," says Ash, "we need your speed."

She huffs as he places me on her back. I flop over on her, barely able to hold the reins, and Ash slips my feet into the stirrups.

"Do you know where you're going?"

My lips part. Already, words are becoming hard to form. "Silver S-Spur . . . Bandera," I gasp. "I'm Going to Die in Sonora" would be a good name for a country song.

Ash squeezes my clammy hand, with too much pity for my taste, and pets Ranga. "Go now."

I steer Ranga into the clear blue sky, heading east to the Texas Hill Country. My watch ticks heavy on my wrist, and I slump over.

"Ranga, no matter what, keep . . . flying. F-fly until you

hit . . . B-Bandera. Fly to Silver Spur Ranch—"

Thank goodness she's been to Silver Spur Ranch before. I place my head on her neck and shut my eyes. My muscles tense as we carry on, against the wind, and on to the checkpoint. My breathing turns ragged, and hot air dries my lips. I want to lick them, but I can't seem to draw my tongue to wet them.

Ranga keeps on as the minutes slow. I want to apologize for pushing her too hard, but I can't form the words. Instead, I think of poor sick Gran, and Pa, who is barely hanging on by a thread. He can't lose both me and Mom to a viper. He just can't. With what little strength I have left, I lightly rub Ranga's opalescent scales.

My eyes flutter open. Beyond us, miles away, I see fields of color: pink evening primrose, Texas bluebells, and red fire wheels. The wildflowers sway in the breeze, surrounding a cluster of dragons, people, and celebratory banners. But my legs feel like they're evaporating, and I'm not sure if they're still in the stirrups. I imagine my mother, paralyzed but fully conscious as she lay dying at my side. She wanted to explain where the antivenom was but couldn't. A familiar terror builds within me. The finish line is so close, but I may not make it. May never see Drake's Dragon Ranch again. May never eat homemade biscuits, hug Gran, or laugh at Pa for getting pork rinds on his shirt.

Ranga dives down, and I can no longer feel the wind against my skin. I can see the end, with sheriffs, the medical team, and locals waiting for my arrival. Draggers rush in and small children wave banners.

But before I cross the finish line, my body gives up, and the last gasps of breath escape my lungs.

CHAPTER
17

Somewhere in Texas

My head pounds and my eyelids blink open. A bright kerosene lantern glares down on me, and an IV sticks out of my arm. It's nighttime and a tiny clock on the stool beside me reads 5:16 a.m. Stitches trail up my mangled arm. My ribs hurt, and I still feel dizzy. But I'm alive—tucked away in a field hospital tent, the sounds of cicadas whirring outside. I sit up and find Ash passed out in a collapsible camping chair in the corner. My makeshift hospital bed squeaks as I shift, and he rustles awake.

Ash's eyes are heavy and lined with dark circles, and his skin seems sallow in the kerosene light.

"Did I make it? Are we in Bandera?"

Ash nods and examines me, crumpled up in his chair with a *Texas Almanac* across his lap.

"What?" I say, cracking a smile. "Didn't think you could get rid of me that easy, did you?"

Ash lays the almanac on the dusty ground and staggers to his feet. He slips his hands in his pockets and exhales a long gust of air. His dark brown hair is a mess, and I can't help but wonder how long I've been doubled up in this infirmary bed. Or how long Ash has waited for me.

The tent is bare, no cards or flowers in sight. Ash is, by all approximation, my only visitor. A spider dangles from the vertical pole propping up the fabric. Not exactly the warm welcome you'd expect when waking up from a viper attack.

"Ranga?" I ask.

"Ranga's fine. She saved your life. You should have let me call the medical team."

"We made it in time, didn't we?"

"Number fifteen."

We're improving. "Has anyone spoken to my family?"

Ash nods. "They've arranged for a supervised call once you wake up."

"Perfect," I mutter. My father won't react kindly to any of this. I can only imagine the fear and worry he must be feeling. I'm honestly surprised he hasn't already mounted a dragon, stormed the race, and taken me back home.

Silence stretches out between us, and I grip the knitted blanket covering me. My fingers claw the loose weave, and I clear my throat. Flashes of Ash scooping me up and sending me to the finish line run through my mind. I wince at the thought, that feeling worse than the pain in my ribs. Despite everything, he helped me.

"Thank you," I mumble, so quietly that I imagine he might have a hard time hearing me. But he grunts. I peer up at him, at the FireCorp logo printed on his tight-fitting polo, and I can hardly believe that I mean it, that I'm grateful for someone who's supposed to be the enemy.

"I guess I finally had the guts to be a decent person," he mumbles back. The canvas door of the tent flaps in a gust of cool night air. Ash rests his head in one hand and laces his fingers through the front of his hair. "Look, I know you shouldn't trust me, but I need to tell you something. Something I've never told anyone outside of FireCorp."

"Oh-kay . . . ," I say, unsure of how to respond.

Ash repositions himself on the foot of the cot. It creaks over and over as he tries out different positions. But none of them seem comfortable enough.

"Have you ever had a best friend?" Ash asks.

I lie. "Sure."

Ash lifts an eyebrow. "A human best friend?"

"Well, not technically." And, possibly for the first time, I realize how pathetic it sounds. I pick at a hangnail, pulling it back too far. "Best friends stay up late and share secrets . . . But I can't exactly share mine, can I? I don't know many dragoneering families. Occupational hazard of not going to a dragon ivy, I guess."

I've never spoken those words, perhaps because being alone never mattered to me before. The other competitors have lasting friendships and shared experiences that I don't. Like Ash, I lower my head.

"Well, when you have a best friend, you *never*—and I mean never—betray them."

I motion for him to get to the point.

Ash fidgets, and the cot squeaks again. "Brayden Boone and I used to be best friends. We did everything together. Played together, studied together, trained together. He was even a member of the FC riding team."

Ash fiddles with the collar of his black FC polo. "But at school, he became my biggest competition, and slowly, he became better than me. At everything: grades, riding, friendships. All Michael wanted was for me to be lead rider of Dragonscale's Junior Team. It was all we talked about in my house: how I would win and how I would beat Brayden. But as tryouts got closer, it became clear Brayden was going to win. He was the better rider. And I hated him for it."

The way he says "hated" feels so familiar. I know what it's like to be that competitive. Bile rises in the back of my throat.

"Then, on the eve of fall finals, Nick stole the principal's prized possession, a miniature snoutgripe named Harlo. Nick suggested that if I planted Harlo in Brayden's locker, I would be the obvious choice for lead rider. So I did. When the principal found the snoutgripe, Brayden was expelled. I was named lead rider the next day."

This is the reason Brayden hates FireCorp. I curl my fingers in the blanket and murmur, "Why are you telling me all this?"

"Because I've never been honest about it with anyone. And I want you to know that I regret who I've been. That from here on out, you can trust me."

I hesitate. "I appreciate that you saved me . . . and that you brought me my compass. But you still drugged my soup, remember?"

"I know. When the school year began, Michael agreed that if I won this race, he'd let me attend any school I wanted next year. No more lousy dragon prep school where he's on the board of directors and I'm circled by FireCorp vultures. No more pointless rivalry with Nick."

Ash rubs his hand on his black jeans and clears his throat. "A week ago, I would have done anything to get free of Michael's choke hold on my life. Including gaining your friendship just to betray you two seconds later. But I can't play their game anymore. Even if it means I'm trapped at Dragonscale forever. I don't want to be the type of guy who cares more about glory than friends."

"Why the sudden change of heart?" I ask.

"Because it was easier when Brayden was out of sight and out of mind. Now, every time I see him, I'm reminded of what I did. And how it's too late. Brayden will never forgive me. I don't think I will ever forgive myself . . . I can't repeat the same mistake with you." Ash's eyes are suddenly more green than gold.

Maybe we're all struggling to do more than just win a race. I nudge him with my leg as if to say, "I understand." The pained look on his face softens.

As we sit silent, the spider dangling from the tent pole sways between us. Ash grabs the spider's thread, disconnects the little guy midair, and gently releases it on the other side of the cot.

Pain radiates through my side as I sit up. "Well, I'm sorry that I was so prideful—so mean. My gran always says you catch more flies with honey than you do with vinegar. But it's just this place. This game. These *people* . . . All I can think of is my family, my ranch, my dragons. I'm scared I'll lose them to FireCorp, who will enslave and torture them until they burn out. I can't let them win."

"But they will win. That's what I'm trying to explain." Ash pulls something out of his pocket and balls his fist. He presses whatever it is, cold and hard, into my palm. When I try to open it, he holds my fingers closed.

"Not until I leave." Ash leans in. "Do *not* let anyone find this in your possession. You need to know what you're up against."

The whisper chills me, and I search him for answers. But Ash reveals nothing.

A field nurse dressed in scrubs printed with cacti and coyotes saunters into the tent and scowls. Ash recoils from me as if from a fiery flame.

"Lie back down, little lady. I gave you the antivenom, but you could be sick for hours, even days. Fever, sweats, nausea, you name it." She turns up her nose at Ash. "And you—it's high time you skedaddle on out of here. She'll be sick as a dog if she doesn't get more rest, and I'd rather attend to my patient in peace."

Ash stands, and I shove my hand under the covers. I'll

have to wait to learn its secret.

"Go on—git!" The nurse shoos him off.

Ash leaves without another word, and I grip the cool object in my palm. I'm dying to open my hand, but the nurse hovers, shuffling around with a fresh bag of fluids and a needle the size of my arm. Inside my hand, the item burns, begging my attention.

"Ma'am," I ask, "do you think I might have some water? Even with this IV, my mouth feels like Kerr County on a scorching summer day." I hope she buys it—anything to get her out of here.

The kind nurse smiles back and pats my leg with a light tap. "Sorry, sugar. You may be sick, but unless you call it quits, the race is still active. You'll have to find water on your own. Wait here, and I'll be back with the doc." As she turns to go, she chuckles. "I've seen many a rider in this tent, and the good Lord knows I'm not supposed to say it, but I hope you beat the tar out of them FireCorp boys. No matter how sweet they act, you just remember, they're the enemy." She taps her fingers along the pole of my cot. "Us small-town girls gotta stick together."

I brighten my face and nod. "Yes, ma'am, we do." Sinking into my who-knows-where-it's-been field hospital pillow, I say, "That check will be mine by week's end."

"Good girl," she says, like I'm a dog who's fetched the Sunday paper.

She scurries out the flap door, and I shoot up, kicking the covers off me. I breathe deep.

Opening my hand, I find a vial filled with light green liquid. Printed across the label are words I don't even need to read:

FLAMEMAW ANDROLONE

And it hits me—I'll never win because I can't. The FireCorp varmints are unbeatable because their dragons are drugged.

These are dragon steroids.

CHAPTER
18

29°45'40.2" N, 99°02'43.1" W

Bandera, Texas

I toss off the covers and scramble out of bed. I have to hide this vial! The soles of my feet press against the dirt floor. I run to the tent flap and peek outside. Coast is clear. I whip around, and the wheeled pole holding my IV bag jostles across the rocky ground. The needle tugs at my skin as the pole slams against the cot.

"Dang it," I mutter.

The stark infirmary tent offers no nooks or crannies, and the vial burns in my hand. There isn't even a tissue box on the folding bedside table to stuff it in. Hiding it under the covers seems like the perfect TV movie way to get caught, tried, and executed.

Beyond the tent, the nurse yells, "She's right this way!"

My breath catches. I dash to my cowboy boots in the corner of the tent and stuff the vial in the toe. The flap door waves open just as I stand up straight.

"You shouldn't be out of bed," says the nurse, holding up a finger. She sets a small tray of medical supplies on the bedside table. "The head sheriff would like a word."

Right behind her, Laudes enters, and her spurs click against the ground. With her high-shined, low-heeled boots, she easily clears six feet. Her warm skin is plump, dewy, and flawless—the only human feature of her otherwise serious face. She is all business in crisp, well-ironed fabric, and she carries a camping chair in the crook of her arm. Guilt burns through me as she spins around, surveying every corner of the bare tent. I sip the drops left in my canteen and set it down, careful not to reveal my trembling hands.

"Not very lively in here, is it?" She turns up the kerosene lamp, letting light pour through the space, exposing every inch of it.

"I suppose not." My heart pounds, and I release a desperate laugh. I tuck farther under my blanket. "C-can I help you?"

"Yes, ma'am, I think you can." The sheriff opens her chair with one swift hand motion and takes a seat in the corner. It squeaks as she presses into it. She pulls a pair of wire-framed spectacles from her breast pocket and buffs them with a blue microfiber cloth. Then, she sets them on her nose as if they're some sort of superpowered Bruce Wayne device. Through the frames, she skims the tent again until her eyes fall on my boots in the corner. "Those are nice cowboy boots. Fine shade of red."

My mouth hangs open. Does she know? Should I confess that I have androlone? When they ask how I got it, what will I say? Will they believe it isn't mine?

The sheriff crosses her legs, which shows off the gun at her hip in an almost elegant way. "Ma'am, are you okay?"

I nod because I can't remember how to form words.

"We haven't been formally introduced, but I'm Sheriff Marigold Laudes. You can call me Sheriff, or Laudes, or Sheriff Laudes—don't call me Marigold."

"Yes, ma'am," I say.

Sheriff Laudes plucks a speck of dust from her lapel and lets it fall to the ground. "The council asked me to reach out to discuss your parting ways with the race."

"I'm not quitting."

"Simmer down. No one is demanding you quit. But if you look around, you'll notice your circumstances have changed . . . I've been asked to reach out to your guardian."

Laudes has clearly practiced this conversation because she knows not to say the word "parents" to me. She takes a phone from her pocket and dials a number. I watch in horror as it rings. "Your gran is on the line."

I shoot up in the cot and swipe the phone from her. "Gran?"

"Hi there, jellybean." The sound of Gran's voice pierces through the wall built up around me, and tears wet my eyes.

I clutch the phone, which feels so foreign in my hands. It's as if the days have stretched out into weeks, and I've forgotten what normalcy is like. "I miss you," I say, sucking back tears.

The sheriff leans in so she's only inches from my cot. She smells like rosewater and fresh leather, and I press away from her, two hands wrapped around the phone as if I could hug Gran through it if I try hard enough.

"They tell me you had a bit of a run-in with a viper," says Gran. "Are you okay?"

"I'm fine. I'm fine."

"You don't sound fine."

"But I will be. How are you?"

I wave the sheriff off, and she barely sits back in her chair. As she adjusts her spectacles, the kerosene light reflects off of them and dances around the tent.

"Just the same as you—fine," says Gran.

"Now both of us are liars," I push. I can't bear to tell her how isolated I feel. That even the people I want to trust don't trust me.

The sheriff twirls her finger in the air, pushing me to wrap it up. "Do you need me to come home?" I ask.

"Heavens, no. I'll be right as rain in no time."

"Gran, I need you to tell me the truth."

"I believe in you. That's the truth." She clears her throat, which is her way of telling me to say something. But I hold steady. I want the truth, the whole truth, and nothing but the truth, so help me Jesus. She sighs. "Well, I'm still sick, and your father is intent on wrapping me up in cotton until I get better. He wants you home—but he doesn't understand what it's like to dream anymore. Aurora was the only dream he ever had, and she's gone."

I choke and clench the phone at my ear with both hands.

"I know this is about more than the money, jellybean." Gran sighs, and the air almost whistles through her lips.

"Do you think Mom would have wanted me to forfeit?"

Gran chuckles through a dry, throaty cracking. "Not in a thousand years. And you know what, honeybunch, I believe you can win this whole darn thing. Show those lily-livered galoots how the cow ate the cabbage. They already called me before this—tried to tell me I needed to convince you to come home. But there's not a snowball's chance in Hades I will let FireCorp off that easy."

Gran's words fill the reaches of my heart and overcome the darkness that's made a home inside it. But the light is short-lived. I can't win. That's the problem. In the end, I'll let her down.

I wipe a tear from my cheek before the sheriff notices. "I love you, Gran."

"I love you too, pumpkin. More than anything, I wish I could be there for that grand finale feast and to watch you take off on that last leg. When you come home, we'll set that trophy on the mantel and dance around the living room like it's the last day on earth."

We hang up, and Sheriff Laudes takes back the phone.

"My apologies for the lack of privacy. They've given me strict instruction to watch you." She leans over, elbows on her thighs. Her nails are unpainted but uniformly oval and buffed to a high shine. "And I am sorry to hear your gran's been ill. Met her once at the Kerrville Dragoneering Fair. She's a good woman."

I chuckle. "I never realized how small the world was."

"Truer words have never been spoken, Miss Drake." She

stares me down. "Have you decided whether you plan to keep racing?"

"Yes. And I'm not stopping."

Sheriff Laudes nods as if she anticipated the answer. In a humanizing moment, she takes off her hat and sets it down in her lap. Her voice softens. "In a race without choices, this is the only one you will get, Miss Drake."

She's right; this is my exit. The androlone makes the choice clear. I *should* choose safety. I *should* choose home. That's what a smart person would do.

"I understand." I lean forward in bed, and my braid hangs over my shoulder. Picking at my nails, I allow a question to form. "If someone was breaking the rules of the race, what would happen to that person?"

"Why?" Sheriff Laudes raises her chin and inspects me as only a dragoneering law person can.

"I—" I cut off.

"You're not asking for yourself, are you. There's something fishy going on. Isn't there?"

"Well . . ."

From her pocket, Laudes pulls out a small notepad with an FC emblem emblazoned across the back. She slips a pen from behind her ear and hovers it over the lined paper.

The doors to my soul slam shut. Sure, the notepad may

just be a freebie promo item, and she may not be one of *them*, but the familiar black-and-yellow logo pulls me back to earth. I can't reveal anything to this woman without the FC blazing down my back.

"Nothing," I say.

Sheriff Laudes clicks her pen several times, waiting for me to say more, then leans in. "If you have information about someone—anyone, no matter who they are—disobeying the code of conduct, you are honor bound to report it. People who break the rules must be held accountable."

I'm two feet away from a cold vial of fast-acting steroids stuffed in my boots. All I'd have to do is glance meaningfully at them, and she'd probably check them. If Laudes demanded every dragon take a blood test within the next three or four days, the steroids would show up. I'm sure it'd be just that easy. Then I could tell Ash she caught me and dragged out the truth. But I hold my tongue. What good is honesty in a world sponsored by FireCorp?

I shake my head.

Marigold sighs and puts her notepad away. But I can't let her disappointment affect me. She tips her hat, then taps her watch as she gets up to leave.

And the alarm sounds for the next leg of the race.

CHAPTER
19

29°45'40.2" N, 99°02'43.1" W

Silver Spur Ranch, Bandera, Texas

I rip the steroids from my boot and stuff them in my pack. My arm sings with pain, so I dump the entire tray of medical equipment—Band-Aids, a bottle of antivenom, a syringe, and some gauze—in my bag. As I rush out of the tent, my pack weighs me down like never before. Draggers crowd me and I push through them, head pulsing and stomach sour from the lingering effects of coral viper venom.

"Miss Drake—you made it. How are you feeling?" asks someone, shoving a recorder up to my lips.

A second cuts in front of me. "Will you still compete?"

I push them out of the way and don't respond. Dear Lord, where is Ranga? The dark sky is barely streaked with dawn as I spin around, searching for her.

Another eager dragger shoves past his desperate colleagues. "Do you think you'll survive if you head out there?"

"I—" I can't think.

Someone grabs my arm and pulls me to my left.

"You look like roadkill run over twice. And your belt buckle still isn't shined." Karbach whips a long arm into the air, keeping back the other draggers, and whispers, "I'm this close to breaking a story about FireCorp. Keep a close eye on them." He points into the distance. "That way!"

I feel as if I'm about to be sick, and now I'm desperate to talk with Karbach about what FireCorp rumor he's unearthed. Does he know about the steroids? But the alarm sounds again, so I push those questions down. I spot Ranga in the distance and race for her.

When I reach her, she chirps, and I throw my arms around her slender neck. She wriggles with delight and curls a loving, shimmery wing around me. For a moment, her warmth calms my stomach.

"I'd be dead if it wasn't for you," I say, hugging her neck and reveling in the sleek feeling of her skin. "Thank you, girl. I'm sorry I got so angry in Sonora. Forgive me?"

Ranga chitters and rubs her head along my side. Her

scales burst with washes of iridescent color.

"Are you ready for another ride?"

Her magenta tongue hangs out of her mouth, and she does a little dance. That's a bona fide yes.

I struggle onto her back, my stomach pinching as I do, and we glide to the starting line where the nineteen other riders who've made it to this leg are waiting. Ranch hands double-check the camera on Ranga's bridle. I doubt it will film much in this darkness, but die-hard fans across the country will tune in nonetheless.

Laura ignores me as I make for the line—which means she's still angry about the viper. Perfect. I want to run over and warn her about FireCorp. The vial of steroids is in my pack. All I have to do is show it to her and hope—or, as Pa would say, pray—that she'll remember that FireCorp is the enemy, not me.

"All right, riders!" blares the announcer. "On my mark, race for the hologram. Complete your mission and race to the next stop. Intact."

How encouraging.

My head swirls, but I'm grateful that this time, I probably won't be met with the image of a dead loved one.

The announcer lifts a .45-caliber revolver to the heavens. "Ready . . . Go!"

Bam!

The shot echoes across the plains. The locals whistle and cheer as we dash to the platform. Rion is first, and he dismounts to slam the red button. Johnny Adams, 1970s rock star of the dragon rodeo circuit, flashes before us. He croons the poem as if he never died in a hollowhorn-roping accident:

> *Greek poems under clear, blue sky.*
> *Old rocks where buried creatures lie.*
> *For fire fades and cannot thrive,*
> *where water demons come alive.*

This is the least confusing of all the poems, because if you've grown up in a dragoneering family, this is a well-known nursery rhyme. We're hunting for the South's oldest dragon:

The three-headed hydra of East Texas.

Every rider takes off in the same direction, each one of us knowing exactly where we are headed. Per race rules, we will need to avoid crossing over major cities like Austin, so Caddo Lake is nine or ten hours away. It's the longest flight we've made, and spending that much time on a dragon's back is a stretch for any rider.

Ranga and I maintain the lead, but my body aches. Gray overcast replaces the bright morning sun as we speed on, all twenty of us advancing to the same legendary destination. If coral vipers are dangerous, then hydra are sheer terror: humpback whale–sized beasts with three heads and long, thick necks as powerful as the fabled brontosaurus. With the steroids, the FC will be able to challenge the hydra head-on with ease . . . But how effective will Ranga and I be against the creature? Aches travel through my limbs, worse than any flu, and my body begs for water. But my canteen is empty, and as we reach the hour mark, my stomach turns.

The other dragons race at my back. My stomach lurches again as I focus on the horizon like someone in the middle seat trying to avoid motion sickness.

Ranga feels my struggle and slows up.

"No, girl—keep going." I flick the reins, but my hands start to shake. My throat swims. No—

I vomit off the side of Ranga, and spittle dribbles against her. She shudders and banks toward the ground as I see stars. I don't want her to stop, but I need a break. She lands, and I practically roll off of her. Again, my body heaves, and I curl up in the fetal position. Time keeps ticking—five minutes, ten minutes—and I struggle to my feet, but I can't catch my balance. I suddenly wish I had listened to Laudes. How can I go on like this?

Ranga huffs, and, overhead, the other riders pass us: first Laura and Colt, followed by the Bhattis, Rion, the Grousewood boys, and, of course, FireCorp. Again, I try to stand, and again my stomach turns. Bile rises in my throat, and my stomach growls with a painful emptiness.

"Ranga—please." But instead of spurring me on, she nuzzles me and tucks me under her wing. I huddle there, my thoughts drifting to the other riders between waves of sickness. My mouth burns for water, but even if there was a creek nearby, I couldn't walk to it.

Minutes stretch out. How many, I'm not sure.

My eyes flutter open and I rise to my feet, finally able to stand. The other dragons are gone—so far beyond me in the distance that I can't see them through my goggles' binocular function. A tear rolls down my cheek as I reach into the saddlebag for toothpaste to rub on my teeth.

As I do, the cold vial of green liquid I haven't given up caresses my fingers. Keeping out of the brindle camera's sight, I take it from the bag and hold it in my palm. It's a heavy stone. A gem of green that sings to me. Calls to me.

There's a curious blank mind space that happens when

I'm about to do something I know I shouldn't. It's an eerie calm spot, the eye of a whirling storm where I stand numb at the center and watch as my thoughts spin out beyond me. My head swims with all the things I couldn't say to Sheriff Laudes or Gran or, well, anyone. All I can do is act. And that's what I'm afraid of.

I lean against Ranga's compact frame, the cool bottle of steroids resting in my palm. Her breath warms the air, and she nudges against me, burying her nose into the crook of my arm. I run my hands along the purple spines on her back and caress her cheek.

"I just don't know what to do anymore, girl." I grab my bag, hobble to my feet, and walk away from her, careful to avoid the camera. I hold the vial up to the sunlight creeping out from behind thick clouds and read the words once more. The black print stares back at me on the label:

FLAMEMAW
ANDROLONE

The hazy sun casts through it and forms a prism that shines onto my tattered T-shirt. Its colors sing of promise, and I consider the possibilities. What's one more cheater in a race full of cheaters?

From my bag, I pull the syringe stolen from the nurses' station.

Can this needle even pierce Ranga's skin? And how much would androlone help in such a short period? It's fast acting with a short half-life, but how fast? Still, using it seems better than not using it. I breathe heavily and shove the syringe into the bottle. I shake as I do, trembling not only at the thought of being caught but at the grave consequences of lowering my integrity. Can a person come back from this? Can Ranga?

I stare mindlessly as I draw the liquid into the syringe. Once it's full, I set the bottle down and spray liquid into the air. I've heard that you have to get rid of air bubbles. I flick the needle, because that's what I've seen people do in medical shows, and try to swallow the lump in my throat.

Shielding the needle, I spin around to look at Ranga. Her eyes are dull, and she hugs the ground as if she knows . . .

What is wrong with me? This isn't how races are won. Not by the Drakes. I drop the syringe on the ground and race back to Ranga. A tear falls from my eyes and down my chin, then I begin to sob.

"I'm sorry, girl. I wouldn't—I'm sorry."

The autopilot mind space evaporates. I'm left with my thoughts and the all-consuming knowledge that I won't win, I can't win, but I may still die trying.

I saddle Ranga like a real cowgirl and set my sights on the distance. Not to the race, but to other solo riders who have no clue what they're facing. I clasp the vial, rip the foil from the top, dump out the liquid, and then slip the bottle into my pack. It could be the key to reminding my fellow riders—including Laura—who the real enemy is.

Ranga and I take to the skies as a gust of cool, moist air surrounds us.

Clouds roll through as we ride for Caddo Lake and the sky turns increasingly gray. We barrel into falling rain, and I collect a few drops in my canteen. Ranga and I close the gap between us and the other riders, but I sense Ranga's hesitation as we approach them. A massive wall of clouds and lightning brews in the distance, directly where we're headed. I place my hand on the emergency beeper issued by the race, feeling for a vibration that might indicate a weather-warning message. Large, doped-up dragons like the FC's may be fearless against a storm, but even if they bust out Kevlar riding suits, it's unlikely they can withstand a thunderstorm's sixty-miles-per-hour gusts of wind.

Or, at least, so I think.

With only twenty riders left, only half of us will make

it to the final leg. I sink down in Ranga's saddle, using her body and armor of scales as a shield while we ride hard and fast. The rain grows stronger and streaks across my goggles, obscuring my vision. I click on my thermal imaging. Ahead, all of the other dragons slow down.

Then, they stop.

A funnel cloud collects in the distance, swirling from the mass of storm clouds, lightning, and rain.

It forms into a tornado that cuts across the desert like a whirling monster. From this distance, it appears slow and graceful, but I'm no fool. Flurries of dust and debris fly up around it, and Ranga pauses midair, flapping her wings to keep us steady as we watch the unthinkable giant spin through the landscape. Bypassing it will be impossible without adding hours to my time.

"You're doing great, girl!"

Ranga chirps, and I lean into her.

The storm around us picks up speed. Rain droplets trickle into my parched mouth, but they feel like bullets as they hit my skin. Ranga is protected by reptilian armor, and I wish I had something more to cover me than my threadbare *Drake's Dragon Ranch* jean jacket. Suddenly, my emergency tracker vibrates.

Beep beep beep!

I unclick the device and barely shift my eyes from the tornado in the distance to read the digital lettering:

TORNADO WARNING: GROUND YOUR DRAGON. MANDATORY STOP. 1 HOUR.

Every rider in the race is receiving this message. Few weather events can stop a dragon, and tornadoes are one of them. Fiddling with my magnification knobs, I scan the distance. A mile or so off, I watch the other dragons split into three groups and touch down. As the rain licks my goggles, I wonder: Which group is Laura in? This may be my one chance to talk to her before we encounter the deadly hydra. She was cold at the starting line, but will she trust me when she finds out what I've discovered? I secure my device on my belt and pull back on Ranga's reins.

We glide down through the rain and proceed on foot. Ranga's feet suck on the sludge.

"I'm sorry about the mud, Ranga." I squeeze next to her. "Reminds me of the time we got rained out during our Marfa camping trip."

She huffs as if to say this storm is worse.

"Just remember, after all of that, Gran made us a feast and Pa got you that new saddle. Wait until we win this race. Big things are headed your way, girl." I pat her wet side.

Ranga chirps and drapes a wing over me like an umbrella as we walk. Too bad I'm already soaked to the bone.

I shiver as we close the distance—even the Texas heat can't make a rainstorm comfortable. My boots fill with water. Beyond, Rion's dragon, Jet, is a marble-white beacon in the dark and stormy atmosphere. Squinting, I can just make out Quetzal's orange, fiery hues. I reach the outskirts of the group and pass the Bhattis' pink-and-purple nightfrilled racing nesters.

"They won't be very excited to see you!" says Viv through the rain. She shines a flashlight on her chin and makes ghost sounds. Rose joins in.

I ignore them and pull Ranga by the reins to the group of unsponsored riders. She is willing to come only so far, and I let her hang back.

Rain soaks into everything. My hair, my shirt, my boots. How quickly I've gone from dying of thirst to hating water. The storm swirls around me as I trudge through the mud to the group cowering under a tarp. Their dragons hover around them, heads tucked under their wings. But they can sense my presence and growl as I approach. Laura coos at Quetzal, a positive sign. Maybe it will be easier than I thought to convince her I would never sabotage her in this race.

Colt, Rion, Laura, and Brayden loom under their makeshift tent, propped up on one end by two sticks. I stand outside, waiting for someone to say something. But the group is hushed, as if they no longer have anything to discuss. Guilt creeps along my skin, not because I've done something wrong, but because they think I have. The hairs on my arms stand at attention as I avoid meeting Laura's eyes. But her stare burns into me, worse than any brand.

Finally, I speak up. "May I join you?"

Silence goes taut until Colt scooches aside, leaving me a spot.

Hands in my pockets, I crouch down beside my would-be alliance.

"So . . . ," says Colt. He fluffs his poncho around him. "How many stitches did you get?"

"Only a dozen or so." I lift my arm. "Could have been worse."

"Lucky you made it out alive," says Laura.

The circle's energy lets me know she hasn't kept any secrets about what happened in the cave. The realization leaves my mouth dry. I clear my throat and part my lips to speak, but Laura beats me to it.

"How fortunate that you were under the watchful eye of a Carne boy," she mutters.

My stomach twists as if I might be sick with viper juice again. I hadn't even considered the message it would send to have Ash linger by my bedside on the last rest stop. Hadn't considered that this would only make my plight worse. And now I'm caught between a rock and a hard place. Ash saved my life . . . but he's still a part of FireCorp. Even after he gave me the steroids, *I'm* still not certain I can trust him—how could I expect them to? In the midst of this once possible alliance, I feel more alone than I ever have. I curl my toes in my soggy boots. The wind blows through the tarp in a haunting gust.

Brayden scowls, but behind his eyes, I see . . . pity. He clears his throat. "I'd be careful if I were you, Cassidy. You don't understand what you're signing up for."

"But—" My voice cracks as I search for words.

Ash steps from the rainy shadows.

"I think you're in the wrong camp," snaps Brayden.

"I came to talk with Cassidy," Ash says.

Now the suspicion spreads, and thunder bursts in the distance. He couldn't have chosen a worse time to show up.

"Of course you did," says Laura.

Brayden shifts his weight. "Or maybe I should pull her

aside and tell her what happened first."

"Look, I'm sorry, Brayden," pleads Ash. "I don't know how many times I have to tell you. I made a mistake."

Brayden turns cold and silent. He pulls his hood over his head, pushes past Ash, and takes off into the storm.

The rain pummels the blue tarp, and the solo riders all stare at Ash as he crouches down across from me. Coast clear, I rip the vial from my pack and shove it into Laura's palm.

"Ay no, ¿es lo que creo que es?" she asks under her breath.

"What is it?" asks Colt.

"That's why none of us can get a win—why the FC dragons are so savage and impossible to beat in head-to-head challenges." I point at the vial. "They're hopped up on flamemaw androlone."

Laura reads the bottle more carefully, then hands it to Colt, silent.

Colt's eyes widen as he palms the bottle. "Where on God's green earth did you get this?"

Before I can speak, Ash does. "From me." He leans forward and flicks rain from his fingers. "I know you don't trust me, nor should you. But that's androlone. And they're using it."

"You mean *you're* using it," says Laura.

Ash rubs his hands together to warm them and gives a half nod.

"And that's why they will keep beating us." I lean down and whisper, "Unless we change our approach."

"And how would we do that?"

"Fight together—ally. Protect each other like FireCorp does."

Rion grunts. "Fine time for you to say that."

"Look, I was wrong—and this changes everything."

"You mean *if* it's real." Laura snatches the bottle back from Colt. "Now you're consorting with the enemy, and you have this great secret? I want to believe you—really, I do. But how am I supposed to do that when he's by your side?"

"Then let me make this easier for you," says Ash, rising to his feet.

"Don't go," I say, tugging at his pants leg. I turn to the other riders. "We're trying to warn you. You may not believe anything I say—I swear on my life, on every dragon I've cared for, I did not sabotage you during the viper task, Laura—but even if you won't believe that, believe this." I gesture for her to hand the vial back to me, and I hold it up again. "If they're willing to poison their dragons with flamemaw, what else are they willing to do?"

Rion rubs a hand through the tight, barely there curls on his buzzed head as if it will help him process what he's just heard.

Teeth chattering from the cold, I lean toward him. "It's what you said in the first place: we're outmatched and outplayed—each of us. Every FC member wants to win, but they'll prioritize FireCorp over the individual every time if it means coming out ahead. The rest of us are just fighting for scraps. The race is a numbers game. A strength game. And none of us stand a chance . . . not unless we band together."

The ragtag collection of solo riders remains silent, mulling over my words. Waters runs in a steady stream off of the edge of the tarp.

"Some of you run rescues, just like I do. Even if you don't believe me, trust me on this." I push up my sleeve, revealing the gruesome stitches that make me look like Frankenstein's monster. "The only reason I survived was because Ash put me on Ranga and sent me on to the next leg. He told me about the steroids when I was doubled up in an infirmary bed. And I would never lie about dragon abuse. Never." I make eye contact with all three riders.

They don't respond, and a distant thrum of thunder rolls across the plains.

"We tried," says Ash. He steps out of the tent and into the rain.

"Wait!" I shout. The tarp crinkles as I whip around and face him. Water streaks down his FireCorp-branded rain jacket. "Show us."

"Show you what?"

"Prove that the FC is using steroids."

"You have the vial," he says, exasperated. "What else do you want?"

I stand tall, the tarp brushing my head. "If they're using the steroids at every break, then they're using them now. Maybe even as we speak. Take us to them. Prove it."

Ash hesitates.

Suddenly, I'm confronted with my own gnawing mistrust of him. Maybe I've imagined a connection because he's manipulated me. *Again.* Maybe I'm just a pawn in his game, and we're all being set up to fail. I hold his gaze and let him sense my suspicion. "If you back down, there's no chance they'll believe you," I say.

He sinks into his sleek rain jacket, the hood creating a dark void as he considers the threat.

"She's right," says Laura. She stands beside me and I feel a flicker of solidarity. "We need solid evidence. Take us to the FC camp."

"That's a dangerous idea. Maybe we should wait until the next rest—"

Colt points to his watch. "Thirty minutes until we're allowed to take off. It's now or never, fireboy."

"Exactly," says Laura. "Otherwise, we'll assume you're setting us up to get caught."

The three of us boldly stare at Ash, who cracks his knuckles.

Rion breaks the silence. "If you all were wise, you'd leave this alone. Toss that bottle and forget the whole thing. If you're caught with it, they'll expel you from the race."

"What is your obsession with following the rules?" I snap. "We're talking about dragons being tortured here."

"Not everyone has the privilege of choosing what rules they obey," Rion snaps back. He zips up his lightweight camp rain jacket until the collar kisses his defined jaw. "Not everyone can be a special white girl with famous parents."

I bark back, "You claimed you'd be a good leader, and when it comes down to it, you run for the hills? I guess Hollowton Prep boys are just chickenhearted riders in blue uniforms."

The second I've said it, I know I am wrong. I don't know what it's like to be him, and I never will. But before I can apologize, Rion gives a curt bow and leaves us in the tarp.

"Perfect," says Laura, and I half expect her to leave as well. "What's it going to be, *Ashton*?"

Ash strides out into the pouring rain and calls back, "Follow me."

I bolt for Ranga, whose head is tucked under her wing in a makeshift shelter. Colt and Laura do the same with their dragons.

Ash spins around. "No—leave the dragons," he shouts through the crackle of thunder. "They're too big. The FireCorp crew will be checking their trackers for anything larger than a deer."

Laura points at Ash as if her threats could wield magic. "I'm not leaving our dragons here alone, unmonitored, while we walk into a trap."

Ranga blinks at me as I clutch her reins. She doesn't want me to leave her either. I stroke the ridges on her cheekbones.

"I'll watch them," says Colt. Water drips off the edge of his cowboy hat. "But if the tracker beeps and we have the all clear to go, I'm gone."

Laura stiffens. "That's fair." She turns to Ash. "Show us the way."

CHAPTER
20

"Do you trust him?" Laura asks as we trudge through the rain, keeping our distance behind Ash.

The water sucks at my boots, which I'm certain won't retain their former glory. "Dear dragonfire, I hope so," I say.

I'm thankful that, at least for the moment, she's decided to trust me. Hanging my head, I pull beside Laura as we walk. "I didn't mean to screw up the viper task for you," I mumble. "I promise."

She soldiers on through the mud. "Then why don't you just apologize instead of making excuses?"

I sink into the muck as I realize I haven't actually said I'm sorry. Gran would be so disappointed. I plod in front of

Laura and clear my throat. "You're right. I should've been more careful . . . And I should have waited my turn. I'm sorry, Laura. I really, really am." Water drips from my chin.

Laura nods and knocks into my shoulder. "Thank you."

We continue in silence through the pouring rain until we approach the FC's camp, the boom of thunder overhead and the sun hidden behind a thick blanket of clouds. Again, their setup is superior to ours, with actual tents and rain cover, but even they don't have a fire.

Their mounts are nowhere near their circle of tents. Which is strange, given that steroid-pumped dragons would make an excellent barrier against the rain and wind.

Ash pulls down his swanky thermal imaging goggles and scans the area. "The dragons are out that way." He points into the darkness. "Nick keeps the androlone in a black case. They bribed the sheriffs to let the case pass through."

I bristle. "Does Laudes know?"

"If she did, I doubt he'd still be in the race. She's had an eye on Nick from day one."

We creep through the brush, my bones cold from the rain, as Ash gives us a pointed lecture about staying close and following orders. His intensity stokes my nerves. Laura and I exchange glances as he runs over the extensive list of things we can and cannot do. Don't startle the dragons—they'll be frenzied with androlone. Don't speak; don't underestimate what FireCorp will do if they discover us. We crouch down by a boulder.

I flip down my goggles and twist the magnification knob. Two FC riders stand guard beside a muzzled Spanish ravager. The ravager—who usually looks so terrifying with her traffic-cone-sized spikes—trembles. Her scales pulse between dark olive and black. Nickolai approaches and opens a heavy pack.

Spinning the dial on my goggles, I zero in as best I can. Nickolai wields a needle—twice the size of any I've seen—and jams it between the ravager's scales.

I clamp my eyes closed, but the image is seared into my mind. As Laura squeezes my arm, I try to remember that injustices like this are why I'm here, why I'm riding this race.

"You've seen enough," says Ash. "We need to go."

"No," I say. Rain streaks across my vision. "We have to help the dragon." I move to creep out from beyond the boulder.

Ash grabs my arm to hold me back. "Are you insane?"

"We can't leave her to be tortured." I pull my arm free, then step beyond the boulder—only to have Ash jerk me back by the tail of my shirt.

"One day, your recklessness is going to get you killed!" says Ash.

His words remind me of Pa's, and I rip my shirttail back from him. "Stop trying to protect me," I snap.

Ash slips his hood off his head, and streams of water trickle down his face. "I know you're not weak. But you don't understand what they're willing to do to protect FireCorp. You wouldn't even be here if it wasn't for me, so please, let me handle this. I'll tell them the solo riders are spying on us. They'll stop if they think they're about to get caught. You two head around that way—back to your camp." He points to another rocky area with boulders and takes off into enemy territory. His territory.

Laura grips my arm as Ash approaches the guards. "Let's go," she says.

"Not until I know the ravager is safe," I say.

Laura nods.

Ash glances over his shoulder to see if we're following directions, and I shoo him toward the guards. Ash may have saved me from the viper, and I believe he wants to help, but I am not sure how far his bravery extends. My heart pounds as he approaches the two guards, who seem less than friendly about his sudden appearance.

Laura's mouth hangs open, and her ragged breath sucks droplets of water in and out. She closes her lips as I grab her arm in a show of solidarity. I try to remember the breathing exercises my school therapist taught me after Mom died. But what good is air in situations like these?

Ash and the guards bicker back and forth. But all I can hear is the drumming of rain in wide puddles and cedar leaves.

My heart jolts as the guard reaches for his holster and pulls out a flashlight. Laura and I drop to our bellies as he sweeps it across the ground and through the brush. Closer . . . closer . . . until the light almost touches us. Trembling, I cover my head with my hands. My braid drags in a puddle, and the taste of mud fills my mouth.

Finally, the guard puts the light away, and I lift my head. He calls out for Nickolai, who grabs Ash by the collar. I can't hear a word they're saying, but I can tell that Nickolai is about to snap.

"We have to help him," I whisper.

I scramble forward and Laura keeps in step. Nickolai shoves Ash to the ground and looms over him. Mud drips from my hands as I run.

Wreeeeeerowwwwwkkk!

A roar echoes across the desert.

Massive wings burst through the sheets of rain. Rion's dragon descends on Nickolai. The rain pummels him as his dragon, Jet, screeches and spews fire. Water droplets turn to steam around him, and Nickolai flees into the darkness. Jet lets loose another warning cry as the guards scatter in opposite directions.

Jet's wings lash the air and he howls. Atop him, Rion is a model of strength and valiant bravery. But just as Rion turns to head back to our camp, Valeen's draconian hybrid, Scarlett, tears across the sky. Scarlett attacks Jet, who twists in the air to avoid her. Tails fly and wings beat. Flames lick in our direction.

"Jimminy Christmas!" I shout. "He helped! He said he wouldn't, but he helped!"

I pull Laura alongside me and run as fast as I can, away from the fire and toward the cover of a massive boulder. Thunder echoes as Rion and Valeen battle it out in the sky. But Jet doesn't stand a chance against Scarlett's razor-sharp claws and synthetically powered muscles. We lean into the safety of the boulder. Jet flees, and Scarlett chases after him.

"Are they gone?" asks Laura.

"I think," I say. "Thank goodness for Rion."

But the boulder moves beside us. A hot stench wafts into

my nostrils, choking me. Ever so slowly, Laura and I spin around.

Ash's massive wyvern, Juliette, stares back at us with bloodred eyes. She growls, and her broad wings, black as oil slick, shudder with surprise. The boulder wasn't a boulder at all: it was a dragon. Juliette's mammoth tail and car-sized head flank us on either side, holding us in a terrifying horseshoe of dragon muscle, teeth, and tines.

"Hi, girl," I whisper, barely managing to form words.

Juliette glares and hisses, sending a shock through my body. From the quiver of Laura's lip, I know she shares my terror. Juliette hunches in an aggressive pose and smoke swirls from her pointy nostrils. It doesn't take years of dragon-wrangling experience to know that we will become dragon barbecue if we run. Our only option is to befriend her as quickly as possible.

Juliette growls as I inch toward her sleek, spiny head. I reach out my hand and begin to sing. Drips of rain fall from my lips:

Sweet angel, sweet angel,
fly away home, fly away home . . .

Juliette sniffs me up and down, and my clothes waft

in her breezy breath. She bares her teeth, glistening with saliva, and I press into Laura.

"It's okay, girl. I'm not here to hurt you," I say, placing my trembling fingers under her chin.

Just as she's relaxing, another dragon shrieks in pain.

Juliette's spines prick along her back. She lifts her head and wails at the sky in response—a commiserating and angry cry. As the throaty howls continue, Juliette narrows her crimson eyes and circles Laura and me. My heart drops to my stomach. I smell smoke.

Laura grabs me. "We have to make a run for it—now!"

My feet are locked in place, weighed down by more than the water in my boots.

"Now!" Laura says once more.

But I'm paralyzed as heat rises around us, and Juliette's head rears back to strike. Laura grabs my shirt to pull me away, but as we try to run, Ash knocks us to the rocky, wet ground.

He locks eyes with Juliette and holds up his hands. "Friends, friends!"

She jerks back, stunned, then screeches at Ash. The roar is so powerful his jacket whips around him.

"Friends!" he repeats, dropping to his knees and planting his palms on the ground in a sign of submission. Laura and

I press farther into the ground, now understanding why Ash knocked us to the ground.

Juliette inches toward us and roars once more before relaxing and nuzzling Ash.

Relief spreads over Ash's face. He grabs my shoulders so tight it hurts. "You have to go. There's thirteen minutes left until the weather break is over."

Another pained dragon howls in the distance. Juliette whimpers.

"They're rushing to juice up the dragons," says Ash.

I hesitate. "What about Juliette? You can't leave her here."

Ash twinges at my question. "I don't have a choice. Michael said it's this, or send her to work in the mines."

All three of us shudder. Perhaps it's not just dragons who suffer in this system—it's dragon lovers too. And if there's one thing I can't abide by, it's dragons being hurt. Without thinking, I wrap my arms around Juliette and coo a lullaby. She tenses at first, then relaxes, just like Ranga.

"I'm sorry, girl," I say. "I really am."

"Not a wise idea to do that with a dragon that's not yours," says Ash, eyebrows arched.

I release Juliette and stroke her chin. "Maybe not. But everyone deserves a little love."

Ash smiles meekly.

"Time to go," urges Laura.

But as we turn to dash back to our camp, we find ourselves face-to-face with Nickolai Grigori.

Nickolai stares down at us. He wears a lightweight rain jacket that's zipped up to his chin. Beneath the hood, his long blond hair is pulled back tight. Nickolai moves more like a robot than a human: stiff, imposing, and muscular. He grins, cruel and menacing.

"Here for a party, I see?" The cold monotone of his voice floats in the echo of thunder.

"Just enjoying the local scenery," I say.

Laura coughs a warning that I need to quiet down.

"Find anything of interest?" he asks, motioning to the wilderness.

Before I can answer, Ash interrupts. "They were looking for food."

"Come now, moy brat. No need for lies and deceit." Soviet tones lilt in Nickolai's words. "After you clung to this one's side in the infirmary tent, I knew you couldn't be trusted. And here I find you, sneaking around with your peasant friends. Ty predatel'."

"Peasants are European." I wear the mud streaked across

my cheeks like war paint. "Where I come from, we prefer the term 'pioneers.'"

"Well, Miss Pioneer, I'll use language you understand." Nickolai turns on a mocking southern accent. "We don't take kindly to trespassin' round these parts."

Ash inches forward. "Leave her be."

Nickolai adjusts his cuffs like a man far older than seventeen. "No, brother, that is what you should've done."

"You're no brother of mine," says Ash.

Nickolai turns up his nose and sneers. "Funny thing. Unlike me, you've worked your entire life to be ignored by Michael. But I can guarantee you've just shot to the top of his priority list. Excellent work."

Laura shields Ash alongside me. "We know who you are and what you've done."

"We will report you," I say.

Nickolai snickers. "Who will you report it to? The sheriffs of this FireCorp-sponsored competition? Try again."

In the distance, a coyote howls and Nickolai flinches.

I smile coolly. "There aren't many coyotes in Connecticut, I take it. How about a lesson?" I say. I circle him, slow and steady. "Coyotes are interesting animals. For the most part, they hunt small prey alone. But they're known to team up and take down larger prey as a pack." I pick something out of my nails. "Much to learn from coyotes, you know."

Nickolai chuckles. "Ah, yes—the promise of a team. Let me ask you this: How long do you think we've trained? How many hours do you think we've spent coordinating, learning one another's moves? Our success aside—and believe me, a FireCorp rider *will* claim the glory—we can afford to team up because we ride only for the honor of winning, not money. None of you can *afford* to team up."

His chilly words spread over me like ice, blue as Nickolai's eyes. He turns and advances on Ash. "We may need to put on a show for the cameras, brother, but I will be delighted to tell Michael how you turned on us mid-race. Perhaps I'll finally get the recognition I deserve. My thanks to you, brother. Do svidaniya."

Nickolai leaves us and the air whips around us in a cool gust. Laura and I try to comfort Ash, but he mumbles something about facing his own consequences and slinks into the rain to collect Juliette.

CHAPTER
21

Laura and I race for Quetzal and Ranga, mud spritzing up around us as the clock winds down. We find Colt already on his dragon. Rain drips from the brim of his cowboy hat.

"Glad you two made it!" shouts Colt. His dragon fans her wings and chitters.

"So are we," I say. I try and fail to wipe the rain from Ranga's saddle before jumping on her back. "Have you seen Rion?"

"I saw his dragon tear across the sky with Valeen not far behind," says Colt. "Since he flew more than a few hundred feet, he'll be slapped with a time penalty, for sure. What happened?"

"He did what I thought he wouldn't. He stood up to

FireCorp," I say, proud of Rion's bravery.

"Well, I'll be." Colt scratches his head. "And the androlone?"

"They're definitely using it," says Laura.

"So we're doomed," says Colt.

"No—but their dragons are if we don't do something." My watch beeps. "Let's go! Be on the lookout for Rion!"

We take off to the gray skies as a fierce entourage heading for Caddo Lake, and our dragons' wings unfurl in wide sweeps that bash the rain.

At over twenty-five thousand acres, Caddo Lake, just outside Louisiana, is one of the largest flooded cypress forests in the United States. The area is fiercely protected by the Texas Parks & Reptilian Wildlife Department, and dozens of warning signs dot the area. Massive trees with bulky roots spring from the swamp. As we skim the top of the bayou's forest, alligators peek up at us through the trees.

We arrive in Caddo Lake around five p.m., just as the rain subsides into a slow drizzle. Since we were only forty-five minutes outside the bayou, the flock of twenty competitors arrives at roughly the same time. Landing a dragon in a swamp isn't easy, so we leave them scattered in the forest on solid ground. The doped-up FC dragons take the driest spots and terrorize the rest of us to ensure we're farther from the task.

The swamp echoes with low, rumbling growls that must be from the hydra. Draggers watching the race won't see much from our camera-outfitted bridles, but the game designers have attached video equipment to the limbs of hundred-year-old trees.

I slide from Ranga's back with more reluctance than usual. I hug her neck, and even though her scales are a dull gray, she doesn't whine.

"I'm proud of you," I say.

She nuzzles me and lets me leave without a whimper.

Strangely, a few FC riders stay with their mean black dragons. The dragons tremor with agitation and they snap at me as I pass through the perimeter they've set up. I now feel stupid for not realizing they were on steroids before. There's nothing natural about their constricted pupils and twitching muscles.

The ground sucks at my boots and makes squelching sounds as I shuffle toward the bank. On my right, Colt, Rion, Brayden, and Laura stand together, wide-eyed. The Grousewood boys and the Bhatti sisters concoct their own plan from afar, and to my left, Nickolai leads the FireCorp riders. Ash wavers just beyond an invisible line dividing the independent and FC riders.

A thirty-foot airboat with a massive propeller fan on the back is anchored in the bank. I'm certain the next clue is on the boat. The water below is dark and impenetrable, and even though the boat is not far from solid ground, it's the first time none of us rush to it, instead waiting for someone else to crawl into the water.

"Ah, heck," says Colt. "I'll take one for the team."

Colt rips off his shirt and tosses it in the mud. He's covered in dozens of tattoos, including an intricate dragon breathing rainbow-colored fire that snakes around his shoulder.

Laura and I stand on the muddy bank as Colt wades to the boat, shoulders peeking out from the water. I half expect the hydra to jump out and take him, but she won't bother unless she's disturbed—or unless we invade her nest. Colt heaves himself onto the flat-bottomed boat, which bobs, sending fat lily pads in the water rippling across the swamp. He raises a fist in a show of solidarity, then kicks the deck to set off the hologram.

Kyle Bennington, the redheaded seventeen-year-old who shocked the world when he was drowned by an amusement park hydra last August, appears this time. He speaks in a southern drawl that stretches his vowels like taffy:

Invasive lilies choke the creek.

Retrieve a bulb with your best technique.

The words echo across the water, and I remember an article about blue lilies some moron planted in Caddo Lake. Apparently, they're a huge threat to the hydra's habitat. This is a conservation mission.

"There's gear!" shouts Colt. He lifts up a metal canister and a scuba mask.

Ah, crickets. I chuck off my boots and dive out into the water as the others do the same. We race out to the boat, and the swamp floor makes a steep drop so I can no longer stand on it.

The boat rocks as nearly two dozen of us haul ourselves onto the metal body. Colt has already masked up and jumps into the water.

I rifle through a treasure chest on board, pushing other riders out of my way, and grab a mask and an unfamiliar canister.

"What is this?" I ask Laura as the Grousewood boys shove us to the side.

"A portable air canister . . . ," she breathes. "I've used them before. It should last for an hour."

Protruding from the canister is a long hose with a rubber

mouthpiece. I thumb it in disbelief. "Are they serious? We're dragoneers, not scuba divers!"

Masks on tight, the Bhattis bite down on the mouthpieces, jump into the water, and disappear into the boggy darkness. The Grousewood boys do the same. The rest of us linger on the bobbing airboat, gazing out into the mysterious black water.

I'm supposed to go down there and nab a lily from the nest of *the three-headed hydra*?

Just perfect.

To my right, someone pops open a flare, and I jump at the burst of light. It buzzes with crimson fire, releasing smoke and sparks that fill the darkness. The ominous waters stir. The red glow lights Valeen's alabaster face. She chuckles and tosses it into the river.

My mouth hangs open, which is a good thing because I'm about to hurl so many southern curse words in Valeen's direction that Gran will be able to hear them in Pecos. Who knows what she stirred to life under there? No sneaking up on it now.

Ash clips an air tank on his belt, then barks at Valeen, "Do you have to make everything more difficult, Grimsbane?"

"You're so cute when you're angry, Carne." Valeen kisses

the air, then pulls on her scuba mask.

I advance on Valeen. "You'll kill us all."

"No. I'll kill *y'all*." Valeen points at the unaffiliated riders, spurring on her mocking tone. She sidles up next to Ash and leans into his sinewy arm. "We train with hydras at Dragonscale. And I could find these lilies blindfolded. Best of luck to you."

She grabs Ash by the wrist, and this time he doesn't relent. Instead, he jumps off the opposite side of the boat, abandoning Valeen and FireCorp. Good for him. Valeen grits her teeth before diving into the river. Nickolai and two other FC riders jump in after her, followed by the rest of their lackeys.

Ignore them. Focus. What would Aurora Drake do?

My breath catches in my throat as the remaining riders dive into the swamp. Every rider for themselves.

Dear sweet daisies and daffodils . . . I hitch my portable tank to my belt, bite down on the rubbery mouthpiece, and pull the mask over my face. Oxygen fills my lungs as I breathe in. One breath, two breaths, then . . . I dive into the water.

My ears fill with the muted sounds of chaos. Blackness envelops me as I swim deeper, and I twist the tiny headlamp attached to the mask. *Breathe slowly*, I tell myself.

Don't panic. Breathe slowly. I repeat this over and over as trails of bubbles rush to and fro in the water. The tank will last an hour—no more. One hour to find a bulb and escape with my life.

As I dart down, legs kicking furiously, I peer through the darkness, pushing aside tendrils of spatterdock and duckweed. My limbs fumble, more used to land than sea, and I do my best to push on. The water grows chilly as I dive deeper, kicking down . . . down . . .

Down . . .

I feel something slice through the water. A rush of bubbles surrounds me, and something grips my leg. The slimy tentacle wraps round and round, pulling me deeper underwater. I bite down harder on the mouthpiece, terrified that I will lose the air canister that's keeping me alive. I take a heaving breath and try to slow myself, but I can't. The tentacle keeps pulling me.

As I flail and thrash, another figure moves past me. Rose is caught in a slimy arm and rips through the water. Forgetting about the competition altogether, I break free from the tentacle and swim for her, hoping I can pry her from the hydra's clutches. I reach out a hand and Rose's fingers graze mine . . . Then something bashes into me, jolting me to the side. It severs the rubber hose connected to my air canister. I watch in horror as the mouthpiece sinks into the murky water beneath.

Air. I need air. I kick my way to the surface.

Overhead is chaos. The hydra's slimy, tree-sized tentacles thrash in the water, splashing algae all around. Without even trying, I know I can't hope for a fluke like I did with the wurm. And who can sing underwater, anyway? At least there's no sign of the three gargantuan heads. Yet.

I crawl to shore, escaping the madness. A few yards away, an alligator is doing the same thing. But Rose hasn't risen from the marsh. I have no idea where Laura is—I didn't see her under the water at all, and she's not up here. Still no sign of Rion. Other riders fight with flailing tentacles. I lift my head to the open sky. I can run—should run.

FireCorp riders pop up from the river's surface, one by one. Each carries a slimy bulb with a network of roots that trail to the ground. Ash isn't with them.

Valeen sashays over, unfazed by the fury. She yanks off her goggles. Her wet bob seems almost fashionable as she shakes her head. "Tsk-tsk, Cassidy—time is running out." She holds up the dripping bulb and wags it in my face.

Maintaining composure, I glance at her air canister on the ground. Nickolai notices and flashes a wicked grin. "I think not," he says. My heart drops as he collects the used air canisters from each of his fellow riders and stuffs them into his pack.

Massive bubbles gurgle in the swamp, as if the three heads are exhaling beneath the surface.

Nickolai cracks his knuckles. "Happy hunting. Let's ride."

Valeen and Nickolai dash for the forest to mount their dragons alongside a few other FC riders. They rise over the cypress canopy and take off. I turn back to the onslaught, knees weak and arms trembling. The air kisses my wet skin, and I rub the charm on my bracelet. What would Aurora Drake do?

I have no idea what Aurora Drake would do.

Laura pulls herself onto the bank, and Colt pops up beside her. They're both soaking wet, but only Colt has a bulb in hand. Laura staggers toward me. Colt takes off in the other direction and disappears into the trees.

Neither Laura nor I say a word. We exchange empathetic glances that convey it all: perhaps this is the last leg for both of us.

Just beyond us, Ash snaps out of the water like a trained Navy SEAL. But unlike the other FC riders, he is bulbless. Perhaps Valeen decided he wasn't worth waiting for without a lily.

Ash surveys the scene, and I can tell that he's analyzing

what it means that the rest of the FC has left him. He counts the remaining dragons with his fingers.

"Fifteen left," he says. "There's still time."

Laura turns to me, dripping wet. "Do you have a plan?"

A plan. Yeah, my plan is to stay alive. But now isn't the time for sarcasm. Several riders are scattered on the bank, and the other half must be in the thrashing water amid the treacherous waves, tentacles, and murky roots. Everything happens so fast I can barely think.

Rose pops out of the swamp and staggers into the forest on the opposite side of the lake. Then, three massive heads the size of oil barrels rise from the water. They drip with algae and bits of moss, and their bioluminescent eyes glow with a cool, eerie blue. Each head has rows and rows of serrated teeth like a great white shark. Our group rushes farther into the cypress forest, where the forty-foot necks cannot reach us. The shrieking, massive heads flail, and the sound of breaking tree limbs mix with the screams of other riders.

I squat down on rank soil and gather my composure. "Three heads, three of us," I say.

"Make that four." My head spins around as Rion rushes to our side.

"You're alive!" I shout.

Laura tosses her arms around Rion as he drops into the dirt, soaking wet and breathless.

"We couldn't find you after the tornado stop," says Laura. "What happened?"

"Valeen's hybrid injured Jet—clawed his wing right down the middle. I left him hidden in the forest so she wouldn't attack him again." Rion's face is grim as he stuffs a muddy bulb in his pocket. "But that doesn't matter now. I want to help."

"We'll be okay," I say. "You already have your bulb, and you need to help Jet. That wound will fester, especially out here."

"I won't leave the rest of you here."

I squeeze his arm. "You've already helped us more than you know. Even though I acted like total beef jerky, you stood up to FireCorp. And that's what matters."

He glances at Ash and nods, and I feel a surge of admiration rush through me. Rion rises to his feet.

"No chance you have your air canister, is there?" I ask.

Rion shakes his head. "It's at the bottom of the lake."

"That's fine—go," I say. I suck in a breath as Rion makes for the forest.

Laura holds her canister to her chest. "If you two can fend off the heads, I can get the bulbs—one for each of us. Maybe not faster than fifteen other riders, but I can try."

Ash retrieves a lightweight mass of rope and aluminum from his pocket. "Michael instructed us to bring bolas—and now I know why. He must have bribed someone for insight about this leg." He holds up three cords with metallic orbs dangling at either end. "Juliette and I can muzzle the heads. But you have to keep them distracted."

I grit my teeth. Ranga is fast—but is she fast enough?

"I can do it," I say. I hope.

"I guess it's one for all, then," says Laura.

We break apart and Ash and I race for our dragons. When I find Ranga, she's pinned to the ground in a massive black-and-red net. Freaking FireCorp. I struggle with the net and Ranga cries out, but I feel powerless to unhook it from her spines.

"It's okay, girl—just hold still. I'll get you out," I say frantically. I squeeze my arm through the netting and pull the bowie knife from my pack. Working as quickly as I can, I cut her free.

Ranga cowers, but I jump on her back and don't acknowledge her fear. There's just no time. Once in the sky, I pull her reins and guide her to circle the bank. Ash is already hovering above the chaos on his dragon. We dart back and forth, just beyond the hydra's reach. As we turn for another loop, I hear a bloodcurdling scream.

"No! Stop!"

I whip around to find Brayden ensnared in the hydra's grip. A gargantuan tentacle wraps around his body and lifts him into the sky. One of the hydra's heads snaps at Brayden, and for a moment, the entire world goes still. The thrash of water, roars, and screams fade into the background. Across the clearing, Brayden's dragon cries out. But the goldenscale is also pinned to the ground with a massive net, powerless to break free and save his rider.

Ranga releases a burst of fire that startles the hydra.

I jerk her reins and make for Brayden, shouting, "Ash! Ash!"

But Ranga and I aren't fast enough this time. The hydra drags Brayden underwater, then back up again, playing with her food. Brayden sputters and cries. Ranga releases more fire as we dance around one of the heads, hoping to distract the hydra. But the hydra barely registers us. As its tentacles coil tighter around Brayden, Ash breaks into the clearing. Juliette soars down like a mighty steed into battle.

Brayden claws the air, tangled in the hydra's powerful arms. "Someone! Please, help!"

Ash picks up speed, whirling down, and Juliette roars her battle cry. But the hydra squeezes Brayden tighter in her powerful grip.

I clench my reins, and my body goes numb.

"No!" shouts Ash.

He drives Juliette down, and she claws at one of the hydra's many plate-sized eyes. The creature screeches, and Juliette takes out another eye. Then another. Partially blinded, the creature drops Brayden and flees back into the deep. Normally I would hate anyone for injuring a dragon, but I forget everything I believe about dragon conservation as I run to Brayden. Even the West Texas Dragon Wrangling Association will forgive a rider for injuring a dragon in these circumstances.

Ash and I dismount in a stable patch of marshy land and sprint through the network of trees to Brayden's side. I know instantly that he's in bad shape—he's probably broken a dozen bones. Ash's face contorts into a desperate grimace. I crouch over Brayden helplessly, a whirl of emotions stirring in me.

"Are you okay?" I ask.

"I—I can't move," says Brayden, his lips trembling. His brow is pouring sweat, and I dab his forehead with my bandanna. "Where's my dragon?"

Only a true dragon rider would ask that at a time like this.

"He tried to get to you in time. So did I," says Ash. "I'm so sorry. So, so sorry."

Ash takes Brayden's hand as tears flow down his cheeks.

"I . . . know," says Brayden between coughs.

All three of us know that Ash is apologizing for so much more than today's events. Brayden closes his eyes, and I pray he stays with us. Not just for him, but for me. Selfishly, I don't think I can bear to watch another person die. Around us, other riders escape with their bulbs, but at least half the riders are still hunting.

"We have to get him back to the checkpoint," I say, turning to Ash. "Now."

"I don't think we can move him," says Ash. Examining Brayden, I realize Ash is right. It won't be safe to load him up on a dragon in this state. And even if we do get him some sort of medical care . . .

"Stay here," I say. I run for Ranga and pull her face up to me so the livestream camera is aimed directly at me. "Um, this message is for the game designers. I'm not sure if you guys can see this, but we have a man down. We can't move him. Brayden needs medical care. Immediately." I leave Ranga in the marsh, promise her I'll return quickly, and head back to Brayden. When I return, I find the two boys sharing a quiet exchange and I sit back a few feet to give them space. I hope that this is Ash's chance to make things right. Just in case . . .

Farther down the bank, Laura rises from the water. Her shirt is bulky and covered in mud and algae. She joins us at Brayden's side and mutters, "Madre mía."

I wipe my nose with the back of my sleeve. "You should go," I say to her.

But instead, Laura drops to her knees in the mud beside Brayden. She empties her shirt, and four bulbs fall out. "I grabbed what I could."

I suddenly realize tears are streaming down my face, and I wipe them with my dirty forearm.

"For those of us who fight together." Laura hands a bulb to Ash and a bulb to me. She hands the fourth to Brayden, who clutches it to his chest.

His eyes remain closed, and I can tell he's struggling to breathe.

"You should both go," says Ash. "I'll stay here with him until the medical team arrives." He grips Brayden's hand a little tighter. "I hope that's okay, Brayden."

Brayden wheezes and nods his head.

"Take his goldenscale to the rest stop with you. I'm

273

worried his dragon may attack the hydra when he finds out what's happened. And that'll just make things worse."

I want to wrap my arms around Ash and tell him it will be okay, but I don't because I can't make any promises. In situations like these, no one can.

With heavy hearts, Laura and I free Brayden's golden-scale and together we race for the finish line.

CHAPTER
22

30°20'00.4" N, 96°49'19.4" W
Dime a Dozen Ranch, Dime Box, Texas

At eleven p.m., we arrive in Dime Box, Texas, as cicadas buzz in the distance. Below, "BBQ HERE" is spray-painted on a particleboard sign, and a distant floodlight flickers over an old convenience store. In the ranch just beyond, a winding dirt road leads back to a campground centered around a bonfire. A sleepy tune of a harmonica lilts in the air. There's no sign of the festival or feast we're expecting. If it weren't for the collection of juvenile spin-thrushes, I might not know this is the checkpoint.

The purple-and-cyan spinthrushes chirp and chitter, and as we pull in, I notice they are joined by the announcer, a few draggers, and a handful of locals. Otherwise, only Valeen and Rion—who are on decidedly opposite sides of the camp—appear to have arrived just ahead of us. Veterinarians crowd around Jet and Valeen's hybrid for health checks. The other dragons and their riders are nowhere to be found.

As we draw closer, mournful faces reveal that they've seen the whole thing through our livestream cameras. The somber twang of a harmonica melts away mid-tune as Laura and I touch down with Brayden's goldenscale behind us. The announcer sets down a beer bottle and steps forward to greet us.

Bloodsucking journalists swarm in, but I notice Karbach maintains a respectful distance as he snaps away with his camera. The goldenscale's gold-flake skin is the color of tarnished brass, and a ranch hand takes his reins. Like a pro, Laura presses back the draggers and begins answering their questions with calm restraint.

I slide off of Ranga, who winces. I know she can feel the heavy mix of emotions.

Valeen rushes to Brayden's dragon. "Where's Brayden?" she asks.

She hasn't been here long enough to hear the news.

I watch Valeen crumble as the coordinators explain what's happened. Suddenly looking younger than her red lipstick and spidery mascara suggest, she wraps her arms around Brayden's goldenscale and sobs. I suddenly realize that Brayden and Ash aren't the only ones with history. I slump over in the grass. Rion pushes his way through the draggers to my side.

Valeen looks out to the crowd of locals and ranch hands, some of whom are crying and others who seem to revel in the drama. Her lip quivers, then she suddenly locks eyes with me.

"What are you looking at—*mother killer*," she says between clenched teeth.

Before I can process what she's saying, I'm on my feet. Valeen's mascara-streaked eyes narrow as I launch in her direction.

"What did you say?" I ask.

"You heard me."

My vision blurs as flame curls deep in the pit of my stomach. The memory of my mom—her last shallow breath—mingles with the image of Brayden imprinted in my mind. The inferno within me rises into my chest and seeps through my veins, taking over the rest of my body. My fingers coil into fists. Waves of fury roll off me as blood rises in my cheek, my ears, my lips.

Valeen's face is a target; her red lips are a bull's-eye. I pull back, fist balled, and aim. The fist flies . . .

Rion leaps to my side and rips me away. He holds my arms in place as I thrash against him.

Valeen inches back but hisses through her teeth, "Your own mother died because of you. Ash is lucky if he's not next. You don't know what you've done, setting him against us. Setting brother against brother. You're a selfish piece of backwoods trash."

"Let me go!" I say, blood burning through my veins. "Let me give her what's coming to her." She may be tall, but I can guarantee that lugging around saddles and doing *actual* chores has prepared me for a showdown.

Valeen backs away, and her sour expression drains of color. Spurred on by her fear, I break free and claw toward her.

But Rion yanks me back again and holds me so tight it hurts. Shaking, I peer out over his bearlike arms.

"Don't do it," Rion whispers. "She's not worth it. Trust me."

Cameras take their shots and reporters prattle into recording devices. Karbach shakes his head at me as if to say, "Listen to Rion, you idiot." Acting foolish in front of dozens of camera people anxiously recording my every move certainly won't help my cause. I make for Ranga and rest my head on her shoulder. At least we will have time to breathe.

I spin around to face Valeen, who's clamped once more on the goldenscale. "If you come near me during the grand finale feast, Valeen, I swear—"

"A-actually, ma'am," says the announcer, "this leg isn't over."

I lift my head, exhaustion weighing it down. "What?"

Laura breaks from the reporters and joins me by the announcer.

"I know this is a difficult time, but—uhh . . ." He swallows and adjusts the brim of his hat, "This is just a touch point so we can assure you have what you need for the next task. Do you have your lilies?"

I pull mine from my saddlebag and toss it at him as if he's the enemy.

The announcer catches it in his hand, scowls, and walks it back to me. "You'll need it for where you're headed."

I cock my head, gripping the slimy bulb. Even the muscles in my hands feel sore. My stomach gnaws with hunger, and the sourness makes me feel like I might be sick all over again.

The announcer points to a hologram platform and my shoulders slump.

"We're still racing." I suck in a sharp breath. *No.* I'm dying for sleep, food, and a moment to rest my head.

Laura groans and trudges to the platform. She kicks it, and this time, it's not a rider that appears but a dark tunnel. Small figures rush out of it, thousands of them. Tiny specks fly up into the air and disappear beyond the edges of the hologram.

"Dragonettes," says Laura. "Do you know this one?"

I nod and my neck pinches. "Old Tunnel State Park outside of Fredericksburg, I'm guessing. Look at the hole—it's an abandoned railroad tunnel. Home to three million Mexican free-tailed dragonettes." Which, if I'm honest, I don't like one bit. Small creatures are harder to control than larger ones.

"Dragonettes aren't the only thing in that tunnel," says Laura. "A massive airrage also lives there."

Of course it does. I sigh. "Let's go."

"Unless—" says the announcer, cutting off.

"Unless what?" I snap.

"Unless you'd like to, umm, take a break," he says. "No one would fault you kids if you did."

"Cassidy and I are fine," says Laura. She grips the sleeve of Rion's T-shirt, which is crusted with mud and wrinkled from the dried lake water. "Come on, Rion."

One of the vets snaps off a white latex glove. "Mr. Carter here is having his dragon's vitals checked," she says.

"Jet is dinged up pretty bad," says Rion. "I'll be along in a bit. Just go."

For the first time since this race started—maybe for the first time in my life—I don't fight back.

Laura and I ride side by side for two and a half hours to Old Tunnel State Park. We are swift and silent as night, speaking not a word to one another because I'm afraid that if I do, I'll cry. I stroke Ranga's scales and hope she doesn't hate me for roping her into this dangerous adventure. She flashes her brightest turquoise shade to let me know that she's okay, but I can't help feeling guilty. As my mind reels, I also wonder if Valeen was right—

Have I doomed Ash by befriending him?

I recall Nickolai's icy threat at the tornado stop. I sip on rainwater from my canteen and chew on my last strip of beef jerky, pretending the meat is the grand feast we will have on the last leg.

If I make it to the last leg.

CHAPTER 23

30°06'01.5" N, 98°49'09.7" W
Old Tunnel State Park, Kendall County, Texas

Around 1:30 am, we touch down in a grass-laden gorge that spreads into a wide-open field. At one end, a shadow-shrouded tunnel is carved into a rocky hillside, the remnants of an eroded railway tunnel from the 1940s. Stars wink overhead and hundreds of fireflies blink on and off like Morse code in the field. Colt and the Grousewood boys laugh around a small fire just beyond the hologram platform. The FC riders are nowhere to be found. Laura and I slide off our dragons and head for Colt. A jackrabbit hangs upside down on a spit over the fire.

"Hey there, ladies. Nice of you to finally join us," says Colt in a jovial way that grates against the pain in my chest. Neither Laura nor I joke back. Colt's face twists. "You two look like you've seen a ghost. What's wrong?"

"Brayden got hurt." The words are matter-of-fact, as if I'm a war reporter delivering stats to a far-off commander.

"What?" Colt sits up straighter, arms perched over his knees. "Will he be okay?" The Grousewood boys go silent.

Laura unties the bandanna around her neck and shakes it. Dust flies in the air. "I don't know. The hydra got him."

"Sweet heaven above." Colt takes off his white Stetson cowboy hat in a sign of reverence.

The Grousewood boys follow suit. It's suddenly no wonder that Buckle & Grousewood have been courting Colt for years—he's western classic, down to the bone.

The night air swirls around me and I glance at the tunnel. "Why aren't you racing?"

Colt slides his hat back on, and I can tell he wants to ask more questions. But because he's kind, he doesn't. Instead, he pulls out his lily bulb and dangles it before us. "We have to put the bulbs in some sort of box in the tunnel. Which I am guessing will be much more difficult than it sounds once the airrage returns. The ol' boy who lives there is out feeding—he won't return until dawn, and the platform says we have to wait until six a.m. to enter."

My body relaxes just a bit, thankful, at the very least, for a moment's rest. In a rare Texas Dragon Race gesture, the

Grousewood boys offer us a bite of their rabbit. Laura and I take a quick bite, then untack Quetzal and Ranga so they can hunt. We fill our pots with water from a nearby river and forage for what little food we can in the dark. But I feel weak and give up after finding only a few sour mulberries. If I can make it through this leg, at least I'll have barbecue and ice water waiting for me at the celebration feast.

Hearts heavy, Laura and I lay out our blankets and plop down beside Colt. I draw my knees up to my chest and rock lightly. The Bhatti sisters touch down a few minutes later and saunter to our circle. A twinge of relief runs through me—at least they weren't lost to the hydra as well. Rose runs a glittery cowboy boot along the ground.

"Rion is out," says Viv. "Jet's wing was too mangled after his run-in with Valeen at the tornado stop. They had just dismissed him when we made it to Dime Box."

Her words deliver a second gut punch that mingles with the achy hunger in my belly.

"Valeen las va pagar por esto," says Laura.

Colt jams a stick in the fire. Usually, being down two contestants would be helpful to anyone still riding. But when one is a friend and the other may not make it, it feels like less of an accomplishment.

"Can we join you?" asks Rose.

Colt motions to the fire and I scooch over. Viv and Rose sit next to me, their movements in time with one another. Without a word, I know they've learned about Brayden at the pit stop. Now, even they seem joyless.

Inky night lingers overhead. The wind whistles through the gorge, and crickets chirp all around us. But reptilian moans waft through the air. Instantly, I recognize the howls from our experience at the tornado stop. The FC must be here, and they're probably "disciplining" their dragons.

As the howls ring out through the gorge, Laura pulls the saint's candle from her pack and sets it on one of the rocks surrounding the fire.

"When my abuelo went to the hospital, we lit a candle to petition the saints for his good health," says Laura. "I don't know if it works, but since my tía gave me a votive of Saint George, patron saint of dragons, it seems only right that we light it tonight." She dips a twig into the campfire and catches a flame that she shields with her hand. Her face glows with soft firelight, and she leans forward to light the candle.

My chest aches for Brayden as we take a holy moment to reflect or pray or whatever people do in these sorts of situations.

But my thoughts drift, and I remember that we have yet to confront the last leg, which will surely be the most dangerous. I wonder how my father will feel if I die during it, and suddenly I regret not inviting him to join us for the final feast . . . even if he disapproves. Fear creeps along my skin. They say that teenagers believe they're invincible, and perhaps that's mostly true. But now, as I glance around the circle of somber competitors, I think we all understand the consequences.

Colt slides his pearlized mandolin from its tattered case and strums a soft tune. As he plays, I close my eyes and lift my voice to the night sky.

Welcome, heroes, to Heaven's door,
saints and sinners too.
It's open wide forevermore.
When we ride, we ride for you.

A thousand angels could not compete,
no matter how hard they try.
This is the final ride, so sweet,
the end, our last goodbye.

Together we lament as the candle burns, swaying with

the music. The field of fireflies winks in and out, sometimes matching the tune. And as we carry on, Ranga drops down to join us, lured in by my song. Quetzal follows. And the Bhattis' twin dragons. Before we know it, each of our dragons is crowded around us in an unbreakable fortress. Ranga nudges my back affectionately.

When the music peters out, I clear my throat and rise to my feet.

"Brayden isn't the only one suffering in this competition," I say. "I've watched the way that each of you treat your dragons. You love them. They're an extension of you—family. But the FC treats them like machines. Playthings. That philosophy shouldn't win this race. Dragons are incredible, misunderstood creatures, worthy of wonder. We can show people what it means to treat them with love."

Suddenly, I feel like a vulnerable kid instead of a seasoned dragon rider. Ranga chitters and flaps her wings, sending embers flying into the air. I run a hand along her opalescent spines before lifting my chin to the group.

"This isn't about winning for money or personal glory anymore. We need to win because dragons deserve better. And we can't afford to let each other fail. Every time we try to best one another to get ahead, we strengthen FireCorp's position. We show them we're willing to sell one another out . . . And for what? Their pocket change?" I stand taller. "They don't even need the money—for them, this is a power game—one more way to prove that FireCorp owns this industry and every dragon in it."

This time, no one whispers among themselves. Instead, each rider weighs their options, just as I have. Like a true cowgirl, my mother believed in being independent. But I'm not her. And I probably never will be.

"When we first arrived, Rion suggested we ally together to beat the FC, and I laughed—we all did. But we were wrong. A boy is fighting for his life. And elsewhere dragons are being tortured. They don't deserve to be treated that way."

Laura stands beside me, the flames reflecting onto her scuffed legs. "More than anything," she says, "I want that shiny first-place trophy and the title of First Rider. But things have changed."

I stare into the candle's flame once more. "Ash may be Michael's stepson, but he's given us vital information: the FC is using androlone to amp up their dragons."

"And you believe him?" asks Viv.

"Laura and I both witnessed what they're doing at rest stops. They transform their creatures into something twisted and dark." I pause. "We can't just let that slide."

"Let's tell Laudes they're dosing," says Colt. "We can get their entire team of dragons disqualified."

"This whole competition is bought and paid for by FireCorp," I say. "Sure, there are other sponsors, but the FC is the biggest. If we complain, we'll sound like whiny kids with no proof."

Laura chimes in. "Even if we appeal to have their dragons tested, their lawyers can easily run out the clock on us. The drugs will metabolize and be undetectable in the dragons' blood after three or four days. And I guarantee the FC legal team can hold off the council before they manage to secure a blood sample. Our best bet is to band together and hope one of us can outsmart them."

I brace on edge, waiting for an argument. But this time, no one argues. Colt nods, and Grousewood shares a silent exchange that says they know Laura and I are right.

"We have to work together," I say.

Ranga howls into the night. And Quetzal joins her, screeching and crying to the moon like coyotes ready for a feast. One by one, the other dragons join and form a fierce choir. The seriousness on my competitors' faces shifts, and Colt pops up, his mandolin still strapped across his shoulder. He strikes his mandolin strings with rough, forceful movement, making nothing but noise, like a true country outlaw. This is our war cry. The sound evaporates in the dry Texas air as he yelps, and we join him.

As a group. As a fellowship. As a *team*.

I stay up after the others drift off to sleep and shine my belt buckle until it is as gold and gleaming as the summer sun.

CHAPTER
24

My eyes flutter open as the sun rises over the horizon. I sit up from my warm space nestled against Ranga's stomach.

"Did anyone see the airrage return?" I ask, untangling from my blanket.

"I saw some of the dragonettes return, but not the airrage," says Colt.

I wince. It would've been nice to know how big and terrifying the creature we're about to face is. I've only seen pictures of airrage in copies of *Sharptooth Junior* and dragoneering field guides. From what I remember, they are massive translucent blobs of muscle and capable of squashing a person with their toad-like feet. Worse, their mouths extend from ear to ear, and while they may not be quick to take flight, they can spew flames in seconds.

"We've got a half hour left until we can get in," says Laura.

We pack our things and refill our canteens, preparing for what we assume will be a very long ride to our final destination. I prep Ranga's saddle, making sure she's ready for a swift takeoff after the task. She yawns sleepily, and I can tell she'll enjoy a victory feast just as much as I will. If we make it.

At six a.m. sharp, the entire group rushes into the tunnel as a horde of hungry, would-be victors. All we know is there will be boxes to lock our bulbs in to complete the task. But I can guarantee they won't make it easy. I shove the bulb in my pocket and hope the airrage doesn't wake up.

The FC wears dark fire-retardant jumpsuits and helmets with blacked-out visors. Ash, who must have arrived sometime in the night, dons the same gear. But he's decidedly separate from FireCorp and remains on the outskirts like a loner. I wave for him to join us so we can hear more about Brayden, but he declines. I guess breaking from FireCorp *and* publicly joining us is just one step too far.

I power up my goggles' night-vision setting as we all dash into the cave.

Hundreds of wriggling dragonettes cover every inch of the cave, and as we glide through with flashlights, there's the sense that they may attack at any moment. To the untrained eye, they look like bats with fuzzy brown bodies and piglike noses. But the scales hidden in the fur and the slitted emerald eyes remind us that these creatures feed on more than moths and mosquitoes. The stench of dragon guano is strong enough that I tie my bandanna around my face like a horse-thieving bandit.

Cassidy Drake and the Tunnel Gang, at your service.

We crowd through the narrow passage together—FC, Grousewood, and unsponsored riders alike. Personally, I've had enough of mysterious caves for a lifetime. My only saving grace is that this time, I'm not waltzing toward a Texas coral viper. But while there may not be venom, this dragon is a true fire-breathing nightmare when awakened. Maybe none of us will make it out alive.

Not that the Bhattis look bothered by that possibility at all. They almost skip down the dark tunnel, reaching up to the tiny dragonettes as they walk.

"Sweet babies," Viv coos.

My skin crawls as Rose strokes one and places it on her

shoulder. I keep moving, guided along by Laura and Colt. Breaking for it, the FC pushes ahead of us like a swift pack of Olympic racers. My heart jolts as Nickolai forms an impenetrable wall between Ash and our group. The rest of us race to catch up, and the dragonettes stir with millions of fluttering wings. They sing spookily, like vampiric songbirds, trilling and chirping as we rush through the passageway.

The stench grows as we reach the end of the tunnel and the sleeping airrage who lies in wait. Clustered on the ground lie the twenty bread-box-sized containers we are supposed to leave our bulbs in, each marked with the name of a participant. Even Rion's and Brayden's boxes are there. The game designers had no idea they would never see this task. Since everyone has a box, I guess the race will continue after this . . .

On top of my container is a palm print reader, meaning only I can open it. That's why they took our prints before the race started. I place my sweaty palm on the box, and the lock clicks open. Inside is a second box made of wood and metal, a glory of steampunk crafting with dozens of gears and knobs. I fiddle with a couple of them, searching for the box's opening, but nothing. Beside me, the Grousewood boys crowd together in a small circle, holding their boxes in the center.

Laura pulls me to her side, and Colt joins us. We hold up our boxes and compare them.

"It's a puzzle box," says Laura, flipping the contraption around in her hand. "I've watched videos of people trying to solve them online. We'll have to slide the planes and twist the gears in a specific combination to unlock them."

I thumb the laser-cut edges and tiny knobs. "The boxes are all the same, which probably means they have the same moves to open it."

The FC is already hard at work on their puzzle boxes, crowded together and swiftly copying one another's moves. Laura, Colt, and I fumble with our own boxes, spinning and turning the knobs and comparing notes as we go.

"Grousewood!" I say, eagerly waving them over. They hesitate but stay hunkered down in their own group.

Colt snorts and spins his box in his hands. "So much for teamwork."

I grit my teeth and ignore them. "Bhattis?" I ask, less confident.

They share a silent exchange and dash for us. We expand our huddle to let them in. The tiny dragonette leans off of Rose's shoulder as we tinker with each of our boxes. We're three clusters: us with our madcap collection of anxious riders; Grousewood, who won't help; and the FC, who work as a coordinated pack of chess players dressed in riot gear.

The airrage snores, and a putrid gust of air swirls through the cave. In response, the dragonettes chirp in a haunting wave that echoes down the corridor. I'm too busy twisting gears and sliding planes on the box to clamp down on my ears.

There's a loud, slow scraping noise as the airrage shifts like a massive dog in the middle of a dream.

"Faster," says Colt. We crack several of the moves, but still, the box won't open.

Across the cave, Myra whispers sharply, "I've got it!"

My stomach twists as the entire FireCorp group rumbles with excitement and opens their boxes. I crane my neck but cannot decipher any of the moves they've used. Frickety frick. A strong, familiar, almost urine-like smell mixes with the carnivorous stench of the airrage, perfuming the air with sickly noxious fumes. Even with my goggles on, my eyes begin to sting.

"What the devil is that?" asks Rose.

"Concentrated ammonia," I breathe, ice in my words. "Smelling salts. We use it on the farm for waking up dragons who've passed out. The boxes must be filled with it."

"Which means—"

"Which means every time a box is opened, more ammonia will flood the tunnel, and the airrage won't be asleep for long," I snap. "So we need to figure out this puzzle, drop our lilies, and blow this Popsicle stand!"

The FC stuffs their lily bulbs in their boxes, slams them shut, and powers out. I half expect Ash to stop and help, but Nickolai pushes him forward.

"Pay attention," Viv snaps in my direction.

I keep fiddling with my box as the tunnel rumbles.

Yeeeeowwwwwww!

Two gold flashing eyes wink open and the cave fills with smoke.

My heart drops into my stomach.

"I've got it! I've got it!" yells Laura, no longer bothering to stay quiet. She shows us how to twist and slide the various planes and gears to unlock the puzzle box. I fumble with my gears. Across the cave, the Grousewood team hesitates but keeps fiddling. The box opens as the dense smell of concentrated ammonia fills my nose. I press my lily bulb into it, careful not to breathe deeply, and slam the box closed just as embers from the airrage's mighty throat light up the cave.

"Go, go, go!" I shout.

We scramble up. The Grousewood boys keep tinkering

as the flames grow and the airrage lurches from the dark, shrouded by shadows and curling smoke. Its face is amorphous, and two long slits stretch from its gaping jaws to its tire-sized amber eyes. The flames in its belly broil underneath translucent muscles, glowing through the network of veins and its salamander-like skin. It huffs and roars to the ceiling.

Yrrrreeeeowwwwwwwkkkk!

The dragonettes screech even louder.

I dash for Grousewood. "Let me help you," I say, squatting down.

Colt pushes me aside. "I've got this. Find the next clue. *Go!*"

The dragonettes swarm around us, and I dash for the light at the end of the tunnel. Millions of them spiral out of the dark in a stunning aerial display that blocks the tunnel. They fly into the back of my head as they scramble to avoid being roasted. Coughing and wheezing from the smoke, I keep running as fire explodes behind me. I feel like an action hero darting out of the tunnel to freedom.

Outside, the hologram platform has sprung to life with another famous dead rider spouting a poem, but I can barely focus on it. Laura and the Bhattis are already on their dragons, waiting for us. The tunnel puffs with smoke.

The Grousewood boys and Colt are nowhere to be seen.

"Where's Colt?" shouts Laura, her voice a hard edge.

I shake my head and stare at the tunnel. No Colt. No Grousewood boys. I hold my breath. This can't be. The dragonettes swarm out in a squeaking, writhing mass. Seconds drag on as my heart pounds in my chest.

Suddenly, Colt staggers from the smoke with Grousewood. One of the Grousewood boys hangs limply off of Colt's shoulder.

"Sweet heavens," I shout. "Is he . . . ?"

"He's fine!" shouts Colt. "Passed out, but fine. Go, or I'll sew you to your saddle!"

I nod and rush for Ranga, leaving them behind. Once saddled, I guide Ranga to the hologram platform to riddle out the clue with Laura and the Bhattis.

"Ranchitos Las Lomas!" shouts Rose, interrupting me before I can review the poem. "That's the location of the pre-finale feast."

I smile—I've been to Ranchitos for dragon events many times. Together, Laura, the Bhattis, and I take to the skies. Even with the steroids, the FC's lugs of meat won't beat our smaller dragons during the four-hour flight. I croon "Keep on the Sunny Side" by June Carter to Ranga, and at her insistence, I sing it all the way through twice more during our ride.

This time, we arrive at the finish line first, earning a place as competitors in the final leg of the Great Texas Dragon Race.

CHAPTER 25

For this final leg, the ranch hands collect our dragons for a full round of medical checks. The race is now an even split, with five FC riders qualifying—Ash, Nickolai, Valeen, Trevor Price, and Myra Holden—and five unaffiliated riders: Laura, Colt, the Bhattis, and me. Ranga whimpers, and her opalescent spines pulse as I hand over the reins.

"We'll take good care of her," says a kind man who's missing an eyebrow. A scarring pattern spreads over his cheekbone and under a black eye patch. His badge says "Diego."

"It's okay, girl," I coo.

Diego pulls out a bloody T-bone steak from a plastic

sack at his side and dangles it on a pigtail hook. "We've got treats!"

I pat Ranga's smooth scales as she takes the meat in one toothy bite.

"Plenty more where that came from," says Diego. "Nothin' but the best for the finalists—and we wouldn't want any visitors to become dragon meat. Even if they did sign waivers."

By the time the sun sets, a full brigade of people eager to see dragon riders will have descended on the campgrounds like ants on a dollop of honey. Since the last leg is the most publicized, and dragon riding has recently been under so much scrutiny, I expect they're making a grand show of dragon safety and rider welfare. Especially now that the world knows a boy is fighting for his life.

"Any word about Brayden Boone?" I ask Diego.

"Not out of the woods yet, but I think he'll make it." Diego smiles encouragingly, and I heave a sigh of relief. "Now head on back. I've got your girl."

Beyond a guarded partition, an eager gang of reporters jockeys for my attention.

"Cassidy! Cassidy!" they yell.

Spurred on by the hopeful news about Brayden, I wave, resulting in a few cheers. I kiss Ranga on the nose, promise to see her soon, and make my way to the riders' private area.

Valeen is waiting to check in next, and she scowls at me as I pass. Ash is just behind her in line. A brutal black eye covers the right side of his face.

"Jeez-oh-Pete," I gasp, walking up to him. "What happened?" I lift my hand to touch the splotchy purple-and-blue streak in his eye socket.

"Do us a favor and leave us be, Miss Drake," Nickolai says as he comes to stand behind his brother. He cracks his knuckles, which are red and swollen. I scowl.

"I think Ash can make his own decisions," I snap.

Head held high, I look to Ash, hoping he will correct Nickolai or stand up to him in some meaningful way.

But Ash's eyes flick to the swarm of cameras beyond the fence. "Just go," he whispers.

The words cut right through me, and my fingernails press into my palms. I try to remember that this is Ash's FireCorp mask, but that's what sours my stomach.

Beside Ash, Nickolai stands proud. He laughs—no, he cackles. "Yes, perhaps Ash can make his own decisions."

I don't bother to conceal my disappointment. Instead, I march off to the winner's circle, where the hungry reporters wait on edge. The Texas sun pours down on me as they shove microphones in my face.

"You've made it to the last leg. Do you think your mother's success—and ultimate death—is what drove you to this point?"

"Are you still glad you decided to compete? Even after you watched Brayden Boone get so terribly injured?"

"Do you think you stand a chance at winning?"

As much as I've craved a spotlight to speak out against dragon cruelty, I'm suddenly tongue-tied. My mind reels from too little sleep, and the emptiness in my stomach clouds my thoughts. "I will win," I say, heaving my pack onto my back. "And I won't need to use the treachery of a team like FireCorp's to do it."

A reporter with too much bronzer and a pretty floral dress pounces like I'm a bone she's about to clamp on to. "FireCorp donates millions of dollars to dragon conservation around the world. How does that level with your way of thinking?"

I balk, suddenly wishing that I were dealing with Karbach instead of this stooge. "They only give that money for good PR and tax write-offs," I say, less eloquently than I would have liked.

"Now, now, Cassidy," says Valeen, cutting in front of the reporters. She turns on the most delightful face I've ever seen her wear, and even with melted mascara, she exudes charm and class. "Stooping to cheap shots? I would've expected better from you."

I inch back and swallow a dry lump in my throat.

"FireCorp has always been, and will always be, a model dragoneering agency," recites Valeen. "They are proud to sponsor this year's race and I am honored to be a part of the FireCorp team alongside Nickolai, Trevor, Myra, and Michael Carne's son, Ashton."

The reporters eat up the well-rehearsed line like flies swarming cow dung. Barf.

Valeen's easy rapport with the press is just one more reminder of how disadvantaged I am and why simply accusing the FC of using steroids isn't the way to stop them. At least not now.

I march off past the reporters' area and back to the restricted section for riders and ranch hands. Security guards check us in at the partition. Beyond it, the private zone is fortified by miles of barren ranchland and barbed wire as far as the eye can see.

For this leg, we have access to the ranch's cowboy showers, so at least we'll be camera ready. Bones aching and muscles sore, I take a cold dunk that is both exhilarating and awful. Cleaner than I've been in days, I towel off and make my way to Laura's makeshift camp.

Across the field, Ash ignores the world and kicks back liquid from his engraved Yeti. Three hundred yards away, Nickolai lingers around his camp, laughing with Valeen, Myra, and Trevor Price, the fifth FC rider to make it this far in the race. All I can think of is the black case of steroids somewhere in Nickolai's tent. At least Ash gave us that info before he decided to transform back into a chilly jerk.

I fan out a blanket beside Laura's.

The campground beyond our private rest area has transformed into a busy carnival, complete with streamers, fresh pies, and fried Snickers bars. The news of Brayden's survival has spread like wildfire, and they've even set up a donation area where visitors can contribute to his medical bills. Seven yellow greatfrills zoom overhead like fighter jets at an air show. They puff smoke as they barrel through the cloudless canvas of bright blue.

At this moment, I miss Gran so much. Pa too. In all my dreams of competing, a finale feast without my family was never in the picture.

"You can spend as much time with my family as you want," says Laura. She's decked out in a CalDrac Institute T-shirt from the freebie bag. "My abuela doesn't speak much English, but she'll love you just the same. I'll even translate a few of her stories—she's seen more wild dragons than anyone I know."

I thank Laura and plait a long fishtail braid with my damp hair. Braids are an all-purpose hairstyle that goes with everything. Whether you're celebrating a victory *or* pissing off an evil, multibillion-dollar corporation like FireCorp, braids work.

And I plan to do both things today because I have nothing left to lose. Somehow, I'm going to make sure the FC can't use those steroids on their poor dragons.

The camp bells chime, announcing the opening of the gates.

"They're here!" squeals Laura, scrambling to her feet. She deftly applies her lip gloss despite having no mirror and smacks her lips.

"For such a tough dragon rider, you sure act like a girl," I say.

"Cassidy, we *are* girls. And I plan to look my best for the cameras, because screen time leads to scholarships." Laura sets a hand on her hip. "Do you know that my mom got a second job so she could pay for a trainer to help me last year? And my dad came to every qualifying race, no matter how early. I'm taking advantage of every angle I can, because my family has put in a lot of time, energy, and money to get me here. You should do the same."

I smile. As much as I'd like Laura's help in a plan to stop the FC from using the steroids, I know this isn't the time to bother her. She's on her own mission.

Laura pinches her cheeks, accentuating the blush of her high cheekbones. "Now, if you'll excuse me, I'm off. Come with!"

"I'll be there in a bit," I say, thumbing through a tattered field journal. "Just reviewing a few more plays."

Laura sighs. "If you can't win by now, you won't win at all. Which, by the way, is wonderful advice, because even if we work together, I will still kick your butt. Nothing you do now will give you my first-place trophy." She pockets her lip gloss as live music strikes up.

"You wish." I chuckle. "Go have fun. I'll be there soon."

Laura takes off past the partition dividing us from the public grounds. The afternoon bustles as everyone attends to arrival tasks. A golf cart carrying a load of fireworks takes off on a dirt road, out into the desolate field within the restricted area. The driver chatters to someone on his walkie-talkie.

What dragoneering event would be complete without a brilliant fireworks display? Especially one sponsored by FireCorp. I'll be surprised if they don't flash their logo in red and yellow bursts. With FireCorp's heavy presence, I try to imagine how I'll manage to get the case of steroids out of the FC's clutches.

But I'm parched and fresh out of ideas, so I make my way to the festivities and the free VIP drink station. The buzz of families leaves me feeling empty, but I pour myself a lemonade and sway to a western swing cover of Willie Nelson's "On the Road Again."

"Cass?"

I spin around, and lemonade sloshes from my cup. "Pa!"

The sun hangs over him like a glorious beacon. Bursting with warmth, I run to Pa and wrap my arms around him. He squeezes me tight in a great bear hug, crushing my ribs. He holds me back and studies me.

"You're a mess," he says. "What have you been getting into?"

"I couldn't even explain if I tried." I hug him again, tighter this time. "I can't believe you came."

"Well, after I received your invitation, I had to."

I smell a rat. "I never sent you an invitation."

"No matter—I'm here now," says Pa. "Can we grab a seat?"

"Sure can."

I lead him through the crowd of children with fiery

pinwheels and balloon animals shaped like various dragon species. The smell of cherry-topped funnel cakes hits my nose as I guide us to an open picnic table beneath a mammoth red-and-white tent. The band plays a cheery song, and for the first time, I feel in tune with it.

Pa pushes a rusted cookie tin my way. I open it to find a sad cluster of pecan sandies.

"I know they're your favorite." Pa scratches his forehead. "And since Gran wasn't there to make them, I felt it was only right that I try. I would have brought sun tea if I thought there was a cold chance in Hades that either of us would drink it."

The happy music fades into the background as he mentions Gran, and the sad expression on his face anchors me to the earth.

"How is Gran?" I ask.

My father grimaces. "She says she's fine, but I can tell she's in a lot of pain. The docs aren't sure if it's genetic or environmental, but they keep promising they'll figure out what's wrong soon enough."

Yeah, with a few more pricey tests. I pull out a sandie and bite down. It crumbles in my mouth, but not the right way.

"So good," I say, choking down the dry cookie.

"Who taught you to lie like that?" He winks at me. "It

sure didn't come from our house."

"We have our fair share of liars here." I glance over my shoulder at the cult of FC.

Pa taps on the picnic table. "Made any friends out here?"

Across the tent, Laura passes a corn dog to a small boy in a dinosaur tee. She catches my eye and waves. "As a matter of fact, I have." I wave back.

Pa nibbles on a sandie, cringes, and sets it on the table. "Well, that's a worthy prize."

I falter because I understand what he's implying. "I'm not coming home, Pa. We're almost done—and I've made it this far intact."

Pa grunts. "Well, at this point, it doesn't matter if you win."

"Of course it matters."

"It won't." Pa adjusts his frayed baseball hat so it obscures his features. "I've been in talks with Michael Carne's assistant over at FireCorp. We're signing a deal at the end of this week."

My heart drops to my toes. Surely I've misheard him. I didn't realize the band was so dadgum loud. "A deal?"

"We'll be able to keep the ranch and stay on as tenants. FireCorp will become our new partner." He bats a fly off the tin of cookies. "Even though I don't care for Michael, it's the best option we have."

My head spins, and I search for Michael in the sea of faces. When I find him, he's smiling. Waiting. It hits me that he was the one who invited my father . . . and he's been waiting for the precise moment when my father would break the news. He raises a glass to toast me and sips it, never breaking eye contact.

"You mean our new master," I breathe.

"I've reviewed the contract up and down, and if we want to keep the ranch, this is our best deal." With his ring finger, which bears a dinged wedding band, he pulls his collar and fans air into his shirt. "Turning FireCorp down—turning Michael down—would not be a wise move." He spits out "Michael" like it's an unripe peach.

"But why? *Why* should we be so afraid of him?"

Pa hesitates, and his face darkens as if he's about to tell me some terrible secret. But he takes a sip of sweet tea and mumbles into the cup, "Because he's a cheater. And cheaters always get what they want. If he wants Drake's Dragon Ranch, he'll have it. At any cost."

"What did Gran say? She'd never agree to this."

"I'm not going to bother Lynn with that sort of thing right now, grasshopper. She needs to focus on her recovery. That's why I'm here." Pa slides a calloused hand across the table. "Imagine how much worse off she'll be if something happens to you on the final leg. She couldn't take it in her condition . . ." Pa squeezes my hand. "Come home. For Gran's sake."

As my father clutches my hand, I picture him trying to protect Gran the way he wishes he'd protected my mom. And honestly, I'd love to see her, smell her tacky rosewater lotion, and help her paint her nails some garish shade of turquoise. Maybe my presence can help—if medicine doesn't work, perhaps love does. But I pull my hand back from Pa.

"I can't." My red leather boots are glued to the dirt.

Pa stiffens. "What?"

"I can't go. I have to stay." As the words slip from my lips, I slump down.

"Cassidy?" His voice wobbles as he inspects me. "What's gotten into you? You'd put Gran through hell for a few dollars and some glory?"

I study the table in front of me and follow the trails of the wood grain—anything to avoid looking at him.

"Has the race really changed you that much?" he asks.

I press my lips into a hard line and reach into my pocket. I take out my mother's compass and set it in the center of the table.

Pa lights up and grazes the metal with two fingers. "Where did you get this?"

"Gran. She gave it to me and told me to remember that Drake women never give up."

He turns it over in his hand, lovingly. I'm not sure if he's registering what I'm saying or if he's lost in nostalgia. I reach across the table and place my hand over the compass.

"Dad," I say, "the FC has lied, cheated, and stolen to get to the top. And you should see how they treat their dragons. I can't let them win. Not like this."

Around us, the audience claps in tribute to the previous song. I pretend they are clapping for the truth.

But Pa hangs his head. "Cass, the FC will *always* cheat their way to a win. You can't change them. The best you can do is accept it and move on to bigger and better things."

I inch forward on my bench so that I'm barely hanging off the edge. "You're not listening to me, Pa. I have to choose courage. I can't give up."

"Oh, honey, that may be true." Pa hunches over and hides under his hat as if it's a security blanket. "But sometimes you have to know when to give in."

The words bite as I consider them, and he asks me once more. "Please, come home."

314

I clutch the compass to my heart. "I can't—it's not what Gran would want. She told me that if I followed my heart, this compass would lead me where I must go. Well, Gran is my heart, and so it's time to follow her."

CHAPTER 26

27°40'01.8" N, 99°12'08.3" W

Twin Dragon Ranch, Ranchitos Las Lomas, Texas

Pa leaves before the night's grand festivities begin. He says he has to get back to Gran, and since I'm not going to be there for her, I don't complain. I don't even bother telling him how much it would mean to have him there when we take off for the final leg. Because he already knows. And asking—only to get shot down—will just make me feel more alone.

Gran always says, "A cowboy stays on the job until it gets done, no matter how dark it is outside."

At this point, I am more cowboy than Billy the Kid.

I dart through carnival games and wave at various passersby, some of whom offer sweet hellos. But even though I've become a semi-celebrity, I'm a girl on a mission. No time for southern politeness. The smell of cotton candy hits my nose as I zigzag through the crowd.

I head back to the restricted area and allow the sheriffs to pat me down for contraband—namely, technology that we might be trying to smuggle into the race. All clear, I dash for my tent and grab my goggles. The magnification knob wriggles, and I press it back on until it snaps.

If I can make it to Ash's camp, I'll have a direct line to the androlone. I may not have a plan, but now is the time to improvise. I take off for his tent site.

The Bhatti sisters step out in front of me. Ugh.

"What are you doing?" asks Viv. She lifts her lavender cat's-eye sunglasses, which she's wearing at night for heaven knows what reason.

"Nothing. I, um . . ." I've never been the best liar.

"Oh, we know trouble when we see it."

"So, you might as well tell us."

"There's no point in trying to keep it secret now."

They talk so fast my head spins. "I—"

Rose sighs and smooths her pastel curls, now streaked with mint green. The dragonette she befriended at Old Tunnel pops its head out of her holographic hip bag. "You may think we're just here to play games, but if you haven't noticed, both of us made it to the final round when many other players failed."

"And that's not a mistake," says Viv.

"If you're causing trouble," continues Rose, "I'd be willing to bet my life that it'll be at the expense of FireCorp."

Viv snorts. "Guaranteed."

"So, let's drop the charade." Rose inspects her pointed black nails, which peek out from her fingerless gloves.

"Because when you said you wanted a team, we take that seriously," says Viv.

Rose's lips curve into a crescent moon with hot-pink gloss. "And we want in."

My mouth goes slack, and I'm so surprised I can't do anything but slip my thumbs through my belt loops.

Viv leans toward her sister. "She's going to crack."

"Or screw this up," says Rose.

"Both, I think."

Viv pulls me close by the straps on my backpack. "The key to pulling pranks is making sure that no one questions you."

"Which means you have to be smart."

"Smarter than smart."

"And confident." Rose motions as if casting an aura around me. "And right now, you look guilty."

"Why act guilty when you're doing good?" says Viv.

"Exactly."

Fantastic point. I stand up straighter.

Rose props an arm on my shoulder, and it's covered in designs drawn on in permanent marker. "I never got to tell you: I appreciate that you tried to help me at the hydra. That was classy. So tell us, partner . . . where are we headed?"

Equal opportunity pranksters. That's what Laura called them the first day. Since I have nothing left to lose, I'll bet on that call. It's either that or run back and hide. And that's not the game I'm playing.

I nod my head toward the brushy field. "I'm going to make sure they can't torture their dragons with injections. I'm going to steal the case of steroids at Nickolai's camp. Level the playing field and give their poor dragons a break."

I let the words hang in the air. The Bhattis have been so *strange* this whole time—their own little duo of trouble—that I have no idea what to expect. Rose coos as the little dragonette chirps and crawls out of her bag and onto her shoulder.

Viv smiles wickedly. "Then lead the way."

Without another word, I lower my goggles and guide the sisters to a brushy area just past Ash's tent. We drop between two limestone boulders, and I point to Nickolai's tent. A lanky ranch hand paces around the twenty-yard stretch of FC camp, a stalwart guardian of the hidden androlone. He wears a wide-brimmed cowboy hat and dusty jeans that epitomize the word "cowboy" and takes a long drag of a nasty cigarette, then tosses it on the ground. With the heel of his shoe, he squashes it out.

"I've seen the case Nickolai keeps the androlone in," I say. "If you two can distract the ranch hand when he's the furthest from Nickolai's tent, I bet I can get it."

The sisters regard the ranch hand for a wide minute. They speak in a silent language, exchanging glances that I don't comprehend.

Viv clears her throat. "I usually wouldn't say this . . . but are you sure you want to do this?"

I glare back at her. "You're joking, right?"

"This isn't a prank—this is a declaration of war against FireCorp. And they take no prisoners."

These are fearless young women, and their hesitation sends waves of doubt through me. Am I underestimating what Michael Carne will do if he finds out? Up until now, we've been playing a game of cat and mouse. What happens if I discover he's a lion?

Gazing at the hired-gun ranch hand, I shove down that thought. Even if Michael's a lion, I am a dragon.

I set my hands on my hips. "Honestly, I expected more brass from you two," I say. "But if you're scared, then leave. Because I'll die before I stand by and let them dose those dragons when I could have done something about it. Maybe I just love dragons more than you two."

The dragonette on Rose's shoulder chirps in response.

Viv runs a hand along a star-shaped Sharpie tattoo trailing up her forearm. "What will you do with the case?"

"I haven't gotten that far."

"You know, we peeked at the fireworks platform," says Rose with an edge of curious mischief. She points in the opposite direction of the fairground, out into the barren ranchland beyond the FC camp. "They set it up a few hundred yards out."

"Safe from visitors but not safe from the likes of us," says Viv.

"The fireworks they're using tonight are *real* Spark and Dragon Fyre Council fireworks. None of that lame roadside business for normies." Rose rubs her nose on her dragonette and speaks to it in a babbly baby voice. "They're the best fireworks on earth. Fortified with ground graylark dragon skin. Yes, they are, sweet baby!"

"There's enough on that platform to end Visiting Day with a real *bang*." Viv holds out her fingers and begins to count on them. "Wooden racks loaded with paper cannons of chrysanthemum shellwings. Canisters of bolted crossettes. Dozens of violet diadems."

Rose nods. "I'd say that the platform will be equipped with enough fireworks to set off a powerful explosion."

"Enough to destroy, say, a case."

"Guaranteed."

Waves of excitement ripple through me. Destroying the steroids with the FC's own fireworks display would be ultimate poetic justice. Reckless, sure. But what true dragoneer wouldn't do the same to help dragons in need? I nod, and the sisters give me a rundown, outlining how fireworks coordinators usually leave launch platforms roughly ten minutes ahead of time, giving me a short window to drop the case and make a break for it. Clearly, they've done things like this before. My watch reads 8:13 p.m. That's seventeen minutes until the grand display.

Night vision enabled, we slink through the tall grasses toward Nickolai's tent and crouch down. I hold up my finger to my lips as if to say *shhh*. Nickolai's tent is only forty feet away, and the ranch hand is at the other end of the FC camp.

"If I make a run for it, do you think you two can distract him?" I ask.

Viv scoffs. "That's not even a challenge."

They creep right to cut him off before he circles back and I scurry to the left, through the dried grasses and shadows, until I reach Nickolai's tent.

"Hey, what are you two doing here?" An unfamiliar raspy voice ricochets off the ground.

The Bhattis step forward to meet him, blocking him from coming any closer. They giggle with their schoolgirl personae that I now recognize as a complete and total ruse. I slip into the tent, scuttling for the safety of shadows.

"This isn't your camp."

"It's a free country," says Viv.

"Last we checked, anyway," says Rose.

I panic and rifle through the tiny tent. Sleeping bag. Canteen. Maps. Saddlebag. And underneath the sleeping bag, the briefcase. I pop it open to find five vials of liquid, one for each of the FC's five contestants. My heart pounds in my throat, and a light breeze wafts through the tent's flap door.

"What's in the tent?" he asks, shining his flashlight into it.

I squeeze back and avoid the light, case in hand. I feel the tent's seams for another zipper or a slit to escape through, but the fabric is an impenetrable wall. I press farther into the corner and grab the bowie knife dangling from Nickolai's saddlebags.

"Let me through, or I'll call the sheriffs."

Rose chuckles. "Get 'im, Stasi!"

I hear the high-pitched squawks and squeaks of a free-tailed dragonette.

"What the—!" shouts the ranch hand. "Get this thing off of me!"

I hear him flailing around, and I jam the tip of the knife into the nylon and slash it open. Case in hand, I dive through the opening. My cowboy hat slips off my head, but there's no time to reach back into the tent and retrieve it. I crawl on the ground through grass and gravel, making my escape.

Don't make noise, don't make noise, don't make noise . . .

I hit the shrubs just beyond the tent and ditch the bowie knife. The Bhattis take off in the opposite direction, back toward the festivities, with the ranch hand on their heels. Dear God, I hope the ranch hand doesn't radio for backup. My watch reads 8:24 p.m., which means I have six minutes left. Six minutes to race across the field, get to the platform, dump the case, and run away unscathed. My muscles are tired from too little food and restless sleep, but I power through, legs burning as I run.

Four minutes.

I run through the thicket. Branches scrape my legs and catch on my holey jeans. My mind reels and I hope the Bhattis are warding off anyone who might catch me. I turn on my goggles, fiddling with the wonky dial, and try to zero back in on them. But the spinning doesn't work, and I can't seem to make them out.

Worthless goggles.

I dash to the shadowy platform, which is a tangle of fuses and hundreds of fireworks, each bigger than the last. As my eyes adjust to the darkness, a spectacular red explosive labeled "CHINESE NIGHTCLAW" commands my attention. It's the largest by far, which means it will have the most firepower. I place the case beside it.

But suddenly, I hear a strange electronic popping sound, followed by a loud *grumphhhh!*

The platform creaks and I spin around to find a sleepy grylock firejaw. He's lumpy and green, with a tiny head, and looks sort of like an obese Stegosaurus with miniature wings. He yawns, and a puff of smoke trails out of his mouth.

Something crackles again, and over a tinny speaker, an encouraging voice says, "Okay, Ernie. Get ready."

This must be the grylock's trainer. The grylock's nostrils

emit a spray of sparks.

Of course they aren't lighting the fireworks with man-power. They're using a dragon.

Normally, I wouldn't be afraid of a grylock—they're gentle, dim-witted herbivores that move painfully slow. But this grylock is about to light these fireworks and turn the platform into a Cassidy barbecue. As I slowly back up, my foot catches on a tangle of fuse and I fall over onto the platform. I try to scramble to my feet, but I can't get up. My ratty jeans are caught on something on the platform.

Jimminy. Freaking. Crickets.

"Ohhhkay, bud," I coo to the grylock, "just be still." I wrestle with my jeans.

Again, the little speaker crackles. "Showtime, Ernie!"

I tug at my knee, and for a moment, I forget how to breathe. The grylock, on the other hand, huffs in a big gulp of air and fire brews in his throat.

"No, no! Ease up, little buddy," I warn in my sweetest southern voice. "*Please* don't light the fireworks."

The grylock holds the massive gulp of air in his lungs and gives a befuddled look.

The speaker hisses, "Fire away!"

"No, Ernie, *no*!" I shout.

But the dull grylock doesn't even register my command.

Instead, he breathes onto a large fuse and tucks his head under his arm. Then I smell burning.

The fuse's lit tail rapidly travels across the platform. It burns wildly, inching closer to the explosives. I rip my jeans free and land on my back from the force. The fuse touches the first firework. It explodes off the platform, and sparks kiss my back as I scramble up out of the dirt. I run faster than I ever have, back toward the safety of camp as explosions take to the air.

Colors burst in the sky as I sprint back toward the fairground, avoiding the FC camp. The bald sheriff nods at me as I exit the restricted area, but doesn't ask questions, which means maybe I haven't been caught.

A big band plays swing music, and around me, children clap as the fireworks shoot into the night sky, then explode in flares of vermilion and acid green. Everyone oohs and ahhs to the tune of sonic booms. I find Laura on a patchwork blanket, loved ones jammed all around her. I plop on the blanket's edge, catching my breath.

She leans my way. "Where's your dad?" Her feathery earrings flutter around her face. "We've been waiting for you." She gestures, and one of her nephews hands me a Styrofoam cup of sweet tea.

I take the cup and try to steady my nerves. "He's gone,"

I answer. As I straighten my braid, my stomach sinks . . . My hat is in Nickolai's tent. And it's too late to turn back now. I take a deep calming breath.

Bursts of color explode in the air, leaving trails of smoke scattered against the canvas of black. My heart thrums, but I can't focus on the dazzle. Each time, the echo of another blast sends me reeling.

I keep listening, waiting. Waiting for the nightclaw's blast of gunpowder to let me know the FC dragons are safe for one more day. I glance across the lawn and spot Michael sitting alongside a woman dressed in muted colors. With her dark hair and high cheekbones, I immediately recognize her as Ash's mother. She and Michael don't touch, but his posture is still protective. She's just one more prize like his dear Ashton.

The fireworks overhead burn impatiently, just like me . . .

Pop! Pop! Pop!

The nightclaw shoots into the sky and sends a loud echo across the plains. Families crane their necks and cheer. The cigarette-smoking ranch hand darts across the field. With my hat in his hand, he squats down and whispers something in Michael's ear. Michael becomes visibly tense, which Ash's mother ignores. From across the sea of blankets, I catch his eye.

I raise my Styrofoam cup to the sky, toasting him as he did me, my look even smarmier, for I am filled with white-hot rage. Michael's nostrils flare, and I know he's no idiot. His plastic smile melts into a scowl. He knows what I've done.

I lift the drink to my lips and take a sip.

Best sweet tea I've ever tasted.

CHAPTER 27

Around six a.m., I awaken to the toothy grin of a terrifying yellow dragon. It glares at me with massive purple eyes, then grips me by the T-shirt.

"Wha—" I stutter.

Beside the imposing dragon, a sheriff prattles on, "Cassidy Drake, you're charged with tampering with your fellow competitors' belongings during an official race break. Anything you say can and will be used against you by the council."

Well, crap on a cracker. "But I—"

"This dragon will serve as your escort during official council proceedings."

The dragon growls and bares her pointy chompers at me.

Flaxen-tailed guardians like this one are ruthless when it comes to safeguarding their treasure. And this time, that treasure is me.

Laura tries to claw the dragon off me, but the creature bats her off like an unwanted fly.

The sheriff hoists me onto a saddle atop the flaxen-tailed guardian, and she hums with anger as I settle on her back. There's no need for restraints because if I run, this dragon will keep me with her at all costs until her owner releases her from the task. I place my hands on her spines to steady myself, but she growls again, and I grab the saddle horn.

Clanging bells ring through the air, signifying that it's time to begin dressing our dragons.

Poor Ranga. We won't even see takeoff, which somehow makes it worse. I curse myself for thinking I could get away with messing with the FC.

Pa was right—I won't win the race. I won't even finish it. Now *that* would bother Mom.

But at least I didn't give up. And at least the FC dragons are free of androlone for another few hours.

The behemoth dragon lumbers through the VIP area as stars overhead give way to the early morning light. Muffled chants drone on in the arena beyond, and as we inch forward, the words become clear.

"Cas-si-dy! Cas-si-dy!"

"Drake! Drake! Drake!"

My jaw falls open. I can't see anyone from this remote part of the camp, but the crowd knows I'm missing. And they care.

Their call-and-response bounces back and forth as the dragon lurches toward an old practice arena. Its iron gates swing open, and at the other end, a makeshift panel of five men and two women waits for me at a long table. Next to the head of the council sits Michael. The flaxen-tailed guardian leads me to the table and shakes me off of her back. I fall to the dirt beside her.

I look up from the dust and scowl at Michael. "Did you hear my fan club?"

He doesn't even acknowledge me.

The flaxen-tailed guardian grabs my shirt by the teeth, lifts me into the air as she hisses, and sets me in a chair. She doesn't back away and instead hovers over me, reminding me that I am her captor. Laudes stands beside the council's table but doesn't make eye contact. I'm not sure if it's because FireCorp owns her or because she's disappointed in me. I hate both possibilities.

The head of the council clears his throat. "Cassidy Drake, we've called you before the council to discuss your expulsion from the Great Texas Dragon Race." He passes papers down the row on either side of him, and the various council members inspect them carefully. "As you know, interfering with a fellow competitor's property during the finale feast is strictly forbidden. And according to a ranch hand, you rifled through and damaged Nickolai Grigori's tent and stole his bowie knife at approximately eight seventeen p.m. last night." His slow drawl pulls his vowels out extra far, like poisonous honey dripping down a spoon.

I hesitate. "I—"

"You were attempting to sabotage FireCorp, weren't you?" interjects Michael.

"I most certainly was not." Unless you consider stopping a doping scheme sabotage, that is.

"Is that so?" A cow-pie-eating grin spreads across Michael's face. "Then tell us, Miss Drake, where's your beloved cowboy hat?"

Well, crap on a cracker. "Uh—it's a dangerous race. We've been through hell. I don't know where I lost it."

Unhappy with my tone, the dragon behind me huffs a hot breath onto my back.

"Sheriff Laudes, the evidence, please?"

Laudes walks forward and places my cowboy hat on the council's table. The head councilman holds it up.

"We found this hat inside Nickolai Grigori's tent. It is yours, isn't it?"

I feel my face flush as he dangles the hat before the jury.

Shock ripples through my body, but I keep stone still . . . I curse myself for leaving the hat and toasting Michael across the field with that stupid cup of sweet tea. What a reckless way to tip my hand. He must've connected the dots and concocted a way to make sure I'd be unable to compete. At least he doesn't seem set on destroying the Bhattis' chances too . . .

Michael folds his hands neatly on the table, his wedding band catching the light. "You may think you're invincible, Miss Drake, but you're just a small-time rancher who's out of her league."

At the end of the table, a gray-haired lady who looks as old as Gran and nearly as scrappy noisily fiddles with her papers. Another councilman a few seats down stiffens and scratches his nose. My lips turn up at the corner. While most of the board members are corporate sponsors or owners of large ranches, a few are unaffiliated. One of Michael's advisers coughs into his hand, a quick reminder to keep on task—and remember his audience.

Michael adjusts the knot of his tie, while I imagine strangling him with it.

My mouth is dry, and I cross my arms tight against my chest. "There's a lot more to this story. FireCorp has been breaking the rules since day one."

From the judges' incredulous faces, I can tell no one is about to believe a word I say. Dang it. I should have come forward about the steroids the second I learned about them. Stupid, stupid Cassidy.

Michael leans over the table and points at me. "As if anyone would trust you now that you've been caught red-handed. You, Miss Drake, are not the brightest star in the sky."

I raise my chin and glare back at him. "You're right—I'm the ever-loving sun."

I swear the older woman on the end chuckles.

My guardian, however, is not so pleased. She puffs loud bolts of fire into the sky, and even the head councilman ducks under his table. But not me. I keep my composure. I won't be scared of this dragon any more than I'm afraid of Michael Carne.

With a creaking jolt, the arena door at the back bursts forward.

"Stop!" says Laura. Laudes nods to her as she passes.

Ignoring the gargantuan fire-breathing dragon at my back, Laura walks right up to the panel and puts her hands on the table. "As I've mentioned several times, I would like to provide testimony for this case."

Michael scoffs and gestures with wide arms. "This girl can't be trusted to give testimony—she's barely thirteen and Cassidy's closest ally."

"And a man with clear motives against the defendant is sitting on the jury." Laura stares him dead in the eye and walks back from the panel, creating an audience. The flaxen-tailed guardian keeps steady watch, as if Laura might try to spring me from capture at any moment. "If he's allowed to vote against her, then I should be able to speak on her behalf. Especially if you want to avoid the *appearance* of favoritism. The press has already scrutinized the decision to allow sponsors on the council. And in case you haven't noticed, it's a media circus out there. Besides, my parents are right outside. So if there's an issue with my age, you can take it up with them."

I now know Laura has probably been more than a member of the debate club. With her confident stride and shoulders pushed back, I bet she's the freakin' captain.

Michael shoos her off as the panelists argue. "This is highly irregular," he says.

"This entire thing is irregular," says Laura. "And there's a massive crowd out there to witness it all. The hundreds of fans shouting Cassidy's name won't be thrilled when they discover you've refused to allow her fellow competitors to speak in her defense. It's going to be a PR nightmare."

The panel whispers among themselves as Laura holds firm on the invisible line she's drawn herself. I sit up, straight as an arrow. A massive yellow tail slashes in front of me, reminding me not to get too confident.

Finally, the chairman relents. "We will hear this supposed testimony."

Laura reaches into her pocket and sets a small, empty vial of flamemaw on the councilors' table. "This is androlone, a powerful, illegal steroid. And, according to Ash Hook, FireCorp has been using it since the race started."

I swell with pride as the panel ignites with murmurs. Sheriff Laudes whips out her pad of paper and begins scribbling.

Michael slams his fist on the table. "Ash would never make up such a ridiculous tale."

"Oh, Ash is happy to provide testimony," says Laura. "But strangely, the rest of the FireCorp team wouldn't let him through to join me at this council meeting."

"The girl is lying," says Michael. "Perhaps *she's* the one who's been using androlone since it's in her possession."

"Test my dragon if you want to," challenges Laura. "In

fact, if you plan to bar Cassidy from racing, why don't we shut down the entire race and immediately test all of the dragons for evidence of doping . . . I'm sure it would make for some fascinating headlines."

Laura glows, and in her face, I see absolute and perfect kindness. Winning this race is the thing she wants most. And she's just agreed to forgo it to save me from whatever twisted fate Michael Carne has planned.

Either that, or Laura is making a huge gamble.

I respect both possibilities with equal enthusiasm.

Michael's face is a wall of steel, and I know he's weighing his options. How bad does he want me disqualified?

The lady at the end of the table speaks up. "If we're set on disqualifying Miss Drake, I wouldn't be opposed to further investigation."

Sly woman.

Another councilman pipes up. "An investigation would waste thousands of dollars in rentals, concessions, and employee time!"

"Not to mention the costs of securing the location," says another member. "And how much have we spent on advertising?"

Arguments spark back and forth, and I lean back in my chair, letting the front two legs lift off the ground. The guardian clips me with her snout and reminds me to keep still. I smell smoke on her breath.

Laura paces back and forth. "Families from all over the country have arrived for this event. You've gone to great lengths to secure it and pay for it. Not to mention the ten riders who have given their all to be here." She takes a deep breath and captures each panelist's attention. "And a competitor nearly lost his life."

You could hear a pin drop. Michael takes a breath to say something, but Laura beats him to it: "There are only two options: allow Cassidy to finish the race, or tie up the council in a long drama while disappointing thousands of loyal, paying fans."

My jaw drops to the floor. Laura's confidence hangs around her in a glowing cloud as if she's won the race already. The panel is silent, and Michael, who's become a wall of anger, twirls his wedding ring around his finger. He peers into me as if he can see through my head to the back of my skull.

The head councilman knocks on the table. "All in favor of suspending the race and conducting further investigation?"

Not one hand goes up.

"All in favor of letting Cassidy compete and allowing the

race to continue, as planned?"

Each hand but Michael Carne's lifts to the sky. I lean forward, ready to spring up, and the guardian places a long, clawed hand around my entire body, clamping me to the chair. I grunt as she squeezes, pressing my ribs into the seat.

The head councilman raps his knuckles on the table. "The council has spoken." He rises from his chair, and the other members follow, shuffling papers. "I suggest you two get to your dragons."

But the guardian doesn't relent.

"Michael," urges the head councilman.

His face a wall of stone, Michael lifts a whistle from his pocket and blows. On command, the flaxen-tailed guardian squeezes tightly once more, then releases.

I jump out of my seat and snag my hat. As we rush out the iron door, my braids flying, I turn to Laura. "Thank you."

"It's the least I could do . . . ," she replies, panting as she runs. "You made this a fair fight. And why compete unless you can compete against the best?" She smiles, her perverse streak rising to the top. "Well, second best."

CHAPTER 28

I dash onto the field, which has transformed into a spectacle of fog and lights. Cheers erupt from the stands as people call my name.

"Cas-si-dy! Cas-si-dy!"

"Drake, Drake, Drake!"

Laura shouts as she waves to the crowd, "You're a favorite! They practically rioted about your dismissal."

My spirits rise as the audience chants. Smog-logger dragonettes emit great puffs of smoke, casting an eerie early morning glow around the entire arena. The stadium seats are filled to the brim with spectators and children. The air is full of excited voices and the rumbling of feet. In the middle of the chaos is Ranga, fresh eyed and gleaming with turquoise. I race for her and she giddily flaps her wings.

"Oh girl, am I ever glad to see you!"

She coos and I toss my arms around her.

The sky lights up with an orangey hue, the first signs of morning. Down the line, Ash stands tall in his black leather boots and avoids eye contact with Valeen and the rest of FireCorp. Good for him. He nods at me and lowers the shield on his racing helmet.

"Ladies and gentlemen!" shouts the announcer. "May I present this year's council!"

Michael Carne steps onto the scene first, waving to the crowd like a champion himself. I'm proud to hear some boos lift above the noise. The remaining council members line up in the judges' panel. They all wear purple ribbons, honorary signs of their success as our leaders. Instead of showing reverence, I bend down to fiddle with the straps of Ranga's saddle.

"Cassidy!"

Reorienting myself, I step up onto a stirrup and peer over Ranga's back to find Laura beaming.

"Look!" Laura shouts, pointing to the stands.

In the box just beyond the council sits my father. He claps and whispers with Laura's father at his side. I wave erratically and stand up on the tippy toes of my boots. His presence gives me the final boost that I need to take on this race, protect my friends, and maybe—just maybe—win.

The announcer paces in front of us with a megaphone. Like a head coach in the last stretch of a football game, he bellows, "All right, competitors. In this platform awaits the final hologram. You've been furnished with Dragon-flight bridle cams, compliments of our friends at Buckle and Grousewood."

The crowd cheers as ten massive stadium screens power up. I realize that every screen is streaming Ranga's bridle camera. The screens switch to the other competitors and our names appear in dramatic graphics. Sponsorship logos with everything from dragon gear to soda flicker.

"Ladies and gentlemen, the final leg of the Great Texas Dragon Race is about to begin! I present our ten competitors: Rose Bhatti, Vivian Bhatti, Cassidy Drake, Nickolai Grigori, Valeen Grimsbane, Myra Holden, Ashton Hook, Colt Meyer, Trevor Price, and Laura Torres." Cheers and applause send our dragons roaring and flapping. Gusts of smoke spread throughout the arena.

I can barely make out my father in the stands now, waving at me one last time. I wave back and catch Michael sneering in Pa's direction.

"Riders! Take your marks!" shouts the announcer.

I take a deep breath and straighten Ranga's reins. "Okay, Ranga," I whisper. "We've got this."

Nausea wells in my stomach as we approach the line and stand next to our dragons. Laura is right beside me, and Quetzal shakes her head as if knocking off flies.

"Go!"

The holographic projection of the very first winner of the Great Texas Dragon Race, Earl B. Cody—who tragically died during the second annual Great Texas Dragon Race—flashes to life. He croons a poem as the riders gather round.

Lovers are beguiled,
underneath the rising moon,
beside the northern wild,
bloodshed may be coming soon.

On a nest made all of glass,
chief glory does await.
Kinship helps to beat the mass,
resist the perilous fate.

A race in sandy, trickling time,
no neon flags to spare.

Claim now the hungry winner's dime,
high honors to declare.

I scribble down the words and hope to make sense of the poem later. It's by far the most confusing clue, and the poem's beats are slightly off. I'm certain that's not a mistake. I race back to Ranga and pull down my goggles. Once in the sky, Ranga and I quickly catch up with Colt and Laura, and we assume a tight formation in the air. The Bhatti sisters and Ash take another route, and the four remaining FireCorp dragons trail behind us.

Trembling, I scan my scribble and it clicks: the first letter of each line spells the location. *LUBBOCK RANCH.*

"Lubbock!" I shout to Colt and Laura.

"What's that small ranch about an hour north of it?" I ask. "Sunville?"

"Sunrise!" shouts Colt. "Sunrise Ranch. Big dragon family owns it. Coincidence?"

I grit my teeth. "We ride for Sunrise."

We barrel through the sky, but I make Ranga temper her speed so we can keep pace with the others. She jerks against the reins as if to say, "Let's become the air. Let's forget the world."

"Cassidy . . ." Laura pulls Quetzal in line with Ranga.

"You can beat us all there. Go on without us."

I shake my head. "I'm not going without you guys."

"This isn't a negotiation. You have to do what's best for the team—that's what *we* decided."

Colt butts in between us. "The sky has no speed limit, Cass. Go."

I nod and kick into Ranga. She chirps, thankful for the permission to *move*.

Ranga and I race to Sunrise, my eyes peeled for the "nest made all of glass" in the clue. Speed is everything—the wind in my braids and the scent of desert air whooshing past me fan my desire. Ranga and I are a bullet through the air, and Gran's compass guides us to Sunrise.

Barren earth stretches for miles in every direction, and green farmland gives way to brown soil and windswept deposits of sand. There, in the middle of Nowheresville, Texas, a two-hundred-foot-wide circle of black glassy rocks springs from the earth, forming a dangerous protective nest. The impenetrable ring looks like it's spun from shards of hardened lava reaching for the sky. In the center of the dark pit, a giant snakeskin peeks out from the sand. It is the size of four—no, five school buses lined up, end to end.

An eerie calm pervades the air, and the hair on my arms

stands at attention. I feel like prey—as if thousands of eyes are watching. There's no sign of the neon flags described in the poem, but I'm sure of two things: this is the location of the final task . . . and this will be the most dangerous game of capture-the-flag ever played.

I rotate the dials on my goggles, looking back into the distance. The FC is still hot on our tail, but Laura and Colt hold steady, miles in front of them.

"Quick." I stroke Ranga's spines. "Quick and light."

We swoop over the pit as I search for flags.

I swing my lasso at my side, looping as I get closer. Just as I toss it, the earth quakes and splits apart. A massive brown and spiny dragon—the size of a train and twice as wide—surges out of the sand after us. Its translucent frills extend out, vibrating in the air.

"Up, Ranga! Up, up!"

The gaping mouth launches into the sky and reveals a cavernous throat filled with molten lava. With a gurgling roar, it spews the red-hot substance onto my rope, disintegrating it on contact.

"Holy catfish!"

Ranga recoils, and I hate to admit it, but my skin turns cold.

I yank on the reins, pulling Ranga back, and we narrowly

avoid slamming into the spiky black nest. The scorching lava turns instantly to stone as it cools midair and falls to earth like shards of black obsidian.

A glass-spewing sandragon. Dear sweet succotash.

Hissssss, it warns.

From the safety of the sky, I catch a glimpse of the sandragon's body. The beast is shaped like a thorn-covered horny toad, with a tail as long as a telephone pole. Monstrous raking claws extend from its front legs, and its jaws reveal a gleaming row of serrated teeth, each tooth the length of my leg. Of course, a necklace of green flags is laced around its thick neck. As we retreat, the sandragon gobbles up sand to generate more lava for its next attack. Then it shoves its spiny, armored body into the earth until only its orange, pinpricked eyes remain on the surface. There's no sign of the flags.

Meaning we *have* to engage the sandragon in combat in order to expose the neon-green pennants.

My heart races as I sniff the air.

What is that smell?

I discover a drop of lava burning its way through my saddlebag. I smother the flames with my hat and wipe sweat from my brow.

The fiery lava is sure to penetrate even Ranga's tough

skin. How will I ever capture a flag?

Ranga and I peel down again, and the sandragon's massive jaws widen, spewing more lava. As Ranga tries to escape, the sandragon uses its scorching stream to drive Ranga toward the glassy nest, trapping us between fire and spikes. We flee into the sky. Over and over, I try to lure out the sandragon and snag a flag from its necklace. And each time, I fail, narrowly escaping death.

When Laura arrives, sweat is streaming from my brow, and Ranga's muscles are growing tired. We fly to meet her.

"Where's Colt?" I shout.

"Colt will be here soon . . . and the FC. They're almost here." She lifts her goggles. "Is that—"

"A glass-spewing sandragon? Y-yep."

"Genial," Laura whispers, then flicks Quetzal's reins. They speed around the craggy black ring in a tight lap. Upon rejoining me, she blots her makeup with a bandanna. "This isn't just a protective habitat—it really is a nest. If you look closely, you'll see the babies' eyes poking up from the earth."

I spin my goggles and focus. At least a dozen tiny orange eyes peek out at us from the sand. Sonofagun.

"This mom will viciously defend her babies," says Laura. "When the FC turns this place into chaos, it will be impossible to grab a pennant."

I twist around and locate the FC barreling toward us in the distance, not far behind Colt. "Then we have to work together and snag our flags before the FC gets here." I breathe in, remembering what Laura did to get me into this final leg, remembering that I can trust her. "I'll distract her—you get the flag."

Laura sits tall on her white leather saddle. "Then we switch?"

I nod.

"Deal."

We break apart and dip down into the pit. One after another, we dart up and down, each of us on opposite ends of a lethal seesaw. I dive, neon green in my sights. Sheets of lava spew into the sky. Claws unfurl. The babies screech.

Breathe in. Breathe out.

Hold tight.

As we ride, the broiling lava cools on contact with the air, and the task becomes ever more difficult. We have to engage the sandragon, but every time, her molten brew adds more obstacles to the pit—more shards of glass, more walls to avoid. Meaning that even nimble dragons such as Quetzal or Ranga will eventually be caught in tight crannies of razor-sharp rock. The only break we get is when the sandragon stops to guzzle sand to make more deadly brew.

Adrenaline runs through me, surging with my desire to win. For the first time in days, I remember the thrill of the chase and why I wanted to ride this race before Gran got sick.

Still, no matter how hard we try, nothing works, and the sandragon becomes increasingly aggressive.

"We need another plan," shouts Laura.

In the distance, the herculean silhouette of Nickolai's dragon comes into focus. Valeen and two FireCorp lackeys flank his sides in a brutal formation. I lean back in the saddle, and every part of me feels heavy. My fingers drift to my belt buckle—my now shiny, perfect, gleaming belt buckle. I rock the buckle in my palm.

"I've got it! I've got it!" I whip off my belt and fly alongside Laura, buckle in hand. "Go for it."

"What's your plan?" Laura asks.

"Just trust me."

Laura smooths her ponytail. "I do. Obviously."

I grin back. "Then go—now!"

Laura maneuvers back around, agile on Quetzal like no other dragon in this race.

"¡Vámonos, más rápido!" Her voice rings strong and clear.

Laura dives for the flag, fearless and powerful, a goddess on dragonback. Once more, the sandragon leaps out of the ground, molten glass spewing from her mouth.

Kicking into Ranga, I spur her on, buckle in hand. Dodging lava to my left and a glass barrier to my right, I break in front of the sandragon and flash the belt buckle in her eye.

Errrrekkkkk! Blinded, the sandragon jerks back. She slams into the glass nest but seems unfazed.

Laura barrels down, extending her hand for a flag. But the sandragon releases a molten stream. As Quetzal banks upward, his underside drags against the jagged nest. Quetzal yelps as Laura peels up into the sky and out of harm's way. I make for her, but the sandragon is after me—racing, rushing. I look behind me and see fiery jaws spread. Ranga's tail is only inches from a stream of lava. I panic and pull up, just as the sandragon jerks back and growls. I spin back around.

A lasso forms a noose around the sandragon. Colt's sunny midwestern face gleams back like a proud beacon in the desert. The other end of the cord is wrapped around his dragon's saddle horn, pulling the sandragon back from the flag. She roars, spewing more lava in a violent, oozing stream.

"I can't hold her back forever." The cord squeaks with tension as the wily sandragon tugs hard against the force of Colt's mighty cyan mountain dragon. "We have one more shot."

In the distance, the FC dragons roar, and Ranga trembles.

"Go!" shouts Colt.

I kick into Ranga, and Laura dives just as the cord snaps. Colt's dragon flies back, nearly crashing into the craggy nest. Again the sandragon is on us. Belt buckle in hand, I swoop down for the slitted pupils fixed on Laura. I catch the light and reflect it into the sandragon's eye. It careens back, blinded.

Hisssss!

Brunette ponytail wafting behind her, Laura rips a flag from the necklace.

"I have it! I have it!" She lifts it over her head and waves frantically.

Warmth spreads over me, but it's broken by a chilling sound.

Grrrawwwwwrrrrrrr!

My blood runs cold, and I crane my neck.

Four great FireCorp dragons blot out the sky in a flash of wings, descending like a cloak of evil. Laura and I dart back to assume a formation with Colt, but both our dragons are lagging from the energy they've already spent. Valeen's draconian hybrid smashes into me on the right, and Ranga yelps.

"For someone so small, you're always in the way! Let us show you how it's done," she shouts. "Scarlett!"

Valeen kicks into her dragon, who spews flames on my left. Ranga and I dart into the air, out of the chaos, as the other FireCorp riders descend on the sandragon, pummeling it with fire.

But this time, they lack the extra oomph from the steroids. Their dragons aren't as strong—and their flames aren't as massive.

Which is just as well, because the sandragon is fiercer than ever. The sandragon thrashes, stirring up titanic clouds of dust as she gobbles sand. Across the pit, through the haze, two blazing FC wyverns attack Laura and Colt.

Quetzal cries out as the dragons bash into him. The FC dragons dive into the nest, but the sandragon easily overpowers them. She knocks aside Trevor Price, whose wyvern just isn't as strong without the powerful steroids, and they crash to the ground. I suck in a sharp breath.

As I scramble for Laura, Nickolai and his onyx fireheart wyvern, Sergei, plunge downward. Sergei snaps at Ranga with dripping fangs and chomps down on the tip of her tail. She shrieks, snatching her tail out of Sergei's mouth.

I hear Nickolai laugh as he abandons us and heads back to his prey.

I spin around to find the last joint of her tail is bent at an odd angle. Crying in pain, she races into the sky, away from the nest and the horrifying FC dragons.

"Ranga, wrong way!" I shout.

But Ranga keeps flying, spurred on by an instinctual need to escape. I pull back on the reins, but she doesn't stop. She lands a quarter mile away from the insanity and licks her mangled tail. Ranga's scales are charcoal gray and her eyes are lifeless orbs of fear.

"I'm so sorry, girl," I say, leaning across the saddle and over her body to stroke her dulled scales. "I never should have brought you here."

"Are you okay?" shouts Laura, diving down to meet us with Colt.

I spot the corner of a green flag wafting from Laura's bag, and my heart softens. "You already have what you need, Laura. And Quetzal is exhausted. You should go."

"I agree," says Colt. "Ride."

Laura glances back at the pit broiling with lava, fiery wyverns, and the screeching sandragon. "But we said 'together.' At least let me help fend off FireCorp."

I cringe at the thought of Laura missing her chance. "Then swear to me you'll go the second it's done."

Laura's lips press into a tight line.

"Swear it!" I shout.

She nods.

"Colt, that goes for you too. If you get a flag, ride."

He nods as well.

I stroke Ranga's side. She's the last team member I need on my side. And this time, I will not force her.

"Ranga—I know it's scary, but will you help us?" I ask.

Ranga releases a gust of air and shakes as if expelling her fear. She tugs at the reins, and I know she's ready.

"Then, let's move. Colt, distract Valeen. Laura, loop around and take Nickolai from above. I'll try to grab the flags." I flick my reins and Ranga explodes into the sky.

We speed for the pit as a team, twisting over obsidian barbs and into the onslaught. Colt bolts for Valeen, who cackles as she prepares a massive net with Myra Holden. Laura and I peel apart, taking opposite sides as we race for our targets.

Though I can feel Ranga's resistance, she heeds my commands.

I sit up and straighten my goggles. Nickolai dives into

the fury of dust and disappears into the haze. In a coordinated effort, Valeen and Myra toss a fireproof net over the sandragon. She bursts with molten sand, but the net holds her back. Out of the dust, Nickolai and Sergei peel into the sky.

In Sergei's claws is a baby dragon, barely the size of a kayak. Squeezing it in long, vicious talons, he dangles the fragile baby before its netted mother.

This time, the sandragon sucks in her fiery breath. Her skin turns a dull dark brown and she screeches.

From the bent tip of her tail to the end of her nose, Ranga morphs from gray to the deepest green-tinged black. Sweat drips down my back, and I know, deep in my bones, that if I could change colors, we would match. This poor mother is only defending her nest.

Trevor lumbers forward—his dragon injured but still in play—snags a flag from the necklace, and takes off. I set my sights on Nickolai.

"Ranga," I seethe, "the sandragon needs you."

Ranga takes two heaving breaths as if steadying her resolve, then . . .

"Go!" I shout.

Ranga explodes into the sky. We swoop under Sergei just as Laura attacks him from above.

But Nickolai is too quick. Sergei knocks Quetzal with his long, spiked tail, and Quetzal's wing catches on a spear of black glass. Laura is forced to make a shaky landing beyond the nest. Ranga and I steady ourselves as we close in on the baby sandragon crying in Sergei's claws. I cling to Ranga like a bucking bronco as she latches on to the baby and tries to pry it from Sergei.

Nickolai glares down at us. "Pozhar!"

His dragon releases a fire that bursts on the side of me, singeing my clothes.

"Pozhar, pozhar!" Nickolai shouts again as he whips Sergei.

The hair from my left arm burns away.

Eyes blazing, Sergei inches forward. Heat swells around me . . .

Ash dives onto the scene, knocking Nickolai aside in a powerful thud.

"Fly, Cassidy! Fly!" shouts Ash. Juliette bats at Sergei with her tail.

I see our moment. Ranga loosens the baby from Sergei's grip. The baby whines as we flee from Ash and Nickolai, now embroiled in a fury of wings and teeth.

"It's okay, baby, it's okay," I croon as we dive.

Whhhacccck!

Myra slams her dragon into Ranga and tugs at the baby. We struggle as the little one writhes with fear.

But the Bhattis appear out of nowhere, and this time I cheer out loud. They peel down from the sky like a duo of pink-and-purple rockets. Rose tosses one end of a silvery cord to Viv, and they dart for the FC dragon. They clothesline Myra and knock her from her mount, laughing as they ride.

"Thank you!" I shout.

Emboldened by the Bhattis, Ranga and I dart back into the chaos. To my left, Colt and his magnificent dragon rip the net from the sandragon. A feeling of relief passes over me as Ranga and I swoop down with the crying baby. The sandragon rises from the pit, yellow eyes flashing, and launches for us. I sing rough and throaty, praying the sandragon knows I'm friend and not foe as I offer up the baby.

The sandragon's pupils seize, and in a brief, glorious moment, we lock eyes. Her irises soften as we regard each other, and she eases up. She spreads her jaws wide and flattens her tongue.

I pet Ranga's side. "Release the baby."

Ranga dips farther down and lowers the babe into the sandragon's open mouth. The baby coos as it senses its mother, who gently closes her jaws enough to shield the

359

baby from further harm. I can't reach a flag from here, but I use my knife to cut the necklace, and the remaining flags scatter into the pit. The sandragon shivers in a cloud of dust and scrambles into the earth with her child.

I smile, and warmth spreads through me. I can see Laura, out past the chaos, flying off into the distance. Aside from Ranga, Quetzal is the fastest dragon out here, but he's shaky from his wounds and he jerks up and down in the air. Even if she makes it to the finish line, Trevor is already miles ahead and Myra's titanic FireCorp wyvern isn't far behind. My only hope comes from the sight of the Bhattis hot on their tail with their bag of tricks, waiting to make a comeback.

Below me, Colt swipes a flag from the dust.

"Yes!" I shout, raising my fist over my head in excitement.

"Do you need me to stay?" he shouts. His dragon wheezes with exhaustion.

"Heck no," I shout. "Ride!"

He tips his hat and spins around and takes off after the others. With enough luck, maybe he can keep pace with FireCorp. Or help Laura if Quetzal can't make it.

I turn back to the pit and my fate. With steady breath, I scan the ground through my goggles, desperate for traces of a neon-green flag.

Dirt. Leaves. Cacti.

My heart leaps. On the edges of the pit, my salvation—one lone flag flutters in the wind. Spirits soaring, I flick Ranga's reins and she takes off. Other riders may be ahead of us, but Ranga can outpace any of them. Any time, any day. I sink into the saddle and lean into Ranga.

Valeen pulls alongside me as we dive, her sights set on the same flag. "You know, Cassidy—" She whips her dragon, Scarlett, and inches past me. "Your mother once rode with FireCorp."

My emotions empty out of me and it's as if someone let the air out of the room. But I can't allow Valeen to throw me off-balance. I struggle to maintain my focus.

The flag. Concentrate on the flag.

Valeen whips her dragon again and shouts, "Michael should have destroyed her when he had the chance!"

I fumble, but Ranga is unrelenting. Scarlett snaps at her from the side. Squeezing the reins, I shove Valeen's words deep down.

"We're close, Ranga. So close," I whisper to her, low against her body as we speed. "We can still win."

Ranga picks up speed, and her wings beat the air as we inch past Valeen.

Two hundred yards off . . .

One hundred . . .

The flag flutters in the wind and I can hear Valeen whipping Scarlett with the pop of her riding crop.

But near the ground, just beyond the flag, a cry. My tunnel vision dissolves as I watch Nickolai knock Ash from his saddle. Sergei snarls a violent warning as Juliette lurches forth. But she moves slowly, as if in pain, and Nickolai shows no signs of relenting. I glance back at Valeen, but she keeps zooming toward the flag. I grip the reins. Somehow, they weigh a thousand pounds.

I have two choices—snatch the flag that can deliver my ranch or save a boy who's suffered years of abuse. The flag or a friend. My heart pounds against my rib cage, each beat singing a different claim:

The flag. The win. The ranch.

A friend.

A friend.

A friend.

I break away from Valeen and beeline for Ash.

Across the plain, Valeen's evil laughter lilts in the air. "See you from the winner's circle."

I flick Ranga's reins and barrel headlong toward the growling, violent assault.

Juliette gasps a screeching cry as she tries to escape Sergei's fearsome talons. Unrelenting, Nickolai whips a cat-o'-nine-tails against Sergei, who clamps down on Juliette's wing, midair.

"Stop!" I shout. "Stop!"

We dive-bomb into Nickolai.

Whhhhaaaapppppp!

In a fury of black scales, Sergei spins and lashes me with his massive tail.

I slam backward, toppling from Ranga into the center of the sandragon's pit. Pieces of glass dig into my hands. Spots of light burst across my vision.

Sergei prepares to launch at Ash. But Nickolai's cruel smile turns to charcoal as he glimpses something in the distance and he yanks up on the reins. I spin around.

A menacing wall of debris and dust looms on the horizon. Several miles long and thousands of feet high, the dust cloud barrels toward us, blotting out everything in its path.

"Dust storm," I crack, my breath catching.

Of course we'd face Lubbock's strangest weather events in the middle of the final leg.

The fast-moving, low-hanging brown cloud descends, sweeping from the west. I've seen haboobs, but never from a sandragon pit . . . and never when I'm surrounded by dangerous caverns of obsidian. I secure my goggles tight around my head. "Ranga!"

The encroaching wall of dust whooshes around me.

"Ranga? Ranga?" I choke.

Nothing but the wind talks back. It whips my face, lashing my braids against my cheeks so hard they sting. Dust swirls in the air like something from *The Wizard of Oz* as I pull my bandanna over my mouth.

I hack as the dust encircles us and doesn't let up. Dust storms last only a few minutes, but so much can happen in that amount of time. Ash. Is Ash safe?

The dark orange sky—almost bloodred with haze—stretches in every direction. Dust coats my goggles, I frantically wipe them off, but it does no good. No sight of Ranga.

Underneath me, the ground rumbles like an unexpected earthquake. I scramble to sit up on the uneven, shard-covered ground. *No, no, no.* I struggle to catch my balance as the earth splits open.

Grrrreeeeeahhhhhhkkkk!

The growl thunders in my chest and a silhouetted figure comes into focus.

The massive sandragon, with her blazing tangerine eyes, towers over me.

"It's okay, girl—" I cough into my bandanna.

I stumble to my feet and slowly back away into the cloud, knowing that a labyrinth of sharp edges may be right behind me. I have nowhere left to go but farther into the shroud of dust and the dangerous haboob. More shadows appear. Sharp, high-pitched hissing swells in my ears. Even through the fog, I know the babies are all around me, closing in like hyenas. This time I can't sing with my dust bowl of a mouth, and the mother sandragon coils around me . . .

A burst of fire releases on my side, the heat licking my skin as I narrowly avoid the flame itself. But it isn't the sandragon . . . it's Sergei. The inferno lights the orange sky, transforming it into a red canvas of light.

Between the flames and the sandragon and the endless veil of dust, I imagine this is my time to die. To fade into black forever, just like my mom.

The sandragon walls around me as another burst of fire spews in my direction. Her massive body and armored frills shield me from the horrific flames. The sandragon looks down. She's not trying to hurt me. She's trying to *save* me. I duck into her and the flames retreat.

"Cassidy!" shouts Ash from somewhere above me in the vast, chaotic sky.

I shoot up. Did Nickolai and Sergei grab him? And if

they did, what does Nickolai plan to do?

I run my hand along the sandragon's scales. "Help me." My voice is barely a breath. "Please . . ."

The sandragon cocks her head. Her third eyelids close, protecting her slitted eyes from the dust just like my goggles. She gently wraps a clawed hand around me and boosts me onto her back. The sandragon's sharp spines glisten through the dust. One wrong move and they could spear me alive like giant cactus prickers.

But she's gentle and steadfast. Rising from the earth, the sandragon and I power into the sky, following the sound of Ash's voice. Because she's impervious to the obsidian nest she's built around her, the sandragon easily lumbers over the jagged rocks.

I wrap my hands around two spines and hold tight. Together, we become the atmosphere—and I transform into an extension of her: solid muscle, fused in flight. But I'm flying blind on an untested dragon, and even with her third eyelids, seeing through the haze is impossible . . . unless you have high-tech FireCorp gear. I can barely see two feet in front of me.

I pull back on her spines, driven by nothing but instinct as we chase Nickolai and Sergei. But the sandragon has been on the attack for the past hour, and she's tiring.

As we ride, our pace slowing by the second, the haze stretching across my vision subsides. Through specks of dust, I spot Sergei in front of us, his dark scales shimmering through the powder. Ash dangles from his claws and bile draws up the back of my throat.

The dust gives way even more, and the sandragon inches forward, but she lumbers to keep the pace.

"Release!" shouts Nickolai.

Sergei whips up and lets go of Ash.

My voice catches in my throat.

Ash falls toward the jagged nest as the last pieces of dust whoosh around him.

Down . . .

Down . . .

And the sandragon isn't fast enough.

The world stands still around me, and I reach out, clawing the air as if I can stop him from falling.

Just as Ash is about to hit the ground, Ranga swoops in, faster than greased lightning or a speeding bullet or gosh-darned anything. Her body is a jet in the air. She catches Ash on her back and peels up, away from the nest in a confident glide. Ash clings to her neck.

Triumphant, I try to guide the sandragon down. But her motives are not mine. She jerks up, chasing Nickolai out of the nest. I hold tight, nearly falling off.

Gwarrrrrggghhh! she roars, using her last bit of energy to leap over the glassy barrier. The thinnest shards break under her mammoth body. She's out of sand to create lava, but that doesn't stop her. With fearsome claws, she yanks on Sergei's tail.

Nickolai whips around, and even through his mask and goggles, I can tell we've stunned him.

Jaws barreling forward, the sandragon claws Nickolai's shirt—

And knocks him from his saddle.

Disconnected from his rider, Sergei shrieks as Nickolai goes flying. The sandragon dives down after him. I cling to her as my breath escapes me and watch as Nickolai lands in a mighty thud. Growling, the sandragon knocks a massive wall of sand over him, trapping him half underneath the dirt. I desperately hold tight, squeezing my thighs and arms around her leathery body.

Below us, Nickolai tries to claw his way to safety. In a fury of talons, Sergei fights back, but without his steroid boost and his pack of well-geared FC wyverns, he's no match for the sandragon's size. Nickolai reaches up, hoping Sergei will pull him to safety. Dear God in heaven, this sandragon might kill them both. As Sergei bumbles to save his rider, the sandragon chomps at the earth and guzzles another heap of sand.

Errreckkkkghhh! Sergei cries.

Lumbering and scared, he scoops Nickolai up and drags him away before the sandragon can eviscerate them with lava. As they retreat into the distance, I hear Nickolai howling a pattern of broken Russian.

That's when I realize FireCorp isn't much without their army, androlone, and combat gear. Without their paid-for edge, Nickolai has no flags or prestige to cling to.

Exhausted, I breathe deeply, cheek against the sandragon's skin. She lowers herself to the ground, and I roll off. Her mission accomplished, her babies safe from terror, the sandragon dives back into the nest without giving me another look. I don't even have time to thank her.

I pull my sore body to my feet and, cradling my singed arm, find Ash lying near a motionless Juliette. Ranga does her best to comfort Ash, but there is no comfort to be had.

"Ash?" I ask. My trembling fingers touch his shoulder.

Ash pulls his head from Juliette's still figure, slow and steady. "Is it over?"

"For now."

Ash loops his arms around Juliette and rests a cheek against her scales. I clasp my hand to my mouth, terrified that we've lost another competitor in this race . . . but she heaves a deep breath. I'm so relieved, I nearly lose my balance. Juliette nuzzles into Ash, then blinks, just a little, as if to let her rider know that she's okay. Hurt, but definitely okay. She lumbers to her feet and shakes off the dust.

Ranga chirps at the sky as Ash wraps his arms around her.

"I was so worried," he says. "Never again, girl. Never again."

Beaming, I wrap my arms around Juliette as well. She flinches a bit, then relaxes into my touch. I close my eyes and allow the sound of her heartbeat to fill me with hope.

Ash rustles me from the moment of stillness. "You should've left me to deal with Nick on my own," he says. "All the flags are gone."

My body goes numb and the feeling of relief is replaced with a grave sense of loss. Ash is right. The choice I made cost me everything.

But when I look at this boy with his sad eyes, I'm reminded that Ash has been abused his whole life—just like the dragons who've come to Drake's Dragon Ranch over the years. As he clings to poor Juliette, who may as well be his only real friend, I'm sure that no one's ever saved him from anything his whole life.

I may not have made the smart choice. Heck, it's probably not the choice Aurora Drake would have made if she had been in this race. But I chose to save someone who needed saving. I chose to save a friend. And that's the truth I must hold on to in this moment.

So, although I know we've lost, I load Ash onto Ranga's back. We ride fast and hard toward the finish line with Juliette in tow.

CHAPTER 29

We arrive to the cheers of hundreds and slide off of Ranga. A pack of FireCorp groupies separates Ash from me. In the distance, people are cheering.

And I'm certain that a sponsored rider has won.

I pull off my cowboy hat and shake off the dust. After lugging my pack onto my shoulder, I make my way to the stands, pushing through the crowd. And I feel like I must have dirt in my eyes, because Laura is standing on the top platform with Quetzal behind her, who's draped with fresh roses. Beside her on a lower platform, Valeen grits her teeth and forces a plastic smile of freshly reapplied lipstick. Just below them, Colt stands proud. Newscasters, draggers, and fans crowd around them.

"Laura!" I run to the platform and shout up at her. "You did it! You did it!"

"No, we did it." She jumps down, hugs me tight, and whispers in my ear, "The FC dragons attacked me twice on the way back, but without the steroid boost, we could fight them off. If you hadn't destroyed the androlone, we wouldn't have stood a chance."

Over her shoulder, I see Valeen's scowl and I swear it is absolutely everything. It lets me know that losing to Laura—an unaffiliated, Latina rancher from El Paso—is the ultimate revenge.

Colt jumps down from the third-place platform and hugs us both.

"And where would we be without this one?" I say. "Best lasso work I've ever seen."

Colt blushes as his father pushes through the crowd, then rubs his boy's hair like he's five years old.

"Your son is a fantastic dragon rider," I say as the Bhattis step up behind them, their pastel lipsticks and eye shadow artistically smudged like deranged Arkham Asylum inmates.

"And let's not forget these two," says Laura. "If it weren't for them fending off the FC riders on our way back, we never would have beat them."

"We didn't do anything," says Viv.

"Not that you can prove, anyway," says Rose, glitter-dusted cheeks beaming in the sun.

I grin because we've finally formed the team I knew we were capable of.

"Cass!"

I whip around to find Pa, who wraps me in a bear hug. My arm stings but I couldn't care any less. Finally, he steps back and holds me in front of him as if to confirm that I'm all in one piece. He chuckles.

"You are the stupidest, most reckless, unruly girl I've ever met." Pa hugs me again. "And your mom would be proud."

I hug him back, squinting through the painful bruises all over my body. In the distance, Michael steps behind Ash like a terrible shadow and possessively places a hand on his shoulder. Various onlookers stop and congratulate me for a good game and a race well run.

In between the handshakes and hugs, I lean into Pa.

"Pa," I ask, "did Mom ride for FireCorp?"

Pa grimaces. "That was a long time ago."

"Is that why Michael Carne hates us so much? Because of her? Because she left?"

He tips up his baseball cap as if he's weighing how adult

I am underneath the grime and freckles. "There is a thin line between love and hate." Pa clears his throat. "And for all his flaws, I believe that Michael did love her at one time."

My mouth hangs open and the band swirls around us as the celebration rages on.

Pa straightens the cap back over his brow. "Your mother and Michael were engaged."

Before I can ask any more questions, I hear Ash shouting at the reporters across the scene. He shrugs Michael's hand from his shoulder and cuts through the crowd toward me. The reporters trail him, and suddenly I'm bombarded by a host of microphones and cameras.

"Cassidy, Cassidy! Our viewers want to hear everything!"

"What—"

Pa holds me close as they descend like starving buzzards on lone highway roadkill.

"Ashton Hook said you have information about FireCorp. That you have evidence condemning the organization. Care to comment?"

Ash pushes past the pack and tugs on my bag. "It's okay, Cassidy. You can tell them."

I struggle to catch his meaning, then realize he's motioning for me to open my pack. I open the flap and peer in, and a green bottle of steroids gleams in the sun.

"I would like to comment." I pull out the vial with a grin. "I have evidence that FireCorp is using steroids to dope their dragons."

The reporters blurt a barrage of questions.

"How do we know that vial belonged to them?"

"Can you provide more proof?"

Ash speaks up. "FireCorp has been cheating since the beginning. Cassidy figured it out. And she helped me realize that I'd rather be on the side of good. My dragon, Juliette, is the proof—" He cuts off and looks to the sky as if to stop tears leaking from his eyes. "You have my full consent to test her blood today. And if my stepfather disagrees, well, that should be proof enough."

The reporters separate the two of us in a swarm. As the madness grows, half a dozen reporters descend on a ghost-white Michael Carne. He shrinks behind Valeen and a mess of FireCorp groupies. Across the crowd, Laudes and two other sheriffs seem to have caught wind of the chaos and shove past the flurry of fans and reporters. Realizing his chance to escape as a group of FC loyalists shove back against the press and sheriffs, Michael dashes for the parking lot beyond the festival. A handful of reporters break through the wall of angry supporters and chase after him.

But not all the reporters are interested in Michael, or even Ash.

"Cassidy, Cassidy!" shouts a reporter. "Is this why Michael Carne brought charges against you in the race? Was it payback?"

"Is that why Nickolai Grigori attacked Ash and why you had to save him?"

"Was it because of the steroids?"

I stammer and twirl my ratty, wind-whipped braid as talking heads shove microphones in my face. Thomas Karbach swoops in, white teeth gleaming and cap off the lens of his camera. He cuts off the other reporters and prattles on about the exclusive interview I've apparently agreed to. I'm not sure if he's doing it to shield me from the other reporters or to secure the interview, but I don't care. Across the chaos, Ash winks at me with one black eye.

CHAPTER

31°03′26.0″ N, 102°43′32.5″ W

Drake's Dragon Ranch, Pecos County, Texas

Six weeks later

"Well, grasshopper!" shouts Pa, his face glistening with sweat. "You did good."

I don't feel so much like a grasshopper anymore. Mounted atop Ranga, I lead the mottled rubystinger around the bullpen. Tail skimming the ground, he loops around us, comfortable on the lead. His wounds, now healed, disappear into the amber glow of healthy scales.

"I told you we wouldn't need to sell the ranch to that charlatan," I say.

Pa grins and pulls a letter from his pocket. He holds it over the fencing to get my attention. "Since we have a free moment without high-paying sightseers lurking about, I think we need to have a little chat."

I blush and tug gently on the ruby's rope. "Whoa, buddy. Whoa."

I click my tongue until he gently touches down, his eyes clear and bright. After I unhitch him, he glides off into the sunshine and plays in the blue sky.

I dab my forehead with a bandanna and make for the edge of the fence.

"I happen to have here a letter of interest from Flamespine Secondary School in Tucson, Arizona."

"Flamespine? You don't say." I pull off my fringed gloves and stuff them in my back pocket.

Pa unfolds a letter, clears his throat, and wafts it in my face. "I'm not sure why they made the offer, but it's a full scholarship for your eighth-grade year. Not that I'm keen on letting you out of my sights again. Ever. But you'll get a better education there than you will at Crockett Junior High . . ."

I slip the paper from Pa's hands as he continues his pitch. Deep down, even though I know he hates the idea of not seeing me, he's like any good father who wants what's best for his children.

He scratches the top of his head under his cap with a worried look. "Now, I know a private school isn't exactly your speed, and I know you're a Texas girl through and through—"

"True," I interrupt.

"But Flamespine would give you a proper dragoneering education, just like your mom."

I scan the letter. It's a generous offer. Even with the income we're making from donors and celeb-chasing tours of Drake's Dragon Ranch, Flamespine isn't affordable without a scholarship. What Pa doesn't know is that I actually applied for the scholarship last month.

With Gran's signature, of course.

"Ehem."

I turn to find Gran, who offers me a glass of lemonade with a turquoise-decorated hand. I'm still so glad to see her in good spirits.

"Drink up, grasshopper." Gran's smile warms her skin, which is still sallow despite her blue Dolly Parton–esque eye shadow and pink lipstick.

"As long as it's not sun tea." I hold up the glass of lemonade and let the sun shine through the glass. The sparkle in my nail polish glints. Laura will be happy to learn that the sunflower pattern she applied last week is still fresh.

"I still blame your father for misidentifying that house dragon as a harmless lightrage. How should I have known he was a canyon curlytail with venomous saliva? I figured it was no big deal if he got into my sun tea every once in a while."

Gran's goofy dragon—who's now been banned from living indoors—rubs her legs like a cat and hums, oblivious that he was the cause of all her misfortune.

I pat his head. "Pa and I knew that sun tea was poison years ago. House dragon or otherwise."

"Well, after all that, I doubt you'll ever see sun tea on that porch again." She runs her fingers along the hollows of her cheeks. "Though I swear I may still prefer poisoned sun tea over the Dragon Sisters' awful herbal medicine. Those women are torture artists, not nuns!"

I roll my eyes. "I keep trying to remind you that those torture artists saved your life. After all, they discovered you were being duped by a venomous curlytail when no one else did. If Karbach hadn't suggested they step in, I don't know what we would've done."

Gran gives me a side hug, squeezing me just tight enough that I forget she was doubled up in a hospital just seven weeks ago. She fluffs my loose Dutch braid and whispers into my ear, "Someone's here to see you. Front porch."

The sun hangs low over the house, and I lift a hand over my eyes. On the front porch, lounging in a whitewashed rocking chair, Ash swirls a glass of lemonade in his hands. Sleek black sunglasses wrap around his face and his hair screams James Dean. Oh, Lord. Bet it took him thirty minutes just to get it right.

"What did he say?" I ask Gran.

"Didn't ask. It's your news to unveil."

Dusting my hands off, I leave Gran and make my way to the porch. When I get there, I lean on the railing. "How'd you get here?"

"My mom's in the car." He nods to a black limousine with tinted windows. What a delight she must be. "We used the airfield outside Fort Stockton."

Just a quick trip via private jet. No big deal. I roll my eyes, which Ash ignores. "Any news?" I ask.

I hold my breath as Ash stirs his lemonade, then takes a loud sip. He smacks his lips and sighs. "Michael still won't talk to the press, but we found him."

My breath catches and I ball my fists. "Where?"

He pulls out his cell phone and flips through it. "Here." He hands me the phone, which is opened to a map.

I crinkle my face. "Oman?"

Ash nods. "He told my mother he's 'tending to his affairs.' He claims he's working on some big oil contract. I suppose it's only a matter of time until they extradite him.

Until then, his right hand, Jessica LaPage, is stepping in and toeing the FireCorp party line."

"She wanted Pa to honor Michael's deal to buy the ranch. I'm just glad Pa refused. And that we came up with the cash in time." I hand Ash back the phone as emotions swirl through me. "I listened to her at FireCorp's televised press conference. She's claiming Nickolai acted alone, without Michael's influence. That's crud on a cracker, right?"

The look on Ash's face says yes.

I slump down in the chair next to him and the porch's floorboards creak. "At least Michael's banned from the national racing league while they investigate the steroids. Thank God for Sheriff Laudes. I imagine she's knee-deep in interviews and evidence. Especially after Karbach nailed FireCorp to the wall in that last op-ed. Any word from Brayden?"

Ash shakes his head. "But I hear he's recovering."

The silence stretches out, and I think through everything that happened after the race. I imagine a world where people like Nickolai can't touch dragons, where FireCorp is held accountable and dragons aren't doped ever again. In my bones, I know Michael has bigger dreams for the FC than winning small-time races.

But it's Valeen's final words, before I barreled through

the sky to save Ash, that gnaw at me. I have so many unanswered questions about my mom. According to Karbach, she and Michael were together for years before he proposed and she broke off the engagement. Neither Gran nor Pa has much to say on the subject. But as far as Ash and I are concerned, Michael's hatred toward me wasn't about the steroids or even getting his hands on Drake's Dragon Ranch. It was personal, like he couldn't bear the idea of Ash being friends with Aurora Drake's daughter.

I sip on my lemonade and watch the clouds take the shape of otherworldly creatures. As they morph into dragons I've met only in my dreams, I remember lying on a patchwork quilt with my mom, pointing up into the sky.

Ash leans forward and clears his throat.

I startle out of my haze. "Sorry—what else?"

"If you must know, I'm here about a dragon. I'm retiring Juliette. She deserves the rest. Now I just have to hope Michael doesn't come back and override my decision."

The lemonade mixes with bile rising on my tongue. "I hope she's okay."

Ash nods. "She's tired . . . At least neither Juliette nor I will have to deal with Nick at Dragonscale next year. They'll definitely give him a hard time at Price Military. Even his cruelty won't protect him there." He pauses and wipes the condensation from his glass. "In a weird way, I also hope they help him find some sort of . . . perspective. Or peace. Or something." He flicks the condensation off his hand.

I stop my rocking and try to maintain my composure. I don't need to remind Ash what Nickolai did—the scars Sergei gave him are reminder enough. But I think Nickolai deserves worse.

Ash stirs his cardboard straw, swirling the decorative lemon slice against the glass. "Not all families are lemonade and six o'clock dinners." Across the field, baby knuckers chirp as Pa hand-feeds them corn and bones. Ash entertains a sad smile. "As much as I hate Nick, he's the only other person who knows what it's like to be raised by Michael. And someday, I hope he realizes Michael is the enemy, not me."

I set my glass on the rusted side table and lean back in my chair, so far that I almost tip over. There's not much I can say about families that aren't mine.

Ash sets his glass beside mine and rises from his rocking chair. "I'm sorry I put you on the spot with the reporters." He fiddles with the collar of his fresh white T-shirt, then dredges up his usual haughty tone. "Maybe the illustrious Cassidy Drake will be willing to forgive me?"

The melting sun catches golden flecks in Ash's irises.

I rise to my feet and extend a hand. "Forgiven."

He shakes back and warmth spreads through me. Our love for dragons is a bridge across state lines and a world of differences, and for that, I am grateful.

Overhead, the rubystinger circles beside Ranga, and they land in the gravel driveway. Ranga rubs her head along the rubystinger's neck like a cat begging for scritches. The rubystinger tenses but doesn't flee. His enormous wings spread wide, allowing Ranga to curl underneath him.

Ash slips off his sunglasses and gallops down from the porch. "Where did you get this one?" he asks. He makes a cooing sound as he approaches the rubystinger.

In response, the rubystinger bows his head and lets Ash walk right up to him.

I slip my hands into my tattered jeans and wait as Ash runs a hand along the stinger's side, evaluating the dragon's elongated neck and gleaming scales. When his fingers reach the scar emblazoned on the stinger's haunch, he stops still.

"He was one of ours?" asks Ash.

I nod. "Unfortunately. But he's coming around. There's nothing a little love won't help."

I can tell Ash is thinking of Nickolai as he strokes the

rubystinger's side. "How much?"

"Not everything's for sale, you know." I huff.

Ash's eyes widen. "I, I—"

I nudge him with an elbow. "I'm kidding." The stinger flicks his tail along the ground, knocking Ranga out of the way. "Actually, I don't think Pa will let him go—not yet."

Ash hangs his head and strokes the dragon with the back of his hand.

"But, if you were inclined to wait, maybe spend some time with him while he's in therapy?"

Ash lowers his sunglasses and leans against the stinger, who doesn't squirm. Instead, he settles into Ash's body. Lips turning into a cocky half smile, Ash smooths a lock of hair back from his eyes and crosses his arms. "I'm sure you wouldn't mind me hanging around the ranch."

I flick a braid over my shoulder. "I won't be here."

"What?"

"I'm headed to Arizona with a full ride to Flamespine Secondary."

Ash wags a finger at me. "I thought you were a die-hard Texas girl?"

"I am." I pause. "But maybe the world beyond Drake's Dragon Ranch offers more than I once realized. There are other races to ride, people to meet, and dragons who need my help." The wind whirls around me as newfound truths slip from my lips and fill my soul. I twist my heel in the dirt. "Besides . . . they have a grylock at Flamespine."

"What? You're kidding. No one has seen one of those since—"

"Since the ice started melting in Alaska. Jealous?"

Ash crosses his arms. "Why would I ever be jealous of a lowly Texas ranch hand like you?" He holds up his nose, and we both burst into laughter.

Overhead, the horizon lights up with bright purples and oranges, streaking across the whole plain. "See you soon?" I ask.

Ash nods, spins his fancy cell phone in his hand, and heads back to the hired limousine waiting for him. He waves back, and I tip my hat.

And because all good cowboy stories end this way, I jump on Ranga's back, pulling up, up into the sky, and we fly off into the sunset.

ACKNOWLEDGMENTS

This book wouldn't have been possible without the guidance and support of so many.

Tim, you've believed in me from day one. Thank you for dealing with my endless need to brainstorm. You read the entire book on your phone—and left me midnight notes for consideration. You even turned down the music so I could work in peace. That's true love. Here's to many more trips around Texas . . . and beyond.

I definitely won the "family lotto," and a few deserve special thanks. Mom, your imaginative quilts inspired me to embrace the weirdness of the Wild West. Dad, thanks for your keen insight into how the energy industry might use dragons. Perry, I'm so glad you're the type of brother who loves fantasy . . . and that you married an awesome woman with a flair for words. Sheriden McKenney, your feedback was invaluable during the editing process. Welcome to the family! KayKay, you embody the Southwest like no one I've ever met and were the perfect prototype for Cassidy's Gran. Uncle Brent, thank you for blazing a publishing trail and answering my questions. DeSilva Fam, you guys are the best.

Oh, Laura, what would I have done without you? You truly are the best "Creature Consultant" and beta reader around. Chris, I so appreciate that you pitched in to dream up cool Texas locations where dragons might hide. Kate, thank you for helping me network and for talking dragons and True Grit via Zoom.

A very special thanks to my fabulous agent, Adriann Ranta Zurhellen, who championed this story and inspired me to rework the book for the better. Emilia Rhodes, editor extraordinaire, I'm eternally grateful that you love rescue animals and were willing to love a story about rescue dragons. Thank you for your brilliant editorial vision. Your team has been amazing.

And Texas—this book has been my love letter to the better parts of you. Your complicated past and present are sometimes difficult to witness. But your majestic horizons, hidden beauty, and incredible diversity leave me ever hopeful for your future.